Before the Scarlet Dawn

"Filled with true-to-life characters whose struggles will linger with readers long after the last page is turned, *Before the Scarlet Dawn* is a memorable story of Revolutionary War-era England and America."
—Amanda Cabot, author of *Summer of Promise*

"Rita Gerlach has written a colorful historical with a feisty heroine on a search for survival, romance, and a place to belong."
—Cynthia Hickey, author of the Summer Meadows mysteries

D0354568

Other books by Rita Gerlach

Surrender the Wind

The Daughters of the Potomac Series

Beside Two Rivers (Coming 2012)
Beyond the Valley (Coming 2013)

Before the Scarlet Dawn

Book 1

The Daughters of the Potomac Series

Rita Gerlach

Abingdon Press fiction
a novel approach to faith

Nashville, Tennessee

Before the Scarlet Dawn

Copyright © 2011 Rita Gerlach

ISBN 978-1-4267-1414-6

Published by Abingdon Press, P.O. Box 801, Nashville, TN 37202

www.abingdonpress.com

All rights reserved.

The persons and events portrayed in this work of fiction
are the creations of the author, and any resemblance
to persons living or dead is purely coincidental.

Library of Congress Cataloging-in-Publication Data

Gerlach, Rita.
  Before the scarlet dawn / Rita Gerlach.
     p. cm.
  ISBN 978-1-4267-1414-6 (book - pbk. /trade pbk. : alk. paper) 1. Upper class—Fiction.
2. Fathers and daughters—Fiction. 3. Great Britain—History—18th century—Fiction. I.
Title.
  PS3607.E755B44 2012
  813'.6—dc23

                                                          2011041510

Unless indicated otherwise, scripture quotations are taken from the
King James or Authorized Version of the Bible.

Scripture quotations marked (NIV) are taken from the Holy Bible,
NEW INTERNATIONAL VERSION®. Copyright © 1973, 1978,
1984 by International Bible Society. All rights reserved throughout
the world. Used by permission of International Bible Society.

Printed in the United States of America

1 2 3 4 5 6 7 8 9 10 / 16 15 14 13 12 11

To those longing for forgiveness

Acknowledgments

Many thanks to all who gave me a word of encouragment, a prayer, a hope, in the writing of this novel.

Part 1

Set me as a seal upon thine heart, as a seal upon thine arm: for love is strong as death; jealousy is cruel as the grave: the coals thereof are coals of fire, which hath a most vehement flame.

Song of Solomon 8:6

1

The Hope Valley, Derbyshire, England
April 7, 1775

*E*liza Bloome sat forward from the tattered high-backed chair when someone pounded a fist on the front door downstairs. Her father's Bible lay open on her lap and slipped over her knees to the floor. She bent down to retrieve it, and felt the cold rippled over her fingers through a crack. Wind howled across the downs and moaned through the weatherworn windows. Shivering from the draft, she set another log on the fire and listened to Fiona's shoes tap down the staircase. Whenever the wind rose fierce like on this night, it held the front door fast. Any moment now her father's housekeeper would brace herself against it and the jamb until her strength gave out. As Eliza expected, the door slammed on its lock and hinges. The crash echoed up the staircase, mingling with a man's voice.

The bedroom door quietly swung open.

"Who is it, Fiona?" Eliza glanced at her father, then back at the stout woman standing in the doorway. "Papa is asleep. He should not be disturbed."

"A messenger to see him, my girl. Chilled to the bone, I'd say. Riding over the downs in the dead of night in the wind and cold. It must be important if he went to all this trouble. Should I let him in?"

The log caught fire and the room grew warmer. Eliza drew off her wrap and folded it across the chair. "Yes, I will speak to him."

Fiona placed her hand over the brass knob and set her back against the door to allow entrance to a man dressed in the simple drab brown attire of a servant. He drew off his tricorn hat and gave Eliza a slight bow. A lock of brown hair fell over his broad forehead.

"Is he able to speak with me, Miss Eliza?" He glanced at the frail form asleep in the four-poster bed.

"My father is not well. It depends on who you are, why you've come, and for how long you intend to stay."

"Name is John Travis. I've come with a letter from Mr. Langbourne with strict instructions to put it into your father's hand and wait for his reply."

"On a night like this? It is a wonder you were not blown off your horse, Mr. Travis. I do not think well of Mr. Langbourne for it. He must have paid you well."

"Aye, he did. The wind is harsh tonight, to be sure. But I have a good horse, and Mr. Langbourne deemed my journey urgent. He has heard how sickly your father is. Everyone in the parish has."

Knowing her father was not long for this world, Eliza went to his bedside and tucked in the coverlet. Tonight his breathing was labored, and when she touched his hands, they were cold as the chill wind.

Even in the bronze firelight, his face looked drawn and pale. His hair seemed to have gone white within such a short time, and his body smelled of sweat no matter how much she bathed him. He opened a pair of watery gray eyes and looked at her.

"Who is it, Eliza?"

"A man is here to speak to you, Papa. His name is John Travis. Should I send him away?"

Pressing his brows together, Reverend Bloome paused. Eliza waited patiently, knowing he needed a moment to think. Over several weeks, he had grown forgetful and confused, and relied more and more upon her to help him understand.

"I know no one by that name. Should I know him, Eliza?"

"I do believe you met him once or twice, but no, Papa. You do not need to know him. But he says he has a letter for you—from Mr. Langbourne."

"Langbourne I do recall. Raise me against the pillows, Daughter." He pushed back on his elbows with her help. "There, that is better. Bring him forward and leave us to speak alone."

A shiver passed through her at the last two words. Why would he not want her to stay? What did a letter from Langbourne, a man she had barely spoken two words to, mean? But she did not need to have a conversation with him to know what he thought of her. Either in church, the marketplace, or at a gathering, he always seemed to find her, bow in greeting, and feast his eyes on her.

Once outside the door, she leaned her ear against it and listened. Muffled voices were all she could make out. Seconds later, Fiona, the woman who had nurtured her from the day of her mother's passing, poked her head around the corner. The cap she wore looked white as snow in the candlelight. Fiona always kept her caps starched and clean, and her hazel eyes, set deep within a face round as an October moon, looked just as bright when she raised her brows at Eliza.

"Go on with you, my girl. It is not polite to eavesdrop." Fiona waved her off and moved in front of Eliza with the tray of tea toppling to the left.

Eliza stepped back. "What is this all about, Fiona? Do you know?"

"I won't know a thing until I go in with the Reverend's tea. Now move away from the door. Do not let me catch you peering inside to see what's going on. It would be rude, my dear."

"Then I shall listen outside the door. I have every right to."

"No, you do not, my girl. If your father wants you to know his business, he will tell you. He doesn't need his daughter being so bold as to lay her ear upon his door and listen in on his private conversations."

Determined, Eliza pressed her back against the wall. "Perhaps not, but I think I know why Mr. Travis has come. Langbourne sent him with a letter to Papa to ask permission to wed me. I wish I knew what Papa was telling him."

Fiona rolled her eyes, huffed, and shoved the door open. Before she could close it with her hip, Eliza overheard, "Mr. Langbourne said he knows how dire your situation is, sir, and wishes an answer forthwith."

"And what are the conditions?"

"It's all contained in the letter I have brought. Ah, hot tea. I am chilled, ma'am, to the marrow. Thank ye."

Eliza's breath slowly escaped her throat. She pressed her mouth into a firm line, kept her back against the paneled wall, and stared at the ceiling.

So Mr. Langbourne wishes an answer? No, Papa would never be so callous as to give me to a man I do not know very well, let alone love. He believes in the sacredness of marriage; a holy, unbroken institution in the Lord's eyes, where man and woman make a lifetime commitment to each other in their love for each other. It's a serious matter and not to be trifled with, or bartered for land, possessions, or money.

For a moment, she thought of her mother, how, through the years her father kept his beloved's memory alive, telling

Eliza how he had loved Mary Lanham. Plenty of opportunities presented themselves, but he never remarried. And if only her brother were home. He would see to it that she married the right man and take this burden off their father. Instead, he lived far away, serving in the King's army, committed to finding his own way in the world. In another year, he would be able to resign his service and settle down. But his choice, he said—America. How could Stephen help her from so great a distance?

Unable to bear the suspense, she turned the doorknob and the door opened slowly. Standing in front of her father, Travis turned and passed his eyes over her, as if assessing her from head to toe.

She took the cup from his hand and set it on the tray. "My father is tired. You must leave now."

Her father lifted one side of his mouth into a gentle smile. She hoped he saw her distress. "Thank you," he said. "Tell Mr. Langbourne I am honored by his letter. But it is my daughter who must give him an answer."

Her father's hands trembled while he clutched the letter between his fingers and set it down beside him. The disease that plagued his body caused the tremors, and they seemed to grow worse as the days wore on.

Hat in hand, John Travis nodded and stepped from the room.

"Do not look so troubled, child. This is good news, I should say," Matthias reached for Eliza's hand.

She drew up her chair beside her father and sat. "Let me guess. They have decided to accept women at Oxford and have offered that I come there to study."

She smiled, hoping to ease his melancholy. He frowned instead. "It is nothing of the kind. Why do you jest about such things?"

"To make you smile, Papa." She squeezed his hand. "But I failed."

"Ah, it is good of you, but silly. Women will never be admitted into Oxford or Cambridge. You must read and study on your own at home, as you always have."

"Yes, Papa."

"But not too much, for all a girl needs to know is how to run a house, and you will not find that in the pages of books."

She cocked her head. "Hmm. I do believe I might. But more importantly, love should run a house, not just head knowledge or skill. Now, tell me what Mr. Langbourne has written."

Matthias sighed. "You have been offered a proposal of marriage."

She glanced at the letter and did not let on that she had overheard some of the conversation. "Really? Again?"

"He tells me he will come into his inheritance soon. He says his situation at present is three hundred pounds a year. Later, he will have one thousand pounds yearly for the remainder of his life. For he has been named heir of Havendale, instead of his cousin Hayward Morgan."

"I suppose that is because Mr. Hayward left for the Colonies."

"Against his father's wishes."

"Hmm. He is a bitter man to cast off his true son."

"We are not to judge. Whatever his reasons, Langbourne will own Havendale someday."

Eliza screwed up her nose. "I hear Havendale is unbearably cold. I would not want to live there. And . . ."

He lifted his hand and patted hers. "Have you had any other proposals that exceed this offer?"

"No, Papa. But do not expect me to live with a man I do not care for. Surely he does not love me."

"He says he likes you."

"I cannot accept him."

With a wheezing breath, her father drew himself up. "You will have to deal with him. You will be the one to say no, not I. I wish I could say he is my choice of husband for you, but I am unconvinced of anyone being good enough for my Eliza. However, if you do not have a husband soon, and I should leave this world, you shall be alone and no doubt fall into poverty. That grieves me too much to think of."

Her father's expression grew thoughtful, and Eliza knew to be patient. She stroked his arm in an effort to comfort him. "I could go to Stephen."

Her father shook his head. "He is in the King's army. He would not be permitted to take you. This—" and he held the letter up for her to see, "might be for the best."

"I will pray, Papa, that the Lord will give me the answer I need. After that, I will reply to Mr. Langbourne."

"Langbourne is not a bad-looking man, and he has the means to take good care of you. I know you do not know him well, for you have barely spoken two words to him in all your life. But knowing one another comes in time, and love will follow."

Eliza frowned. "But why would he choose me?"

"For your pretty face and that beaming smile of yours, which would captivate any young man. You are healthy in body, mind, and spirit. Your price, dear daughter, is far above rubies."

She shook her head. "I doubt the health of my mind and spirit matters to Mr. Langbourne, Papa."

"Just consider the offer, child. You might thank me one day for my advice, as you stand over my grave."

Stunned, she could not hold back a whimper at his mention of his grave.

The following afternoon, Eliza saddled the dappled mare kept in the single stall in the stable behind the house. She inhaled the rich scent of hay and lifted her face to greet the sunlight that shot through a hole in the roof.

Before she could lead the horse out, she heard her name and turned to see a horse and rider draw up outside the stable door. Langbourne, dressed in taupe riding clothes and black boots, dismounted. Since the last time she had seen him, he had put on several pounds, and his sandy hair peeked out from under his hat in wiry strands.

He leaned against the frame of the door and tapped his riding crop against his thigh. "Your father has, more or less, consented." His voice sported a tinge of arrogance. "But what about you, Eliza? Have you accepted my offer?"

"No, and not a moment to dwell on it."

"Why not?"

"Because I do not love you."

"Love? That should not matter, at least where you are concerned. I do like you exceedingly, even though I've never said it before now."

She laughed. "Like me? How can you feel anything for me when we have never said more than hello or goodbye in chance meetings either at church or in the village? And I cannot marry a man I know nothing about."

"You shall get to know me, beginning today." He smiled with a glint in his eyes.

She ignored him and cinched the saddle. "And I cannot resign myself to a life of boredom, shut up in some London house, with nothing to do all day but sit and sit."

He moved closer. "I will find plenty of diversions for both of us."

Eliza pulled her horse forward. "I am not of your society."

"You will be. I am taking a risk, I know, by marrying a vicar's daughter. People will say I could have reached higher. But I do not care what the gossips may spread. It is a challenge I relish."

Turning to face him, Eliza lifted her chin. "What do you mean?"

"I should like to change you, take you like a piece of clay and mold you into a wife suitable to my status. With my money, you shall have plenty of silks, and a string of pearls that shall be envied."

"Change me? Mold me? Now I know a union between us would be a disaster. And I do not like silk. It stains too easily. And I cannot abide lavish balls or dinner parties. I am not right for you."

His jaw stiffened. "But I desire you, Eliza. Doesn't that count for something? Is that not what a woman wants? That, and a rich husband?"

She huffed at him. "Surely it is an infatuation on your part. What you see before you on the outside will fade in time."

Frustrated, he breathed out and took her roughly by the arms. "What I see is the most beguiling woman in all the world. You would end up an old spinster if not for your body, which I can only imagine is luscious beneath this dress. And that dark hair of yours—I've thought of it flowing over your bare shoulders. And those violet eyes to tempt me with. Can't you see I want you?"

"I can, and in a manner I do not welcome." She resisted his embrace and pushed him back. His lustful words caused her to wither. She squirmed out of his arms and stepped away.

He slapped the stable wall. "One day you will regret your refusal, Eliza." He mounted his horse and rode off. When he was finally gone, Eliza climbed onto her mare's back and nudged its side with her heel. Her eyes pooled with angry tears that slipped from her eyes and ran down her cheeks. If only he loved her for what thrived deeper than skin, perhaps then she would have considered his proposal. His handsome bank account was not enough to tempt her, nor his promise of a secure future.

Langbourne proved to be no different from the others who had courted her affections. They wanted what they saw on the outside—a body as desirable as an artist's model, seductive lavender eyes, hair the color of black silk, and skin as light and translucent as morning mist.

She reined in her mare and dashed the tears briskly from her face. With a heart that yearned and sought God's plan for her life, she stared at the downs that stretched far into the distance, and drew the cool, damp air deep into her lungs. Determined to make her own choice, she kicked the mare's ribs with her heel and raced it across the windswept heath.

2

The shrill throaty call of a hawk caught Eliza's attention. She halted her horse and gazed at the slow sweep of the hawk's wings as it soared across the clear blue sky above Hope Valley. It hovered a moment, then dove straight toward earth and snatched up a gray field mouse in its talons.

"You see that, Lord?" She ran her gloved hand slowly along the mare's broad neck. "Langbourne is like that hawk. Please, do not let me be that poor little mouse."

Beyond the outstretched wings the bird spread into the wind, the sun pierced a pale beam through a cluster of blue-gray clouds. Eliza marched her horse on, toward the River Noe. Wild comfrey grew along the riverbank, and she dismounted when she spied a spray that was dead from the winter cold. The dried leaves would suffice to comfort her father's malaise. Pinching the base with her fingertips, she plucked the stems from the ground and put them inside a canvas pouch fastened to her waist.

The wind, smelling of rain, damp moss, and turf, rushed through her hair and blew it back off her shoulders. She had been gone too long, she thought, and mounting her horse, she turned back, hoping to reach home before dusk.

As she neared the rocks that threw long shadows across the moors, a long howl rose out of the wind. At first, she hoped it was not a wolf prowling the grasslands far from the forest. Then off in the distance, her eyes caught sight of a spotted boarhound bounding after a rabbit. She nudged her horse on with a click of her tongue and came around a sharp bend in the road where a cart barred the way. One man jumped down and thrust his hands into his pockets—the other drew off his hat and gave her an insolent bow. She went to turn her horse, but the younger man leapt forward and grabbed the halter. The horse snorted and stamped its hooves, as the one man held it fast and the other looked at Eliza with a wide grin.

"Well, if it isn't the vicar's raven-haired daughter. Good day to you, miss."

"Jack Fie, let go my horse."

"Not until you tell me something I've been dying to know. Are you as pure as they say, or have those beautiful violet eyes gotten you into trouble?"

She smacked him across his shoulder with the reins. "Let go, I said!"

"Oh, let the lass be, Jack," said the older man, who clenched a pipe between his teeth.

"Only havin' a bit of fun. Come down, Eliza Bloome, and kiss me."

Relentlessly, he attempted to pull her down from the saddle. The mare twisted, and Eliza pressed her knee hard into its side.

Suddenly, a pistol snapped and lead whizzed straight past Jack Fie's head into his seat in the wagon. His companion yelped. Fie jumped back and hurried to his place in the cart, and with his cohort sped off as quickly as their shaggy work-horse could carry them.

Heat rose in Eliza's cheeks as a man on horseback galloped up to her with the hound hard upon his mount's flanks. He shoved his flintlock pistol into his belt and looked at her with a smile. He wore a dark blue overcoat, tawny breeches, and black riding boots. His eyes were deep brown beneath a strong brow. His hair, dark as the wings of the hawk that flew above, lay tied at the nape of his neck with a black ribbon.

The boarhound barked, and Eliza's frightened mare reared and beat its hooves—its eyes huge and fearsome. Stamping its hooves deep into the sod around the dog, the mare bolted off and went racing across the downs. The rider caught up to her, reached for the bridle, and brought the mare against his boot. It twisted its head with a whinny and skidded to a sudden stop. Thrown from the saddle, Eliza landed on the ground. Dazed, she gasped for breath and slowly sat up.

The gentleman alighted and commanded the hound to be silent and stand down. His shadow fell over Eliza as she put her hand to her brow to steady the dizzy feeling swimming in her head.

"Are you hurt?" His tone hinted of sincere concern, but also amusement.

She looked at him and was struck with the strangest sensation. Flushed, she glared at him. "I do not believe so. Your dog is to blame for frightening my horse and causing it to run off like that. You should control the beast. I could have been killed."

He reached his hand down to her. Reluctantly she took it, and he pulled her up.

"He's really gentle in most instances." Eliza's rescuer slapped his thigh with the palm of his hand, and the hound came forward to have his ears stroked. "You are a sprite of a woman," he went on. "So I imagine you could not control your mare."

His arrogant half-smile caused her blood to simmer. "Normally she is as docile as a lamb. I have never had a problem with her before, not until your animal accosted her."

"Though you are not afraid to speak your mind, girl, you should not be out here alone. Those ruffians could have done you more harm than my dog ever could."

Eliza brushed the dry grass from off her cloak and stepped away. "I do it all the time."

With a quick flick of his wrist, he tossed a stick into the field, and his hound ran after it. "I suppose it is acceptable with your class of person to ride unattended."

She narrowed her eyes. "My class of person, sir, does not sit idly at home staring out of windows. And I would have done just fine without your interference."

His laugh infuriated her to the point that her blood boiled with disdain. "Oh, is that what you call it? I beg your pardon, but I seriously doubt it. A woman is no match for two fellows like that. Where were you going, anyway? To the market for your mistress?"

Proud, she raised her chin. "I am my own mistress."

"By the look of you, I'd say a poor one. If you need work, come to Havendale. My mother may have something for you." He went for his horse.

"I am not in need of employment, sir," she said. "My father and I are well situated at home. I hate to ask, or to impose on you any longer, but would you help me back on my horse?"

He cupped his hands and placed them under the sole of her boot to lift her back into the saddle. "What is your name?"

"I will tell you, if you tell me yours first." No sooner had the words left her mouth than the wind ruffled his hair and she knew exactly who he was by the scar above his left eyebrow.

His face had changed, grown older since the last time she had seen him.

"Wait. I know you. You are Hayward Morgan. I recall the scar you bear. I am the one who gave it to you when we were children. I threw a stone at you for teasing me. Remember?"

His mouth began to curve into a smile, and he touched the scar with his forefinger. She could see the memory rise in his eyes. "How could I have mistaken the raven hair and violet eyes for those of a gypsy, Eliza Bloome? You've grown into a woman since I last saw you."

She drew in a long breath. "Of course you know me. My father has been the minister at Saint Anthony's for thirty years. He baptized you, and your brothers and sister."

"And buried them."

"Yes. It is sad indeed for your mother."

"I have never seen her shed a tear over much of anything. But I am convinced you are right. To lose so many infants gave her cause to make me the last."

It might have been the soft way in which he now spoke that caused her to drop her gaze and her blood to cool. "I am an only child as well. Do you regret it?"

"Certainly. But I do have a half brother. I haven't seen him in years. My father sent him away when we were young, and when he was old enough, he left England for the Colonies."

Eliza shook her head. "Oh, that is unfortunate."

She thought, *How could any woman not show sorrow over such tremendous loss?* "I remember seeing you in church when we were children. Every Sunday you were seated next to her in the first pew. The brass plaque bearing your family name is still there. I suppose someday you will be seated there with your wife and children."

His smile faded into a scowl. "Hmm. I have no such plan."

Eliza stared at him, confused by his admission. Did he not wish to carry on his family's name? Why would he prefer a bachelor life, quiet and lonely, in comparison to a home filled with the pitter-patter of children's feet and the company of a loving wife?

She gave him a sidelong glance. "Hmm. I realize the rich are idle for the most part, but you must have some goal in life."

"I have. And I intend to achieve them all."

Eliza's opinion of him heightened at this view. "You are an optimist. That is an admirable position."

Hayward called to his boarhound as it romped too far. He shoved his boot into the stirrup and climbed back into the saddle. They rode along slowly, side by side, and he turned to Eliza and said, "We never conversed much as children, did we?"

"I was not permitted to speak to you."

"I tried and was punished for it with a riding crop across my back."

"Oh, that is a terrible thing. My father never laid a hand upon me."

"Mine did, and he sent me away to school—said I needed more discipline and to know my place. It was an enormous waste of my time and his money. You had a brother, did you not? Stephen, was it?"

"Yes. He is in the army—in New York, from his last letter."

Hayward shook his head. "Revolution permeates the air in the Colonies. I know enough to be convinced it would be a righteous cause."

Eliza raised her brows. "Indeed? Righteous enough to stand against the King?"

"Yes. I've just returned from Maryland and have seen with my own eyes the stranglehold His Majesty wishes to tighten around the throats of the Colonists. A tax on stamps for legal documents is outrageous, and the quartering of his troops in peoples' homes, against their wishes, is not to be borne."

"You speak of treason."

"I suppose to you I do."

Eliza soaked in his words. She'd never heard any man speak the way he did, and it intrigued her all the more to see what kind of man Hayward Morgan had turned out to be. "You saw things, as you say, with your own eyes. You are that convinced to leave England for good?"

"Why not? There is rich land there, and I have acquired a pretty tract with a mill, near the Potomac. Farmers pay good money to grind their grain. So, I shall do well."

"I would think it would be a lonely life living in the wilderness by one's self. I have heard that the winters there are harsh and the summers unbearable. You would indeed starve."

A curve tugged at the corner of his mouth. "It is true what you say about the seasons, but if you'd only see it for yourself, you would know that the farms and plantations of Maryland are as prosperous as any English estate. If I fail, as you seem to think I might, I have enough set aside to sustain me the rest of my life."

"Are you not angry your cousin has been awarded heir of Havendale instead of you?"

The glint in his eyes darkened. "Of course I am."

"You could contest it when the time comes."

"I could. But I won't."

She stared at him. "I am quite amazed to hear that. You prefer the wilds of Maryland to Havendale?"

"It is said men grow desperate to marry in order to fill the lonely hours. A good wife to bear the burden with is needful if a man means to build his fortune in America . . . I see I confused you when I said I had no plans to fill my family's pew with a family of my own."

"Yes, you did." Eliza shook her head. "But I think I understand now."

"And what about you, Miss Bloome? I imagine you have plenty of proposals."

"None serious save for one. Your cousin has set his suit upon me." Slowly she drew the reins through her fingers.

"Yes, I know. I learned this day that you are not convinced of his intentions. You should marry him. He will have money and property. Do you have other offers?"

She would tease him for his proud look and prejudiced ways. "Hmm. I know of one other—you, sir. You swore you'd marry me when we were children . . . beside the back door of the church when your parents were not looking."

An arrogant light sprang into his eyes and he stared at her a moment. "I'm afraid that for all your beauty, Miss Bloome, you are beneath me. Good day."

Eliza narrowed her eyes. He tipped his hat, kicked his stallion's ribs, and raced off with the boarhound striding hard behind. Wind blew through Eliza's hair and cooled her neck. It stung her eyes. Or was it the sight of him, the words he spoke, and the way he left her that caused tears to well?

As he rode off, she called out to him, "In God's eyes, I am neither beneath nor above anyone. But I am determined to rise above your prejudice, Hayward Morgan."

3

By the time Eliza reached home, dusky sunlight flickered across the glass in the mullioned windows of the old vicarage. Prisms of color, amid the shadows of the trees, quivered in the breeze. She now knew she still had feelings for Hayward Morgan. He made her heart tremble. His eyes pierced straight through her and shook her to her core. His arrogance caused her blood to rise to a fevered pitch.

She admitted his handsome looks drew her to him. Yet, something about his demeanor and cool attitude attracted her as well. Seeing him again sparked an even deeper flame within. Why would she feel this way if it were not meant to be?

She looked up with a start when Fiona called from the threshold of the door. "Oh, my girl." She wiped her eyes with the corner of her apron. "If only you had come home sooner. I did not know what to do, how to find you, and there was no one here to send out looking for you . . ."

A chill swept through Eliza. She jumped down from the mare's back, crossed the flagstones, and hurried through the door. Fiona followed her inside, silent and forlorn as the deepening shades that had overtaken the foyer.

Eliza climbed the staircase as quick as her legs could carry her. She turned and ran down the hallway to her father's bedchamber. She rushed to his bedside. His hands, once strong and protective, lay over his chest. His eyes, once sparkling with fatherly pride, lay closed. She'd never look into them again.

"He went peaceful, my girl," Fiona said in a soft voice. "Without struggle. He called me over to him, asked for you, and then looked up at the ceiling with a light in his eyes that I cannot describe—as if he were seeing Heaven."

Fiona touched her shoulder. "He said to me, 'Fiona, take care of my girl. Swear to me you will never leave her.' And so, I did give him my promise. Then he slipped away content."

Overcome, Eliza dropped to her knees beside the tidy bed and clutched the bedclothes in her hands. "I should not have gone out." The ache, that she had not been with him when he died, shot through her.

A moan crawled up her throat, caught, and then the dam broke. It flowed from every pore, every corner of her soul. It tore, raked. Bitter tears welled in her eyes and fell down her cheeks. She gathered her father's hand in hers, pressed her face against his fingers, and wept.

Through the following days the house seemed empty without Matthias Bloome. The tasks of settling her father's passing were done in tears, but Eliza soon overcame them by drawing on an inner strength birthed from her faith. On the day of his burial, Langbourne sent Eliza a letter, urging her with passionate words to reconsider his proposal of marriage. It would save her from a poor life, he told her. For a moment, she did indeed consider it, but her heart won out. She'd rather live alone and poor than give herself to a man she did not love.

Two other letters arrived by courier an hour later.

> Madam,
>
> Accept my deepest sympathy, and that of my wife's, on the passing of your father, my pastor these many years, a man dedicated to his flock and to the Word of God.
>
> It is with regret, however, that I must inform you that you are required to vacate the vicarage within a fortnight in order to make room for the new minister, his wife, and children. Fiona Goodall is to retain her position as house-keeper, although I must say her work shall grow sevenfold. All furnishings, plate, and books are to remain, per our agreement when your father first came to us years ago.
>
> In such a dire situation as this, I urge you to find employment in the village or on one of the farms. You may call upon my wife for letters of recommendation. She assures me she is able to arrange a position as a servant in one of the finer houses in our county.
>
> Now that you are alone in the world, I expect your compliance in this matter, as well as in the matter, which concerns my nephew and his proposal of marriage—that you do not reconsider it. He is expected to marry someone of good breeding and standing. It is best you seek matrimony on more humble grounds.
>
> Regards,
> Edward Morgan—Havendale

Her face flushed with heat, Eliza lifted her eyes from the letter and stared hard out the window. The downs were green with early spring, and the sky as blue as the wild cornflowers that sprouted from the earth.

"Where is my spring, Lord? Why has life suddenly remained wintry and gray?" The letter quivered in her trembling hand. "No one told me it would come to this, that I would have to leave home so soon."

Her hands shook as she broke the blood-red seal of the second letter and unfolded the page. Addressed to her father, it had come from her brother's commanding officer. Stephen had fallen ill with scarlet fever. His life was over in a matter of days; his body laid to rest in the cemetery outside the walls of Fort Erie. Her brother, six years her senior, left home at the age of sixteen. Now at twenty-seven he was gone, and she at twenty-one was left with no relative in the world, or any hope of seeing him again.

Tears stung her eyes and she tossed the letters upon the bed. Heaving a breath, she stared down at them and struck her palm across her breast wanting to abate the heartache that had taken residence there. "Where am I to go? What am I to do?"

She paced the floor and tried to think. Her mind clouded with grief. *Papa. Stephen. Both gone.* Tears struggled for release. They burned and she blinked them back. Frustration rose and she clenched her hands tightly. The door drifted open, and Fiona poked her head around it.

"What's wrong, my girl? This stumping to and fro is likely to wear out the rug."

Eliza stood still and stared at the floor. "Stephen is dead."

Fiona clapped her hand over her heart. "Oh, dear girl."

"Scarlet fever. At Fort Erie—along the Niagara."

Eliza wiped her eyes. "And there is more bad news. It's in that horrible missive Mr. Morgan sent me, and not a moment to waste after Papa is in the ground. He sounds so sympathetic, but he has a heart of stone."

Fiona stared at Eliza with worry—being much affected by the dreadful turn of events. "Oh, my heart aches for Stephen and that you have lost your brother. And you are right about Edward Morgan. The man is a heartless cad. What's the letter say?"

"That I am to be gone in a fortnight in order to make room for the new vicar and his wife and children." Her throat tightened, and she threw herself across the bed with her arms folded beneath her face.

"Ah, my dear," Fiona said. "Do not cry." She sat down and stroked Eliza's hair. "How could he be so quick to put you out like this, after all these years, with your Papa not long gone? He could at least help you find suitable arrangements."

Eliza lifted her head, locks falling over her eyes. "He told me to seek work on one of the farms or in the village, and that Mrs. Morgan would recommend me as a servant."

"Has he no sympathy at all?"

"Obviously not. And he tells me to find a match on more *humble grounds* and made it plain he would not want me married to Langbourne. I am in agreement with him in that one thing. And there is more, Fiona. He wants you to remain here. Surely he is thinking someone needs to help the vicar's wife with her brood of children."

"I shall do nothing of the kind," Fiona said as she patted Eliza's shoulder. "My place is with you."

"You mustn't argue with him."

Fiona's eyes pooled and her cheeks turned bright red. "I will argue," she said. "I will shout if I must."

"But you have lived here since before I was born. This is your home. You are only saying that because of the promise you made to Papa."

"A promise is a promise, and I intend to keep mine." Fiona tossed her head back in defiance. "Mr. Morgan cannot force me to stay. Mind you, I've set aside a bit of money, and we shall fare just fine. Will that do for you?"

"I cannot take your money. I am to find employment. The chances of you finding a position in the same house as I are slim at best. Now do you see why you cannot get your hopes up?"

"I see your reason, my girl. But I won't go back on my word for anything."

Eliza took Fiona's hand in hers. "We shall figure something out, with God's help we shall. It is hard to imagine leaving the only home I have ever known. But if this is His will, then I must accept it."

"Perhaps you should consider Mr. Langbourne, Eliza. He'd give you a fine house, a bountiful table, and pretty clothes. You'd never lack."

For a moment, Eliza paused to consider Fiona's advice. But she did not love Langbourne, nor did she wish to grow to love him. "It would be sinful of me, Fiona," she said.

"How could that be?"

"It would be wrong to wed a man solely for my own comfort when I do not love him. And it would be unfair to Mr. Langbourne."

Fiona sighed. "True enough. But sometimes a woman has to take what she can in a situation like this."

Scooting off the bed, Eliza strode to the window. "Fiona," she said. "Do you remember Hayward Morgan?"

"That rascal of a boy?" Fiona straightened the coverlet hastily with her palms. "Aye, I remember him—spoiled rotten and proud."

"He has returned to Havendale." Suddenly, Eliza's despair lightened. Her heart seemed to settle to a calm rhythm, as a flicker of longing washed over her. She saw his face in her mind, his smile—the warmth of it perhaps only she could see. Yes, she saw good in him, and, instead of pride, drive and manly strength. She wanted him more than ever. Yet to have him—that seemed insurmountable, unless he changed his view and fell in love with her.

"I met him on the moor," she said, determined to paint him in a different light. "Two men attempted to accost me, and he stopped them. They had come upon me, insulted me, and tried to pull me down off my horse. No sooner had I begun to smack them with the reins than he came riding to my rescue. He fired at them and they ran off like a pair of frightened jackrabbits."

Fiona paused and placed her hands on her ample hips. "Gallant of him. But what does he have to do with anything?"

Eliza turned from the window. "The moment I laid eyes on him my heart soared."

"I am not surprised. Last I saw him he had tremendously good looks."

"It is more than his appearance that draws me to him. He said if I needed help, to come to Havendale. His mother might be able to give me a position. Surely she would help me if he asked."

Stepping away, she threw open the doors of her clothes cabinet and drew out her best dress. A vivid blue, it fit snug against her waist, and the three-quarter-length sleeves hung in a cascade of cream-colored lace. After laying it across the back of the chair, she quickly untied the ribbons on her bodice and stepped out of her day dress. Fiona looked surprised and Eliza smiled.

"I am going to Havendale."

A light dawned on Fiona's face. "Oh, I see what you're up to. You think he'd look on you if you come dressed so prettily?"

"Yes. Although I have viewed my beauty as a curse, and that men have only wanted me because of it, I will this one time use it to my advantage."

"Is that right to do? To lure him in that way?"

"He will quickly see my inner self, do not fear. I mean for Mrs. Morgan to offer me a position. I will win her over. Then I shall be around Hayward more. It was no accident that we happened upon each other . . . in the way we did. I owe him my virtue, if not my life. He is unalterably attached to me."

Fiona gasped. "He will not look on you as a prospective wife if you are reduced to being a servant in his father's house."

Eliza slipped a stocking on. "The fact he made mention of my station tells me he was considering me. His comment was to mask his attraction to me. It has happened before. God has given me the answer, Fiona. I shall win his heart. You'll see."

Fiona snatched the other stocking out of Eliza's hand. "'Tis foolish to think so. You should not get your hopes so high."

Eliza paused. Then she snatched back the stocking. "God knows the way through the wilderness. I think I know what I should do . . . or at least the first step I must take."

"Such a plan may not work. Then what will you do? They'll all be laughing at you for your efforts, and Mr. Langbourne will have naught to do with you afterwards."

Eliza slipped her other stocking on, fastened it about her thigh, and then went to pull on her gown. "Oh, the ribbon on this bodice has come loose, and it is my best gown." With a smile, she handed it to the bewildered Fiona. "Could you mend it, please, while I bathe?"

She had only seen Havendale in passing. Her father had been admitted on several occasions to minister to the family, but only when he was sent for, never of his own volition. As a child, Eliza remembered sitting outside the gates, chin in hand, staring at the old manor while she waited for her father to come out. It had not changed. Blond bricks made up its walls, and a lush green lawn lined with graceful trees and neatly trimmed boxwoods surrounded it. Slowly she rode her mare down the sandy lane with her eyes fixed on the glow of the candles set in two lower windows. A carriage stood outside the door, but company at Havendale would not prevent her from going on.

Once a stable boy secured her mare, she slipped her knee over the horn of the saddle and dismounted with the aid of another stable hand. Gathering her skirts, and her courage, she ascended the stone stairs to the door. She looked at the great iron knocker and hesitated before knocking twice.

A servant opened the door and showed her to a chair in a broad hallway that branched off to the left of her. The house reeked of cedar and old brandy, a strange combination, Eliza thought. Magenta light spread through westerly windows that lined the hall and burnished the mahogany paneled walls the color of port wine.

Twilight deepened, and she feared the lady of the house would not receive her at this hour. Minutes passed, and Eliza grew uneasy. She sat near pale yellow double doors that she surmised led to a sitting room. Behind the doors, she heard voices and light laughter. A maid with a silver tray laden with a tea service stepped past her. Eliza was amazed at how the woman managed to open the door and glide inside. But the maid left the door to the room slightly ajar, allowing Eliza to overhear the conversation within the room.

"I have an announcement to make," she heard Hayward say. And at the sound of his voice, she could not still the beat of her heart.

Then the door drifted back and closed.

4

There were two things Hayward Morgan knew he wanted—land, and a wife to help him build his legacy. She had to be of his class and religion, agree with his political views, preferably have a sizable dowry, come from a respectable upper class family, and be in excellent health and handsome. He had it all planned out, and as he stood from his chair and set his wine glass down on the table, he let his gaze fall on the beauty seated across from him.

The sight of Lilith Marsden's face roused mild, earthy desires in him. He slipped his finger through his neckcloth and loosened it, then met her green eyes. "I wish to speak to you alone," he said, bending toward her ear. "It is of the utmost importance."

"But what about your announcement?" Lilith whispered.

"It can wait." He stretched his hand out to her, and she lightly dropped her fingers into his. She gazed at him with shy surprise, and, with a swish of her skirts, they withdrew through a side door.

Hayward cared nothing what the rest of them in the room thought, but he caught his mother's expression, one that said she would grieve if he were to leave home again. He lowered his eyes and shut the door behind him.

Taking Lilith by the hand, he led her down a narrow corridor that the servants used, into the shadows where there were no windows, and where he thought they were alone. Her face shone through the gloom, and he looked down into it.

Yes, she made a perfect match for him. It had to be destined for them to wed. No doubt entered his mind that his father would approve—not by the way the old man had smiled at Lilith all evening and complimented her to her mother, the widow Marsden.

"Oh, I love surprises." Lilith's jade eyes sparkled.

"I am glad to hear it." Hayward drew her close and traced her jaw with his finger.

"Well, then? Do not keep me waiting in suspense, Hayward. I grow irritated by long pauses." She shook her head with a giggle, and her blonde ringlets bounced around her face.

"I have acquired land—rich land for farming and raising horses if I choose to. I have a fine house and mill."

"Land and a house. Other than Havendale?"

He had not told her his father had disinherited him and settled upon his cousin to gain his estate.

She sighed. "I am exceedingly happy for you . . . and for the fortunate woman who shall be mistress of it. Where is your house? Tell me it is in Derbyshire, for I love the countryside here. Or is it near London? I adore the city with all its distractions."

"No, it is far away," he replied.

Her smiled faded and she pouted. "Oh? Do not tell me it is too far, for that might cause me to be sad, and I do not wish to be sad, Hayward. We have only recently renewed our acquaintance, and I feel quite attached to you. Do you understand?"

"Yes, Lilith." He kissed her temple. "But before I tell you where it is, you must know there is one thing my estate lacks."

Again she sighed when he kissed her jaw. "And what may that be?"

"A lady. And if you decline what I am about to offer . . ."

Her lips parted. "I am listening."

". . . I will be disappointed."

"You hold me in suspense, sir. Tell me what it is you propose."

"I need a wife to guide my house and give me sons. She must be in superior health and of a willing nature, and she must desire above all else to please me . . . in obedience and in my bed." Through the dim light he saw her face flush scarlet. "I see my words have caused you embarrassment. Forgive me, but I have to be forthright."

She blinked and looked shyly away. "Indeed, I forgive you. Please go on."

He drew her into his arms. "I believe you are exactly what I need."

"Oh?"

"My father certainly approves of you."

"And my mother approves of you."

He brushed his mouth over her cheek.

"You mustn't do that," she said.

"Why not? You enjoy it, don't you?"

Her eyes gazed into his. "Yes, I suppose I do. But if you continue, I fear I shall surrender my will and answer your proposal too quickly."

He studied her expression and concluded her apprehension grew out of past experience. "You understand, then, what I am asking you?"

"Indeed, I do. I have hoped for this day. But first, tell me, where is your land, and what kind of house have you? I must know, if I am to live in it the rest of my life."

"I have named it River Run. The fields are as green as what you may find in Ireland, and the river murmurs like a cooing mother. Great forests surround it, and a peaceful stream runs through it. The house is large, and the mill is made of stone from the mountains."

"It sounds wonderful," she said, pressing a finger against his lips to silence him. "But by what river is this fine place? The River Tamar in Cornwall?"

He hesitated, and his muscles tightened. She could not think any further than England? "No. It is called the Potomac."

She stared at him, puzzled. "I do not recall any river by that name."

He glanced away, then looked at her again. "You ignorant darling. It flows between Maryland and Virginia."

She broke out of his arms and stepped back. "What? The Colonies?"

"I just told you it is."

"I do not care if it is in the Garden of Eden. I shall not go there to live. It is a wilderness, and I would be reduced to a workwoman. And there is talk of revolution. I cannot leave my mother. She is a widow. It would grieve her too deeply, and I am certain she would not approve of such an arrangement. No."

"You would be with me." He pulled her back by the arm. "I plan to be one of the richest landowners in Maryland. You can bring your dear mother along, if she is willing."

"The answer is still *no*. I will stay in England where I belong. Buy land here and give me a fine house, and I shall say yes."

Hayward bit down on his lip as she glided away. Once, she turned and looked back at him, lifted her chin, and went on.

The sting of her rejection and her demands coursed through him, and he clenched his fists at his sides. How could she have turned him down? Did insanity run in the females of her family?

He turned in the opposite direction, toward the corner that led into the grand hallway. The light from the windows brightened as he neared the corner. Strange—a mild scent of lavender and rosewater wafted in the air. As he turned, a silhouette of a woman's face, her broad hat, and a cascade of loose ebony curls brushed the wall in shadow.

He stopped short. With a gasp, Eliza arose from a chair.

As soon as she sprang to her feet, heat rushed over her face as if she had come close to a fire. She drew in her breath and wished she could fade into the wall away from his startled gaze and piercing eyes, a step or two farther into the shadows.

The light fell over his shoulders. His brows furrowed, and he stared down at her as if she were a serving wench. Her gown did not match his rich attire. He was dressed in the finest linen, with fine leather boots, and a black crepe ribbon tied his hair back into a ponytail. Perhaps Fiona had been right, she should not get her hopes too high.

He did not look the part of a man bent on living in the colonial wilds. When she tried to imagine him pushing a plow, pitching hay, or milking a cow, a cynical smile spread over her face.

The silence grew louder than speech, and she gave him a slight curtsy and addressed him. "I have come to speak with your mother, sir. You had advised me to do so. Remember?"

He shifted on his feet. "She is engaged."

"I do not mind waiting." She lowered herself back into the chair.

"You are dressed . . . well, not as I last saw you. Your hair . . ."

"I do know the attire of a lady, sir, even though I have no claim to a title or come from a family of aristocrats."

"Aristocrats? Hardly." Hayward paused and cleared his throat. "The servant should not have kept you sitting in the hallway. My mother will not meet with you. We have guests, which you probably realized, as I was speaking to one close enough for you to hear our conversation."

Eliza bit her lip and withdrew her gaze when she saw him catch the action with his eyes, eyes that softened and admired. She stood. "I shall go then, and call on her tomorrow."

"Your reason for seeing her?"

"When you and I met out on the moor, after you chased away those ruffians, you said that if I needed employment, to come to Havendale, that your mother would find something for me. I am hoping she will."

"I learned my father gave you notice. It is only expected that a new vicar should arrive to replace your father. I grew concerned and spoke to her about your situation."

Hope revived within Eliza. "You did?"

"Your father was our family pastor. I did not wish to see you on the streets begging—figuratively, of course—for I doubt you would find a husband in this dire situation. You should not have rejected Langbourne. Men do not easily forget or forgive rejection."

"My opinion of Mr. Langbourne has not changed. I know I should not speak to you of such personal issues, but I will not marry one whom I do not love. I shall come to Havendale and work for your family. There is no shame in that."

He paused and stepped closer. "I am afraid there is nothing here for you, and my father hasn't the money to spend. Haven't you any family to go to? An aunt or uncle perhaps? There is your brother. Surely he would help his sister."

Eliza's hopes were dashed instantly, but she refused to let him see her disappointment. God had some way, other than hers, in mind. "No. My brother, I have only just learned, is dead." She lowered her head.

"I am sorry." He paused, then said, "I wish you good fortune, Miss Bloome."

He turned on his heel to leave.

"Please, Hayward. Do not leave. I will go with you to America."

Astonished, he turned to face her. "What did you say?"

"I will go with you . . . to America. I am not afraid to do it. I can work hard, and I am in perfect health. I have a keen mind, too, and a head for figures. I could help you with the books. And I know how to milk a cow and shoe a horse."

"You overhead my conversation with Miss Marsden," he said, affronted.

"I could not help it. There was no place else to go."

He looked away, his mouth twisting. "It is my fault for assuming no one would overhear. I should have taken her to another room. Did I hear you correctly that . . ."

She met his eyes with a lift of her chin. "What you offered Miss Marsden is indeed beyond what she deserves from the way she treated you, solely because your land is in the Colonies." She saw his jaw tighten but went on. "It is the chance to build a legacy. To find freedom. She is too blind and too spoiled to see the good in your offer."

"You mustn't speak of your betters in such a manner. You are a bold creature."

"I admit I am."

For a long moment, he gazed into her face, and she waited for him to speak. "No," he finally said.

Amazed he would deny her, she looked him straight in the eyes with a challenge. "Why? I have all that you seek. In this instance, I daresay I am far superior than Miss Marsden."

His eyes glinted with superiority. "I cannot wed a vicar's daughter."

"At least, as a vicar's daughter, I have been raised to be a good woman, not spoiled like your lady who just threw you over. If she loved you, she would go anywhere with you."

He laughed. "And you are saying you do."

"Well . . . I suppose I am."

He gave her a short bow. "I am flattered. But there is the matter that I do not love you, Eliza. For all your beauty, some would say it is amazing that I do not."

Stung into silence, Eliza swallowed the lump that formed in her throat. She did not think him cruel, only honest. But what monstrous pride had he! Why on earth would she even consider such a man? At the least, Langbourne wanted her. But not this man. He treated her as if she were a child. She dug in her heels, resolute not to lose his attention. She raised her eyes slowly and forced a sweet smile.

"Do not think me so dull as not to know it, sir. At the same time, I can see you really do regard me with some affection. Can you deny it?"

"Affection or attraction, madam?"

"Either, and the chance of you being in love with me had not crossed my mind. How could you love me? You do not know me well enough, nor have you spent sufficient time with me to know my mind. Most likely, you do not love Miss Marsden. If you were in love with her, you would give up your American dream and give her what she wants."

"This is awkward indeed." He touched her throat and caressed it. The shock it gave caused her to tremble. "You are certainly beautiful and chaste, Eliza, and I have no doubt you are as strong as you say, but you are meanly born."

She slapped his hand aside. "Oh, how dare you speak to me of lowering yourself? If anything, it is I that has been humbled by offering my hand to you . . . my life. Here a highborn woman has turned you down, and I willingly break all the rules by saying I would be your wife, help you build your estate, bear your children, be willing to leave my homeland for a wilderness, and you call me meanly born? Oh, sir, your enormous pride is an affront, no doubt, to everyone who encounters you."

Insulted, the muscles on his face jerked. He grabbed her by the arms and pressed her against him. His mouth went near hers, but did not touch.

"The answer . . . is . . . no." His breath caressed her lips and she whimpered. He released her and stormed away.

Eliza stood alone in the dusky hallway battling tears. She shut her eyes and allowed the droplets to fall down her cheeks, standing alone in a house she now hated.

5

*W*eary of packing her father's clothes in a wicker hamper, Eliza folded the last garment Matthias Bloome had owned and gently placed it on top of the others. She ran her hand over the stark white linen shirt, then closed the lid and secured it.

She pushed the basket against the wall next to the door. Every plate, spoon, and saucer. Every book, and every bit of furniture. Every candle and candlestick. All the linens. All the carpets. Everything, except Eliza's clothes, Bible, brush and comb, and her mother's locket, would be given to others.

The room chilled from the keen wind that blew outside. She drew a wrap over her shoulders, determined not to shed any more tears, but to finish her tasks without grief interrupting her. The tears came anyway, and Eliza wiped them aside. She stood, took herself to the window, and leaned against its broad frame. Heavy-hearted, she gazed out at the land beyond the door of the humble vicarage.

While the sun sunk low, she shut her eyes and listened to a long, whistling breath of wind. A nightjar cried out to its mate. A fortnight had passed since her confrontation with Hayward. Twice since then they had encountered each other, she on foot, and he on a horse she thought matched his arrogance. He tipped his hat to her, gave her a greeting, and then went on. Six agonizing days had passed, and this was her last night in this house. She pondered. Perhaps she had misread those strong inner promptings. Hayward may have forgotten all about her by now. He had said no to her, had he not?

Fiona rushed inside the room. A broad smile brightened her face. "I have been sent a letter," she said excitedly. "It is for a position in London. A wealthy gentleman and his new bride are in need of a housekeeper." She glanced down at the letter, cleared her throat, and adjusted her spectacles. "And they are in need of a chambermaid. This shall do us both well. What do you say?"

"I accept, if nothing else arises by tomorrow. And even so, Hayward may need more time. If I do not hear from him by then, I shall write and tell him where I have gone."

Fiona sighed. "Oh, dear girl. You have not given up hope, but your expectations soar too high."

"I suppose it was foolish of me to go rushing off to Havendale like I did," Eliza replied. "Reckless and desperate. What made me think he would want me?"

"Do not be so harsh on yourself. First of all, was it not Mr. Hayward who told you to come to the house if you needed work? You should blame him."

"He did. But he made no guarantee of anything. Perhaps Mrs. Morgan does not like me. . . . And I did not believe Hayward when he said his father hadn't the means to hire anyone. He is the richest man in the county."

Fiona straightened her back and put her hands over her broad hips. "Don't you see? The gentry do not prefer girls like you to work in their houses. You are a threat to both wives and fiancées. Young men find you beautiful despite your station, and your presence would be a temptation to indiscretion. Believe me, I know what I'm saying."

Fiona folded the letter and stuffed it in her pocket. She then stripped the sheets from the bed and tossed them on the floor. She opened another and shook it out.

"How do you know? Tell me."

"Oh, it was years ago . . . when I was a young girl. I fell in love with my master's son." Fiona spread a fresh sheet over the bed and tucked in a corner. "He was handsome, and enamored with me. We began to meet in secret, but his father found out and sent him off into the army and me packing. I never saw my young man again."

"How sad. And you never married. Was it because of your love for him?"

With a sigh, Fiona shook her head and tossed a pillow against the bolster. "I never found a man like him . . . ever. Oh, there were a few who asked me to wed them, but I couldn't bring myself to do it—to marry someone I did not love."

"Then you understand me, Fiona."

"Indeed I do, my girl."

"You understand why I turned Langbourne down. It gives me ease that you do."

"I never said anything about it, but I did not want to see you unhappy. I held my tongue from your father, but not from the Almighty. But I have been thinking. With your situation the way it is, to leave the house and all, I hate to see you working as a servant. You are too good for that kind of life. Maybe you should reconsider Mr. Langbourne."

Eliza looked away and huffed. "You said that once before. You know I love Hayward. I cannot see myself with anyone but him."

"Now, he is a different story, Eliza. Can you not see how prideful he is? He has a fierce streak about him. I doubt he could love anybody, save for himself. You had good intentions when you went to Havendale. But your emotions got the best of you. I cannot imagine what he thought when you said you would go to America with him. Do you not see how forward that was?"

Eliza stared at the clock on the mantelpiece, the one that had not been wound since her papa had passed away, her mind leaping forward to what she hoped the future would be. Yet she worried. No letter. No message of any kind.

"The sky is filling with clouds," she said. "But I doubt it shall rain. At least not for another day or two."

Fiona stamped her foot. "Eliza, my girl. Did you hear what I said?"

"I did, Fiona." She turned to a box filled with books. "Well, I believe that is the last of it. I hate to part with Papa's books, but I cannot take them with me. They will do the new vicar good. Papa would be pleased for him to have them."

"Eliza, do not put all your hopes in Mr. Hayward. He would have sent word by now."

Eliza opened one of the books and let the pages flutter, closed it, and put it back in its place. "You are right. I suppose I must learn that what I want is not what is marked out for me. And Hayward—he is so difficult to read. One moment his eyes were all storm and tempest. The next bewildered. I cannot say what he will do. I cannot explain it."

That night, Eliza lay in her bed for the last time. Unable to sleep, and feeling anxious, she tucked her arms behind her head and gazed up at the ceiling, at the full, misty beams of moonlight that came through her window.

"Wherever thou shall lead me, I will go," she whispered. "Whatever you have planned for me, I will accept. Only give me the desires of my heart, Lord, for I long for Hayward. I would make him a good wife. I want a home and children, and I know I could make him happy, that he would grow to love me. But if I have been wrong, and he is not for me, help me accept your will."

The clock down the hall struck. Once, twice, on to six, then nine times, she counted out the bells, until they ceased at twelve. Midnight had come. A fox barked somewhere out on the downs, and for one night, the wind lay low.

She threw back the covers, brought her bare legs over the edge, and waited. There beside her door sat her bag. In it, she had packed her clothes and the few possessions she owned. She balled the sheet in her fist and moaned. She did not want to go to London. She did not want to be a lady's maid, serve the idle rich, and endure the congestion of a city.

She stood and paced the floor in her bare feet. Was she being stubborn? Hadn't she just prayed the Lord's will be done in her life? Then why did she feel so downcast? With a will, she tried to gather her thoughts together, and listen to that still, small voice that spoke quietly into her soul.

Wistfully, she drew in a breath, long and steady, and then went to the writing table beneath her window. From a drawer she pulled out paper, and lifted the quill from the china ink-well. Settling into the chair, she dipped the quill back into the ink, then held it over the sheet of paper.

"I must choose either poverty and servitude, or a comfortable life."

She hesitated a moment. Then she lowered the quill and wrote . . .

Dear Mr. Langbourne,

Having received your letter after our last meeting, I am now compelled to reply once more to your proposal . . .

6.

When the beat of horses' hooves and the roll of carriage wheels drew near, Eliza lifted her pen away from the paper, placed it back into the inkwell, and moved to the window. Along the hilltop that overlooked the vicarage, at the crossroads where the moon bathed the night sky deep purple and shone brightest, a gentleman's carriage rambled toward her as a black silhouette.

As the carriage rumbled closer, she watched a lean figure leap down from a horse and sprint toward the house. A moment later, someone pounded upon the front door. Quick as she could, Eliza pulled on her day dress of brown linen instead of her robe. She took her candle in hand and went out into the hall, where she met Fiona. The woman had hastily donned her robe, and her cap sat awry above a pair of anxious eyes.

Fiona puffed out a breath. "At this hour? Who would be so rude as to wake us in the middle of the night?"

"We won't know until we open the door."

"I would not advise that," Fiona said, following Eliza.

Together they hurried down the stairs to the door. Eliza reached for the latch.

"It may be the new vicar and his family arriving early."

"Wait," said Fiona in a low voice. "You cannot be too sure. Ask who it is first. It could be robbers."

Wise words, Eliza agreed. "Who is there?" she called out. "What is it you want?"

"A messenger, ma'am, from Mr. Hayward Morgan."

Setting the candle down, Eliza drew back the bolt and peered outside. On the doorstep stood the boy who had taken her horse the day she went to Havendale.

"Sorry to wake you. But he says it's important, and waits in his carriage to speak to you."

"Tell Mr. Morgan I shall meet with him."

"Eliza?" said Fiona.

"Shh. Mr. Hayward has come all this way in the middle of the night, and it would be discourteous of me to send him away."

With a nod, the boy hurried back to the carriage, where he leaned up and spoke through the window. Eliza snatched her cloak off the hook and swung it over her shoulders. Fiona looked worried. "Do not be anxious for me," Eliza said. "Wait here by the door."

She paused on the threshold to gather her courage and to calm the swift beating of her heart. Had he come to tell her he had changed his mind and wanted her? It had to be. Why else would a man go to such trouble so late at night? Eager, she stepped outside, with her hands hoisting her gown away from the dirt in the road. She walked past the horses to the carriage door. The boy opened it and moved aside.

Hayward held out a petitionary hand. "Will you sit inside with me a moment so we may speak?" This time his voice lacked condescension; it held a tone that said he hoped she would follow his request. "We must speak alone, you and I."

He is taking me away to America with him. She lifted her chin. "I am already prepared to leave upon your father's demand. Has he sent you to rush me out earlier than requested."

His eyes glowed in the moonlight when he leaned forward. "Come inside and I will explain."

Eliza took Hayward's hand, climbed in, and sat opposite him. Darkness lay within the compartment, but still she could make out his eyes, and then his face, as the light from the coach lamps slipped through the window.

She drew back her hood, allowing her ebony locks to gently fall forward. She saw the sudden warm glimmer in his eyes and knew there would be no prejudice on his part or hindrance to what he had to say.

"Ever since the day you came to Havendale and offered to leave with me, my mind has not let go of it."

His description of her proposal chafed her. "I offered to leave with you only as your wife. If you have come to suggest something different, you are wasting your time."

Hayward drew back, looking stunned. "I have not forgotten your exact words, madam. I understood you meant marriage. I have fought the idea, but I must confess to you that I admire, dare I say adore you, though it has been from afar these years."

Somewhat jubilant at his confession, Eliza held back, uncertain whether to believe him or not. This time she decided not to be so anxious. "I see. For years, you say?"

"Yes. I never imagined telling you, but I left you standing in the hall alone. I was very rude to you. No woman has ever stood up to me as you did. Nor has one made as much sense."

"And you came all this way in the middle of the night to tell me this?"

"There is more to why I have come. That was just the preamble."

"The rest?"

"I am leaving Havendale—tonight. I will be aboard a ship bound for America within the week. I am never coming back."

Never? The very word pricked her. "That is a pity. You have only been back such a short while. But it comes as no surprise to me. You made it clear you would be leaving. And so you should, now that you have land and . . ."

He leaned forward and looked into her eyes. "Eliza, stop talking."

The silence grew taut, and she wished she could turn into his arms. But she moved to the door and held out her hand. "I wish you well. Goodbye."

The second she put her hand on the latch to open the door, Hayward clapped his hand over hers and pulled her close. "Not goodbye. Not if you meant what you said before."

The warmth of his hand in hers and his nearness to her caused her breath to quicken. "I do not lie. I meant every word."

His eyes locked onto hers. "For love alone?"

She lowered her gaze. "You may not understand, but it is true."

"But I do not feel as you do. I have no idea what it means to be in love, the way women describe it. I can love you for your beauty, for your passion for life, but a man does not feel as deeply as a woman."

He does not know, Lord, that what he says is wrong. Show him, please, what love means.

"So despite that, will you have me as I am, Eliza, and come away with me? I think it would solve both our problems."

Her mouth parted, but she could not get the words out.

"It will be a difficult life at first—far different from here," he said. "I am willing to accept you as my wife, if you are willing to accept the kind of life I offer you and make no demands on me in the way of lavish living. Though I have money, I must be frugal."

She lifted her eyes, her conviction growing stronger. "I am willing. I am convinced of my course."

"There is something else you need to know before saying yes. My father will denounce me when he learns I have married you."

"But the banns will be posted and he will know beforehand."

"Not if we leave tonight and go to Gretna Green."

"Scotland?"

"It will be a long journey. But we can marry without the restrictions of English laws."

"In God's eyes?"

"In God's eyes . . . Once, I would have agreed with my father that you are not a suitable wife for me due to your class, but then you have come back to haunt my thoughts day and night. Among all the women I have known, I have not met one with your determination or courage."

"I thank you for the compliment. But your mother? I cannot help but think of the heartbreak this will cause her, the pain of being separated from you. She is acquainted with such, I believe."

"Ah, I see. You are thinking of my half brother leaving England to seek his fortune. Though I seriously doubt he shall find it as a botanist."

"With you gone, your mother will have no one."

"Indeed, she will be grieved that I follow in Will's footsteps. But time will mend her sorrow. She has practically forgotten her firstborn . . . She will forget me as well."

Bewildered that this could happen, Eliza said, "I cannot hurt her."

He drew her close. "You are hurting no one."

"Then promise you will try to make things right with your father. You must ease their disappointment somehow."

"I am not accustomed to a woman telling me what to do. But if it pleases you, I shall write to them and explain everything. But there is no guarantee things will change."

"Well, at least you would have tried. I would have thought your father would be proud of the accomplishment you have made in America. Perhaps in time, he will be." For a moment she looked deeply into his eyes. "You are certain, beyond all doubt, you want me as your wife? You will hold to me and no other for the rest of your life?"

"I am a man of my word, Eliza. I take seriously this matter of marrying you." He gently kissed her cheek. Up to this point, she had been only hopeful, not fully persuaded—not until this expression of tender emotion.

"It is exciting to think of beginning a new life in a new land, is it not?"

Eliza smiled. "Yes." She poked her head out. "We are leaving to marry, Fiona."

Wide-eyed, Fiona quickly turned back inside the house. Moments later, and breathless from rushing about, she reappeared on the doorstep with their belongings in hand, dressed with a cloak of old gray wool over her shoulders. "Good thing we were already packed and ready to go, my girl. I hope I have not forgotten anything."

"Quick, Fiona," Hayward said, stepping out and striding to his horse. "If you intend to come with us, then close the door behind you and climb inside."

7

The first scarlet glimmer of dawn crept over the treetops as Eliza opened her eyes. She had dreamt she was back at the vicarage, her father quietly preparing a sermon by the fire in his study. He looked at her over his steel spectacles and smiled, closed his books, and then walked from the room. She followed him, saying, "I am to be Hayward Morgan's wife, Papa." He turned with the Holy Scriptures tucked beneath his arm and smiled. Then the dream ended. She took comfort in it, that he would approve of her choice of husband.

Now that she was awake to the real world, her emotions surged within her—joy one moment, trepidation prickling over her skin the next. They had gone some distance, changing coaches, and making headway over the road northward. She stretched her limbs as best she could inside the cramped carriage. Sound asleep, Fiona's head nodded against her chest in time with the horses' quick steps and the roll of the wheels over roads both smooth and rough. She snored loudly, and Eliza stifled a laugh.

Hayward! She peered out the window. He rode upon his horse toward the rear, and lifted his hand. She waved back and smiled lightly, her heart trembling in her breast. He must be weary, having been in the saddle all through those dark hours with only the moon and coach lamps to guide his mount over the lonely road north.

The sun brightened. The moon descended, and the day drew on. They crossed the River Sark on the toll road near to sunset. Candles burned in the windows, and a narrow walkway made of pebbles went from the road to Joseph Paisley's marriage shop.

"I have no wedding clothes," said Eliza, when Hayward dismounted and approached the coach door. "Does it disappoint you?"

"Not at all. You are beautiful as you are."

The blush in Eliza's cheeks deepened, and she gazed into his intent eyes. "Indeed, wedding clothes would have been a frivolous waste of money," she said, hoping to please him. The gown she wore had been new by a few months, pretty, made of soft brown linen over a white chemise. And when she saw how he cast his eyes over her bodice as it peeked through her cloak, she knew he accepted her as she came to him.

She woke Fiona, and they stepped out into the pale morning light. Eliza held the hand Hayward offered. Her eyes followed the straight line of the path that led to an oaken door. "We shall not wed in a church?"

He leaned closer. "'Where there are two or three gathered in my name, there I am in the midst of you.' Remember?"

She nodded. With anticipation stirring within her, she watched him push open the door and step inside.

"I am doing the right thing, Fiona. Hayward and I belong together, and I will follow him wherever he may go."

Fiona looped her arm through Eliza's. "Mr. Morgan is a fortunate man to gain a wife who loves him as you do."

"I am the one who is fortunate to have such a man. He is as strong as he is brave."

"Do not discount your own bravery, my girl. Your willingness to leave England and live with him in an unknown land is more than most would ever agree to."

"Yes, and you are just as courageous to come with me. Ah, but my heart trembles for him."

"Why?"

"He has yet to feel the pangs of true love, nor the passion and devotion that comes with it."

She watched him turn and hold his hand out to her. She lifted her skirts and hurried forward. The *priest*, as Joseph Paisley was called, greeted them warmly in a heavy Scottish accent. His wispy hair was brushed over his ears. A fleshy, large man, his collar hugged his ample neck. His eyes were large and misty, his cheeks ruddy.

He stood with his legs wide apart, his Anglican prayer book tucked beneath his beefy arm, his gaze upon Eliza as she walked inside. A petite woman came through a side door, dressed in a homespun gown of a shade matching her light russet hair, and stepped up beside the anvil that stood between Mr. Paisley and them.

"Who comes to murry?" said Paisley.

Hayward moved forward with Eliza. "Hayward Morgan of Havendale and Miss Eliza Bloome—Derbyshire."

"Did ye come of yer own free will, Miss Bloome?"

"Yes, sir," she replied.

"And who is witness to this union?"

Fiona stepped from behind the couple. "I am, sir."

Eliza placed her hand in Hayward's, and he closed his fingers over hers. They were warm and strong, and unwilling to let go. The vows were read and repeated, and Paisley struck his anvil. "God be wi' ye! Yer murried!"

Hayward turned Eliza to face him. With shining eyes, he looked down into hers, and placed his hands on each side of her face.

"Kiss h'r, man." Paisley gave him a little nudge on his shoulder. "What are ye waitin' fer?"

And so Hayward bent his head and tenderly kissed Eliza. No man had touched her lips before. He was the first, and she vowed he would be the last. For all her goodness and faith, could she ever conceive of breaking her vows? *Never*. Could she fall if he neglected her, hurt her, or failed to reach the heights of love? *Never*, she repeated in her mind.

As he lifted his mouth away from hers, she gazed up at him breathless, through a mist of tears. With the way he kissed, how could he not love her? His kiss spoke of love. It spoke of devotion.

"You are unhappy, Eliza? Why the tears?"

She shook her head. "Because I am happy."

Fiona stepped forward and looped her arm within Eliza's. She looked at Hayward with the protective stare of a mother. "And see to it, sir, that she remains that way."

Hayward paid Paisley his fee, and he sat down and recorded the marriage. Outside came the pounding of hooves, and he hurried to finish. The door swung open with a crash. With a gait most urgent, a gentleman dressed in a dark brown overcoat and riding boots stormed forward. He stopped short and heaved his chest to catch his breath, then dragged off his hat.

"Stop this at once. Proceed no further!" His stern eyes locked onto Hayward, then flashed over Eliza with a quiver of his mouth that showed disgust. "Tell me it isn't so, that you have gone and married this girl."

Hayward drew Eliza close to his side. "I have, Father. I said I would if she'd have me."

"How can you be so foolish? What are you thinking?"

"On my life, sir, wish us well. It is done. We are man and wife."

"Are you mad? You have deliberately defied me, and you have affronted your cousin, knowing full well he had an attachment to this girl."

Hayward sneered. "I apologize, Langbourne," and he gave him a rude bow.

"Mind your manners, boy," his father warned. Eliza cringed from the way he spoke to Hayward. Why did Edward Morgan despise her?

Hayward stiffened. "I have made my choice. So has Eliza. Do not hate us for it."

Purple with anger and almost choking with frustration, Morgan shook his fist. "How could you be so callous, so rebellious? You have broken Lilith's heart by running off with this girl when it was understood you and she would wed."

A laugh slipped from Hayward on the last word. "Is that what she told you? If she did, she is a liar. I offered her marriage, but she did not like the conditions and refused me. I realized she is too spoiled to live the kind of life I would require. Eliza is far superior to Miss Marsden. What did you hope to gain by following us here, Father?"

"I hoped to bring you to your senses, but I see I am too late."

Eliza followed Hayward's stare, as he looked past his father to the dejected man standing in the doorway. She felt sorry for Langbourne, but what could she do? Hat in hand, Langbourne said nothing. Only his eyes showed emotion, and they were inflamed with unrelenting anger.

"You there," Edward Morgan addressed Paisley. "Undo this."

"What is done in the Lord's name is binding. Leave them in peace."

"My son has rebelled against my wishes. Surely that should account for something in the *Lord's* eyes."

"I believe your son is of an age where God honors his vow, even if you do not."

Morgan shifted his stare to his son. "You have no right, Hayward, to do as you please, no matter what this man says, or vows you have spoken."

Hayward approached him. "Eliza is my wife and now your daughter-in-law. She desires what I desire. A new life on my own land, built by my own hands through my own means. Wish us well, for I do not know when, or if, I shall ever see you again."

His father shook with unrestrained emotion. "I shall never speak your name again. I shall carry out my threat and cut you off from gaining anything from my estate. You are no longer my son."

Hayward made no reply, but Eliza could see how hurtful Morgan's words were. When Morgan jerked away from his son and stormed out, Hayward turned away. Langbourne stood silent near the door. For a brief moment he and Eliza looked at one another—his stare fierce under the sting of her rejection.

"You knew my mind," she said to him. "But for hurting you as I have, I am sorry. Let us remain friends, you and I and Hayward, and please know that you will always be welcomed in our home if you should ever journey to Maryland."

Langbourne's eyes narrowed. He clenched his teeth and gave her a look so cold it caused her to shiver. "I have lost you, but have inherited a fortune."

After Langbourne left, she went to her husband. Was it too late to mend such a breach? Could Hayward leave with this weighing on him—weighing on her? She ran her hand down the sleeve of his coat. "Go speak to your father. Do not let him leave on these terms. The fact that he traveled so far to find us shows he cares."

"He has made his choice."

"Yes, but you can change his mind, if you hurry . . . and . . ."

"You would have me lower myself? You would have me cower and beg in order to gain his forgiveness?"

It was too late. Outside the riders galloped off.

Hayward nodded farewell to the stunned couple standing behind the wedding anvil, then picked up his hat and placed it firmly on his head. The power of his father's rejection shone in his eyes. His jaw clenched, and his hands flexed. Placing his hand on Eliza's back, he moved her to the door and down the path. Eliza gazed at the sky. There were no clouds to hinder a darkening sky, where a gibbous moon hung alongside Venus.

"You love me, do you not, Eliza?" Hayward looked keenly into her eyes; his were the deepest and most soul-searching she had ever seen.

"Yes, I love you, Hayward. I have since I was a little girl. And I will until the day I die."

"That is all that matters to me." He took her hand and led her to the carriage. "Let us leave this place. We have a long journey ahead of us."

8

They traveled on and slept their first night together at a carriage inn, after dining on roasted chicken, freshly baked rolls slathered in creamy butter, potatoes, and carrots—a hefty meal in comparison to what she was accustomed to. She came to him softly, and he held her in his arms through the night.

In the morning, they made their way to the port along Solway Firth. Boats of various kinds and sizes were moored there, and the docks were cluttered with people, crates, horses, and barrels. In Eliza's imagination, tall ships were a thing of luxury and beauty. As she stood on the deck of the *Isadora May*, she took in the height of the masts and the soft swell of the sails as they were lowered and billowed in the sea breeze. The ship made its way out to the Irish Sea in a lusty wind. The planks of the deck quivered with the throng of people. Passengers and crew mingled around her—men, women, and children, all bound for a new land.

With Hayward in the lead, Eliza and Fiona were escorted through a doorway to the deck below. A small cabin, providing room for only one occupant, with very little space to maneuver in and less fresh air to revive the body, would be

Eliza's for the duration of the voyage. With a single cot, a small writing table, and a folding canvas chair, disappointment overwhelmed her when she stepped inside. She turned to her husband and sought the reason why their accommodations were so lowly and not together.

Hayward leaned against the opening. "I do not think I have ever seen anyone look as dejected as you do right now, Eliza. I am sorry our conditions are as they are, but I am right next to you. Fiona's little hovel is even smaller. I had no idea it would be this way."

"The ship you arrived in was not like this?"

"Much the same, I am afraid. I was expecting better this time."

She used humor to bear up under the weight of disappointment. "I suppose we can whisper good night to each other through the wall."

"I suppose we can. And there is no reason to be confined down here the entire time. We will take walks up on deck as often as you wish. Wait until you see the glory of the stars out at sea."

Eliza sighed and drew near to him. She coiled her arms around his waist and laid her head against the breast of his coat. "I shall like that, and will spend very little time in this little hutch. You'll see. I shall make the best of it."

The first month out at sea, gusty winds blew down from the northeast, and the ship cut through the waves at a pace where even the dolphins could not keep up. On the fifth week at sea, fever broke out among the passengers, and the sick were confined to their cabins with only one steward to attend them and a ship's surgeon to administer to their medical needs. Every precaution was made to keep the fever from spreading. Decks and floors were scrubbed twice daily. Chamber pots emptied almost immediately instead of left to linger. The ship's surgeon insisted on it, much to the doubts voiced by the captain that sanitary efforts would do much good.

As the days went by, more grew sick, and the supply of paregoric ran out. Eliza offered the surgeon her help, but he refused her each time and told her to avoid anyone with a cough.

"My servant and I both know how to care for sick people, sir," she told him one afternoon as she stood outside the door of an infected passenger. "My father was a vicar, and we gave aid to the ill in our church. Most could not afford a doctor, and . . ."

"I would prefer, madam, that you stay out of my way." He looked her up and down with a pair of beady gray eyes. She had seen him in the mess, and knew he had no lack of appetite and would scarf down enough food for two. Yet his clothes hung loose over a very lean frame, his face so narrow and thin one could see the bones protruding in his cheeks.

"I will," said Eliza. "But you cannot stop me from giving comfort to those who accept it."

He pursed his lips and narrowed his eyes. "Hmm. Do as you wish. Only do not interfere. I am the doctor here, not you or your servant."

In spite of him, she took it upon herself to visit, along with Fiona, those who were ailing. Together they washed their faces and spooned broth into their mouths. She read to them, talked, and prayed with them. The ship's surgeon took all the credit when anyone recovered.

Hayward grew anxious after the surgeon alerted him to what his wife and female servant were doing. When a man's young wife died, he ordered her to stop. Eliza stood beside him when the woman's body, wrapped in canvas, slipped off a plank into a watery grave.

He heard the grieving husband say, "We were only married a few months." And, "We left Britain to begin a new life in the Colonies."

The captain stood beside him, opened a prayer book, and recited along with the passengers and crew the Lord's Prayer. Hayward felt a sting of dread pass through him when he saw the man cry as the body went over the edge of the ship and splashed into the ocean.

Later that evening, he found Eliza sitting with a woman close to Fiona's age. By the door, he watched her. With care, she put a tin cup to the woman's mouth and helped her drink. Her compassion amazed him.

"You must drink all you can. It will help you get well." She wiped the woman's mouth with a cloth.

"Thank you, Mrs. Morgan," the woman said, her voice raspy and low. "You are so kind and have lifted my spirits. I know I shall recover because of you. I didn't think anyone cared, me being a person of low estate."

Eliza patted the woman's hand. "It should not matter, Matilda. We are all God's children and equal in His eyes. Good news. Your fever has broken."

Hayward snatched Eliza by the arm and pulled her away. "You must stop."

She looked up at him, wide-eyed. "Why? I have done nothing wrong."

"You are interfering with the surgeon's duties. And this fever is contagious. You could catch it. As your husband, I order you not to help these people."

Her eyes filled, and she looked down at the floor. "I will obey you, Hayward. But it makes me sad to do so." And she hurried away from him, back to her modest compartment.

He heard her sob, and would have opened the door and tried to comfort her. But he determined he should not spoil her in that way. Tears were a woman's tool, and he refused to be persuaded by them. If he gave in, and the fever took hold of her and she died, he would be responsible.

Fearing for his wife's health, Hayward approached the captain and demanded other quarters away from the sick. The captain stood on the quarterdeck, his feet set firm with the rise of the ship over another wave.

He refused with a shake of his head. "No, sir. You've paid your fare, and that is what you get for it."

Hayward, too, set his boots firm and stood his ground. "There must be something else besides that hellhole you call a cabin, sir. I insist you remove my wife away from the infection immediately, preferably with large windows so she may have the air."

Annoyed, the captain glanced at Hayward and lifted his face to the wind. Tufts of steel-gray hair blew away from his ears beneath his black cocked hat. His face looked tough as boot leather, weathered and heavily lined from the sun and sea. He smelled of sweat and brine, and rubbed the stubble on his chin.

"What if every passenger demanded new quarters, Mr. Morgan?" Eyes fixed straight ahead, he went up and down on his toes, hands folded behind his back. "What would I do then? And why should I give your wife preference?"

Determined, Hayward dug his hand into his breast pocket. "Because I have the extra coin to make it happen, sir. A gold piece should suffice. Now, will you find her other quarters or not?"

The captain lifted his wispy brows and looked down at the shiny coin in Hayward's palm. "I believe I might. If you would follow my steward, he will show you what we have."

He waved the steward over, leaned to his ear, and gave him an order. "We shall do this quietly, Mr. Morgan. I do not want the other passengers knowing. It would cause unpleasantness. Your wife is favored, sir—the quarters next to mine are reserved for dignitaries."

Hayward thanked the captain and dropped the coins into his hand. He then followed the steward through the door and down a set of steep stairs into the gloom. The lad carried a large iron ring of keys and shoved one into the lock. It clicked, and he pushed open the door. A bed with room enough for two, a table, two chairs, a writing desk, and a washstand, were more than adequate. Windows lined the rear of the cabin, and the steward opened them to air the quarters out.

Pleased he had made such excellent progress in convincing the captain to move Eliza, and that he could share the cabin with his wife, Hayward stepped out and ordered the steward to fetch Eliza's belongings. He found her up on deck.

"I have a surprise, Eliza. I think you will be pleased." He drew her away from the ship's rail where she gazed out at the choppy waves and the seabirds that whirled in the sky.

"What is it?" She looked at him, intrigued.

"You will see." He held out his hand and took her down the steps to the corridor.

When he opened the door and brought her inside to her new lodgings, her face blushed from her throat to her hair.

"We will be together for the remainder of the voyage." He closed the door.

She turned to him, her skirts whispering along the cabin floor. "How were you able to get this? I thought there were no others."

He set his hand on the table and settled back. "Money can buy almost anything."

The sea air that ruffled the ends of her hair drew her to the windows. She knelt on the cushioned seat, and he watched her while she gazed out at the roll of waves that foamed behind the ship. "I feel guilty I have been moved when others are still cramped below."

He sat next to her and picked up a lock of her hair between his fingers. "I do not want to hear about the others. You mustn't run to every problem that arises and try to fix it. Let the ship's surgeon do his job."

Taking his hand into hers, she touched the ring around his finger. "I only wanted to help."

"So did I. And this is my way of doing it. I am obliged to protect you. I was much affected by the loss of that young gentleman's wife. Understand?"

"Yes, I understand completely. Do you not know that I have thought the same about you? I would not want you to fall prey to this either, and if I were to lose you, I do not think I could bear the pain."

Indeed, what would she do if something were to happen to him before they reached River Run? How would she prove to anyone who she was, that she was mistress of his estate? And he had no will as of yet. As this was too bleak to dwell on, Hayward shoved it from his mind and instead gazed at Eliza's pretty eyes.

She held his stare a moment. "But if Fiona falls sick, you must allow me to take care of her. If I were allowed, I would call her *mother*."

Hayward kissed the top of her hand. "We will discuss it if it happens. Which I do not believe it will. Your servant is made of cast iron."

"I wish you would not refer to her as a servant, Hayward. She is my friend, and has cared for me all my life. But you are right about the stuff she is made of. I do not recall Fiona ever being sick. She has always taken care of those who are. You will still permit her to do so, won't you?"

He shrugged. "If she is doing some good, and the surgeon does not mind, of course I will not forbid it. But with you it is different."

Eliza wrapped her arms around his waist. He held her close as twilight fell and entered the cabin. Daylight faded and the sunset bathed the walls pale rose. They were alone, and the scent of her hair and the warmth of her nearness, sent his senses reeling.

He raised her face to his and kissed her lips.

9

*H*igh winds brought them into the Chesapeake Bay on a balmy summer's morning. The sun hung bright over the harbor in Annapolis and sparkled atop the water. Seabirds fluttered their wings in the breeze, darted and dove, and perched on pilings. The town, bathed in gleaming light, looked welcoming, and the clang of ships' bells rang out amid the din of wagon wheels, horses, and people as they moved over the cobbled streets.

Eliza stood at the ship's rail and admired the beauty of the bay and the glory of the colonial city. The breeze lifted her hair from her face. She shut her eyes and drew in a deep breath. The ship laid anchor, and seamen climbed the rigging to furl the sails. She watched them scurry up the ropes as if God had given them the speed of lesser creatures. It caused her to smile, to see the figures contrasted against the crisp blue sky, among the outstretched wings of stark-white gulls.

But an interruption followed, for when the ship's crew began to unload bundles of English cloth, crates of tea, and other goods, the customs officers turned them back. Maryland would no longer receive English goods into their ports.

Hayward and Fiona stood beside Eliza. Hayward addressed one of the officers.

"I have been away for some time. What has happened?"

"Lexington and Concord, sir." The officer turned to leave.

Hayward drew him back. "When?"

"On the nineteenth of April. The first shots were fired as the sun rose."

Hayward glanced over at Eliza. She saw concern in his eyes, but his expression was emboldened. "Are we in danger?" she asked, touching his sleeve.

"The fighting is far to the north."

"But you will keep to your pistol, even if we are as safe as you say?"

He looked down at her and smiled lightly. "In England there are highwaymen. In Maryland, it is no different."

As they moved to the ship's gangplank, Eliza scanned the town. The passengers the *Isadora May* had carried to America nudged past her, sober persons dressed in the common clothes of the working class, who carried a single sack of worldly possessions. Hayward took her hand and moved her forward with him.

Once they were on the dock, he told her to sit alongside Fiona near a stack of barrels. "Stay here until I return. I will not be long." He checked the coins in his pocket, and then handed her a few. "Here, keep these with you."

She drew in a breath. "You are leaving me?"

"I must unload my horse."

She smiled. "Yes, of course."

"And then I must purchase a gentle mare. Fiona can ride her. You will ride with me. You do not expect us to walk to River Run, do you?"

He strode off, and she kept her eyes fixed upon him as he disappeared into the bustling crowd. Fiona placed her hand over Eliza's.

"Not to worry, my girl. He will be back soon."

Eliza sighed. "What if he has come to regret me, Fiona?"

"Why would Mr. Hayward do that?" Fiona craned her head and looked through the throng.

"It is foolish of me to doubt him, I suppose."

"Has he done something to cause you to feel this way?"

"It is what he has not done."

"I should not ask what."

"I thought he would have confessed his love by now. You know life better than I, having lived so long and . . ."

Fiona huffed. "I am hardly in my grave."

"That is not what I meant. What I am asking is what must a new bride expect?"

"Expect nothing and that way you shan't be disappointed."

"Perhaps that is true, but what about love?"

"Love was a one-way street in my situation, my girl. You know that."

"Yes . . . He sleeps beside me, but never speaks of love . . . Oh, what have I done wrong?"

Fiona shook her head. "Just give him time and be a dutiful wife."

A lump grew in Eliza's throat. "I am trying to be."

"Perhaps Mr. Hayward is fighting falling in love with you," said Fiona. "Some men are that way. They are afraid of love. Or they think speaking of it is a sign of weakness. But not to fear. Soon he will come around."

They waited for an hour in the same spot. Though a warm breeze blew that morning, Eliza drew her cloak closer about her until she saw Hayward pass through the tide of people back toward her.

"Look, Fiona, by the fruit merchant's cart. It is Hayward."

She watched him speak to the merchant. The man handed over a sack, and Hayward paid him. His horse pranced restlessly, having been kept in a stall for so long, and was anxious to run. The brown mare beside him snorted and shook her shaggy mane.

Once he reached Eliza, he handed her the sack. Opening it, she looked inside. "Apples. How wonderful!"

Hayward checked the pillion behind his saddle. "You need them after having shipboard food."

She reached out and stroked the mare's nose. "Oh, and she is lovely."

"She is yours," he said. "I got her for a good price. The seller said her name is Nell. Very plain, I would say, so if you want to change it . . ."

"No." Eliza set her gloved hand over the mare's broad neck. "I like Nell."

The breeze coming in from the bay blew tepid, momentarily abating the heat of the day. It moved the lapels of Hayward's coat back, enough for her to see the pistol he had tucked inside the band of his breeches. To protect her, she had no doubt. She felt safe with him, assured of a pleasant journey toward her new home.

Soon Annapolis lay behind them. Shade from the thick canopy of trees stretched over the narrow road. The sun showered silvery dust through the breaks. Within the woodlands, birdsongs echoed clear and sweet, and honeybees hummed over the heads of Queen Anne's lace.

As the sun rose even higher, so did the heat. Eliza, grateful for the shade, dropped her cloak from off her shoulders and gathered her hair to one side of her neck. Mid-afternoon brought the cicadas out of hiding, and they trilled in the trees. So unlike the quiet, windy countryside where she grew up, the many sounds of birds and insects seemed almost deafening. It all delighted her.

"How far is River Run?" The breeze blew her hair back from her shoulder, and she inhaled the sweet scent of wild-flowers blooming along the dusty path.

"At the most, ninety miles." Omega sidestepped and Hayward pulled the reins to the right to settle him. "You only have to tell me if you grow weary, and Fiona, too, and we will pause."

"There is no need for us to stop for long," she said. "For I am anxious for home."

"Are there any soldiers near River Run, sir?" Fiona asked.

Hayward turned his head. "Fort Frederick is further upriver. You are still frightened, Fiona?"

Fiona nodded. "Indeed, sir, for it seems we shall be cut off from the world."

"Do not look so glum. Eliza shall have neighbors, and a ball or two to attend during the season. The land is rife with landed gentlefolk. It shall not be as uncivilized as you imagine."

When they reached the wilderness, Eliza noticed that it seemed a burden lifted off Hayward's shoulders. He appeared happier, less encumbered—less staunchly English and more American. As for the promise of society, she cared not whether she would have ladies to visit or to be visited by, or balls to attend. All she wanted was to make a home out of four walls and to be loved by Hayward.

The chance to help fulfill his dream, of owning the most prosperous estate along the Potomac, pulsed through Eliza's veins. But the question of building his legacy on the backs of poor slaves, whether Africans or white indentures, had not been broached. That day she had spotted a tawny child of no more than eight years of age holding a broad straw fan attached to a pole over the head of a gentlewoman to keep her cool and shaded.

"Tell me you do not own slaves at River Run," she said. "I shall be very distressed if you do, and I meant to ask before but had forgotten. I think it is a terrible institution and an affront to Almighty God. It should be done away with if America is to be a free nation."

Hayward looked at her over his shoulder. "For now, it is a way of life here, Eliza. I have no slaves."

She sighed and set her cheek against his back. "I am glad." Passionate on the subject, she raised her head and straightened her back. "If we can, whenever we can, we should speak up, do something to help our brothers and sisters in bonds. I hear the white indentured servants suffer a great deal as well. I will never understand why people cannot follow the Lord's commandment."

"And which commandment is that?" he asked.

"To love one another. To treat others as we would want to be treated."

"I see I have wedded a virtuous woman." He guided his horse around a bend.

Once they reached the river path along the Potomac, Hayward dismounted and drew the horses down to a stretch of sandy shore where the pools were quiet and they could drink. He helped Eliza down, and she stepped to the bank, with Fiona easing behind her. Under the shade of cottonwoods, Eliza dipped her hands into the gentle ripples. The water tasted sweet and cold, and she splashed her face and neck with it.

Hayward stood near with his pistol in his hand. She glanced over at him and saw how keenly he stood watch, how his eyes scanned the shoreline. She imagined he would pay her little mind if she tested the water, so she sat upon a rock, kicked off her shoes, and rolled her stockings down her calves and off her feet.

Careful not to slip, she stepped over the collected stones, dirt, and sand, and went to the water's edge. Holding her skirts above her knees, she waded out. The silky mud in the riverbed squished between her toes. The current whirled around her calves, and she basked in the cool caresses that rushed over her skin.

"My girl!" Aghast, Fiona waved her back. "So unseemly to hike up one's skirts like that. Not at all what a married woman should do. Draw back, and put your skirts down."

With a turn of her head, Eliza laughed. "There is none to see me save you and my husband, Fiona. You should not expect me to get my clothes all sopping wet. Come out with me, and wash the dust of the road from your feet and limbs."

With a quick arch of her brows, Fiona's mouth flew open. "Not I."

"The water is heavenly in this heat. Your sore limbs will feel the better for it."

"You expect me to take off my stockings, hoist my skirts, and put my bare legs into the river in front of Mr. Morgan?"

With another laugh, Eliza tossed her hair back. "He will not care. Now, come on. It will do you good."

Fiona hesitated and glanced from Eliza to Hayward. He turned away to give her ease that he would avert his eyes.

"I shall not take off my stockings. Just my shoes."

"No, no." Eliza wrinkled her brow. "You must take your stockings off. Otherwise you shall tear them on the stones."

Eliza made sense, and so Fiona hiked up her skirts and secured them. She took off her shoes, then her stockings, and made slow progress out into the river. "It does refresh the body," she said with a smile. She cupped her hands, plunged them into the water, and then rubbed the cool water over her arms and face.

Eliza splashed her, then went further out, and her husband called to her, "Eliza, come back. You go too far. You do not know the river. There are deep pools."

The hem of her dress skimmed along the surface as she waded back, her legs heavy against the current. "You are right, Hayward. I grow too bold."

Surprised by the cautious look in his eyes, she halted. They were locked onto a spot across the river, on the Virginia side where the trees met the river's edge. He stepped forward and motioned to Eliza and Fiona with a quick bidding of his hand. "Hurry, both of you. But make no sound."

Silently, he stepped forward into the water to bring her in. The horses lifted their heads and pricked their ears. Eliza followed the direction of Hayward's eyes. Half hidden from view by the ancient hemlocks and weeping willows was an eagle feather hanging from a crop of coal-black hair, the bare breast of an Indian, his deer hide apron, and the black wolf's mask that covered his eyes.

The Indian stood motionless beneath the shale cliffs that hugged the river. In his hand he clutched a bow, and across his chest stretched the strap of his deerskin quiver. Fear gripped her even though he stood a great distance away.

Hayward led Eliza out of the water to the shore, then brought her back up the bank. Fiona followed after retrieving her stockings and shoes.

"Stay here." Hayward turned back, grabbed the horses' reins, and brought the horses through the line of trees and back to the path. "He is too far to reach us, but there may be others following him by canoe. Why he is this far downriver, I do not know. But it is better we are gone."

He lifted Eliza back into the pillion and then helped Fiona. Through the trees, Eliza watched the Indian. He had not moved; only the breeze lifted his hair and caused his feather to wave. She had an impulse to raise her hand, as if it would win some kind of favor. But she hesitated.

Suddenly the Indian raised his bow above his head and called across the river. Though the loud rapids drowned out his words, they made Eliza's blood run as cold as the undercurrents.

She pressed closer to Hayward. "Do you understand him?"

Hayward dragged the reins through his hands. "He is sending us a warning."

Placing her hands around Hayward's waist and locking her fingers, she felt the kick he gave to Omega's sides. The horse moved on, down the path through the sunlight, where an encompassing forest soon covered them. Fiona rode alongside, her hands still atremble while gripping the reins.

"Do not fear, Fiona," Eliza said. "See how far the other side is? There are no others with him."

"I hope you are right, my girl." Fiona's eyes widened. "On my life, I have never seen anything like that. Oh, he struck fear into me just as if he had shot an arrow into my heart. I pray God there are none of his friends on this side of the river."

Eliza leaned her head against Hayward's back. "Hayward shall take care of us. And God shall protect us."

Then she realized she had left something behind and looked down at her bare feet. "My stockings and shoes. I left them on the bank."

The following day's ride had been uneventful. But near to sunset, Hayward pulled sharp on the reins and Eliza tightened her grip around his waist when a man in a ragged brown coat and stained tricorn hat strode down the path toward them. A lump rose in Eliza's throat when Hayward drew out his pistol and laid it across his thigh. The man, chancing upon them, stopped short. He dragged off his hat and moved to the side of the road. His hair brushed along his neck, tangled and dirty. His clothes hung loose over his lean body, and his eyes were as blue as the river rushing over the boulders below.

"Lord, have mercy," he cried. "You 'bout gave me a froze heart." He pressed his hand over his chest and panted. "Glad you didn't, cause I'd hate to be buried in these woods without being marked."

"And I would have hated to do the burying." Hayward steadied Omega as the horse stepped back. "Where are you headed?"

"Annapolis, sir. I'm going to join the Continental Army."

"We saw an Indian on the opposite side of the river. What news have you?"

The man shrugged. "Most of the tribes have moved west toward the Ohio. But there be plenty of braves joinin' the British. I guess good ole King George thinks that'll strike enough fear into us to get us to bend to his will."

"As fearsome as the Indians are, I will not bend," said Hayward. Eliza then knew her husband was heart and soul for America, that the chance of him joining the Patriots was high. She hadn't given much thought of him going off to fight in a revolution when she first realized she loved him. But it would not have mattered. She would happily take one day with him to none at all.

The man snarled and raised a fist. "Not I, either, sir. Besides, I got nothin' keeping me in the wilderness. I had a nice farm, but Logan's Indians raided us and burned my cabin to a pile of ash. I escaped with my wife and child, but they both died of the fever at Fort Frederick."

Eliza looked down at him. "I am sorry for your loss."

He nodded and blinked. "Thank you, ma'am."

She reached for the saddlebag. "Are you hungry?"

"Thank you, but I have plenty of dried venison in my pouch." He placed his hat back on his head, and appeared to want to move on. He took a few steps, but glanced around the woodlands with his head lowered.

A chill prickled over Eliza's skin when she saw her husband squeeze his hand over the hilt of his pistol. He clicked his tongue and Omega stomped his left hoof, then paced forward. Eliza sucked in her breath when two other men, all in dirty moth-eaten clothes, stepped out of the woods. Through their grins their teeth were slimy brown. Their hands were dirty like their clothes, and their nails encrusted with grime. Each held a musket.

"Friends of yours?" Hayward called back over his shoulder to the man. He cocked the hammer of his pistol.

"Aye," said the man.

The shorter one let out a weasel-like laugh. "Oh, you do know how to tell a tale, John Mayne. You had him believing ye. Oh, Indians burned our cabin, and me wife and child died of the fever. You are a hoot. Should've been on the stage, John."

John Mayne bent over with laughter and slapped his thigh. Eliza stared down hard at the men gathering around them. "You lied to us? Why would you do such a thing? What is it you want?"

Mayne scratched his bristly chin and narrowed his eyes. "There be two things in this world a man wants, ma'am—gold and women. Now, if your man has no gold, silver will do." He dragged his tongue over his lips and ran his lustful eyes over her.

Hayward leveled his pistol. "Touch my wife or this serving woman and I'll shoot you dead. And when that is done, we will move on, not bothering to bury you in these woods. I'll leave your dirty carcasses to the wolves."

The men joined shoulder to shoulder and blocked the road.

Hayward aimed his pistol. "Move aside."

John Mayne folded his arms across his chest. "There be three of us and one of you, sir. I doubt the ladies know how to fire a pistol, let alone carry one."

"Touch a hair on my girl's head and I'll lay you flat," shouted Fiona.

Throwing his hands to his knees, Mayne laughed, along with his fellows. The grin on his face turned into a sneer, and he leaped forward. He swung his musket in an effort to knock Hayward's pistol out of his hand, but missed it by a hair. Hayward squeezed the trigger. A snap of the hammer and the bellow of sulfur sent the bullet whizzing past Mayne's head.

Omega twisted and reared. Eliza held on tight, but unable to stay in the pillion, she slipped off and landed on the ground with a thud.

"Get her!" shouted Mayne. His men hurried forward to grab her. Hayward vaulted from the saddle and slammed his fist into the jaw of the first man he reached. The fiend stumbled back. His eyes rolled in his head, and he fell into the bramble. The other retreated into the woods. Mayne drew a knife and brandished it, the razor edge glinting in the sunlight. Eliza scrambled back.

Her fingers worked fast to lift the hem of her skirts and reach up under her petticoat. From a blue silk garter, she yanked out her ivory-hilted pistol and took aim. Mayne stood in his tracks, wide-eyed and stunned, while Hayward hauled Eliza to her feet.

"Ah, it's but a small ladies' pistol." Mayne shoved his knife back in its sheaf and took a step back with his hands spread out.

"That it is. But enough to do you damage," Eliza said, gritting her teeth. She glanced at Hayward and marked the amused look on his face.

"Aye, she's right." Mayne picked up his tricorn hat and dusted it off against his thigh. He kicked his partner to get him to his feet. Then he swept his weatherworn hat in front of him with a bow. His greasy hair fell forward. "You do your husband proud, ma'am. Good day to you."

Off they scampered down the dusty road without a glance back.

Sighing with relief, Eliza lifted her skirts just above the garter and slipped the small flintlock pistol back in place. She smiled over at her husband, and then smoothed the folds back down.

Hayward shook his head and laughed. "Why is it you have a propensity to attract bandits and ruffians? This is the second time I have had to come to your rescue. But I think you might have done all right on your own with that pistol you keep hidden on your thigh."

A rush of scarlet flamed her cheeks. Perhaps her bravery and skill with a weapon would bring him one step closer to falling in love with her. She fixed her eyes warmly on his. "I saw the knife and had to help."

Hayward put his hands around her waist and helped her back into the pillion. The gleam in his eyes, the soft smile that curved a corner of his mouth, pleased Eliza. He thrust his boot into the stirrup and mounted his horse. "We shall see how you do with a musket once we are settled."

This thrilled her. "I promise, I shall be a better marksman than you, sir, and faster at loading."

"I doubt that . . . But you may try, Eliza."

"You may doubt all you wish. I shall only use that skill in self-defense if I need to. I am not inclined to show off."

Despite their brush with dangerous men, her words brought light laughter to the trio as they passed through the woodlands.

The urge to cling to Hayward even tighter overwhelmed Eliza when the realization took hold that life was precarious in the wilderness, and that the unexpected loomed around every bend. Would he leave her to join the Continentals? How would she and Fiona do out at River Run all alone? The idea caused her to tremble inwardly. She laid her head on Hayward's shoulder and longed to whisper in his ear, *Do not leave me . . . do not go to war. Stay. Stay.*

She then remembered her father's words on the day he told her he was not long for this world. *You shan't ever be alone, Eliza. God will never leave you or forsake you.*

10

*B*linding flashes of lightning raced across the sky. Rain fell as soft as the pine needles it broke free from the evergreens along the road. Within the shelter of trees stood an abandoned cabin used by travelers.

"It is poor," Hayward said to Eliza as he brought her down from Omega's back. "But it is enough to shelter us from the storm."

The feel of her waist against his palms proved enough to cause his blood to race. Her eyes captivated him, and he wished they were alone. He pushed open the door with his boot, went inside, and frowned at the dusty pine needles spread over a dirt floor, and at the leaky roof. At least the last visitor had left a stack of firewood beside the stone fireplace.

He banked a fire while Fiona laid out biscuits and jerky on a kerchief. Eliza spread three blankets over the floor. After they had eaten, and were comforted by the fire, the women fell asleep. Hayward sat opposite his wife, close to the door, where rainwater seeped between the logs in rivulets. Setting his pistol beside him, he studied her face: the closed lids, the parted lips, the blush the fire brought to her cheeks. He barely knew her and yet felt she had been near him all his life.

At that moment, he steeled his heart against falling in love. It would weaken him somehow—cause him to hesitate if called to fight. But it proved a bigger battle than he had imagined. The nights he held her in his arms, caressed her, loved her, and felt her kisses melt into his were like cracks in a dam. Ready to open wider and release the flood at any moment, they had to be held back. God only knew how long she would be his. He knew many settlers in these parts had lost wives to childbirth, Indians, smallpox, and fever. Best to keep his feelings in check to stay strong.

He recalled the hard lesson his father had taught him at the age of twelve. On the day they sent him off to school, his father saw him wipe his cheek with the back of his coat sleeve when his mother embraced him. He grabbed him by the scruff of his neck and pulled him into the stable, where he whipped him.

"That," he said, "is enough to make you cry. Never cry over a woman, you hear? It will make you weak as water, and you shall become a slave. Woman is to be your slave, your servant. She is to lick your boots and always be a step behind you. She is to serve you. Never forget, you are the master."

The words echoed in his mind. But when he looked over at Eliza wrapped in the blanket asleep, he saw a brave spirit. The way she had stood up to those footpads amazed him. And through the entire journey not a word of complaint had passed between her lips. No doubt Lilith Marsden would have fainted from the heat, and at the first sight of a ruffian, and complained incessantly that her comforts were not attended to in a satisfactory manner. Even under this broken roof, Eliza had not whined. And in the face of danger, she seemed more fascinated than afraid.

Lightning illuminated the hovel, and thunder shook the walls. Eliza's eyes fluttered open.

"Are you frightened by the storm?" Hayward said.

"It causes me to tremble. But I think of the Scripture: he has lightning in his fists. I am not afraid."

The Scripture painted a frightening picture in his mind of a wrathful god, a god he did not know, one who could strike him down at any moment with arrows of thunder.

"Fiona does not seem bothered either," he said. "It has been a long journey for her, and she must be worn out."

Fiona snored, curled in a blanket, fast asleep beside the fire.

Sleepy-eyed, Eliza crossed the blanket over her shoulders. "Will it be over soon?"

"Storms are fierce here, and wild like the land. But they pass quickly."

"I can only imagine what the snow may be like in winter. Is there a cold cellar at River Run?"

"Yes, and the forests are rich with game, so we will not lack for meat."

"Hayward, may I acquire cloth? Fiona and I can make our winter clothes. It would be more frugal than going to a dressmaker for me and a tailor for you."

He picked up his pistol and ran a rag over the barrel to polish it. "To begin with, there are no dressmakers, nor tailors, close to River Run. You may have your cloth."

She settled back down and rested her head over her arm. Long he gazed at her, holding her violet eyes, and she said more within her gaze than words could. He set the pistol aside and moved to her. Beside her, he drew the blanket over his body and brought her into his arms. She turned and he could not see her face, only the quiver of firelight in her hair that streaked it with dark red.

He brought his mouth close to her ear and whispered into it. "Now that you have traveled to this wilderness, would you return to England and safety, if you could?"

She nuzzled closer. "Only if I were with you. Where you go, I will go."

❦

In the morning, the storm sped off to the east and the clouds broke open. Ribbons of fog twisted through the bramble and vanished as the heat of the day strengthened.

Hayward had described little to Eliza about River Run, save that he had begun repairs on the old dwelling the moment he set his boots upon the sod. River Run had two lofty stories, gables, mullioned windows with stout shutters, and a fine porch. Window glass glimmered in the sunlight, and the inside walls were painted with soft shades of shell and marigold.

Furniture brought upriver from Williamsburg graced the rooms. He had planned all this for Lilith Marsden. But after he had met her again and realized her childish ways were not the stuff frontier wives were made of, he eventually became thankful for her rejection and the end of any understanding between them.

And he had met Eliza again—the girl he remembered as a barefoot child. She was braver than most men he knew, virtuous, and full of faith, and he finally concluded the Lord of the universe had ordained their union. A poetic belief, he thought, but nonetheless true.

He had informed Addison Crawley, who lived in the cabin in the rear, that upon his return he would bring a new bride to River Run. Addison was to see to it that the house was set in order as best a man could manage. Hayward knew it would lack all the touches of a woman, and perhaps Eliza would think it austere. No matter. He would give her leave to do with it whatever she wished, as long as she did not spend too much money in the process.

The following day, toward dusk, River Run came into view. Situated on a grassy knoll, the house gleamed in the sunlight. The porch shadowed the oak door. The windows sparkled, and on each end were chimneys made of the same stone as the house. Nearby weaved Israel Creek, and a stone mill's wheel moved slowly with the flow of water.

Hayward set his jaw with the air of a man who had come into his own. He had land, a house, and a wife who would captivate his neighbors on both sides of the Potomac with her beauty. He turned and looked back over his shoulder at Eliza, one he had at first not given any thought to, not even the day he had met her on the downs with her silken hair blowing about her pretty face.

How could this girl love him to such lengths that she would follow him into the wilderness of Maryland? Would she have loved him if he had no money or land? He believed she would have, for she was convinced God had brought them together, and she had never inquired into what his yearly income was. If he did not love her, he would, at least, protect and shelter her.

He drew off his hat and set it on his thigh. "Our journey is over, Eliza. There sits our house. I hope it pleases you."

Eliza's warm sigh brushed over the back of his neck as he brought the horse around for her to see the house at River Run. "It pleases me greatly, Hayward. Such a beautiful, welcoming house."

"It is that, Eliza, though not as grand as Havendale, or the plantation houses on the other side of the river. And you see the mill over there?"

"Yes, I see it," she said excitedly. "Oh, I love old mills."

"It will bring us a goodly income when the farmers come to grind their grain."

Eliza turned her head to look at her faithful servant. "Fiona, see our new home? Is it not the loveliest house you have ever laid your eyes upon?"

Fiona halted the mare. "I'm thinking it will be a drafty place, being so old."

"No more than what we were accustomed to."

"There are not enough trees to block the wind."

"We shall plant more. But see how the forest edges the land? Why, that is enough to break the heavy wind. And the creek looks so cooling."

Eliza gripped Hayward's arm and slipped down from the pillion. Lifting her skirts above her ankles, she strode toward the house. When Hayward saw she had no shoes, he stopped her. He swung down off the saddle and turned her round to face him. "Eliza. Haven't you brought another pair of shoes? I shall not have my wife walking up to her new house barefooted and looking so poor."

"I do have another, Hayward. But they are my best and I do not want to ruin them. Besides, I want to feel the grass beneath my feet . . . our grass. It is how it should be . . . at least for today. Say you understand."

He glared down into her eyes, and the chill that perpetually lived in his heart melted. It was a wilderness vast and deep he had brought her to. He could bend to her desire to feel the coolness, the softness of the land.

With a coy look in her eyes, she tilted her head. "You could take off your boots and walk beside me."

He drew up. "I am no gypsy."

"Hmm. I cannot argue with that." She walked on. "But I find it sad, Hayward."

He stepped alongside her, a little more deliberate in his boots. "Why?"

"Well, because you are in this beautiful wilderness, and you will not shake off your blue blood just this once, for a cool walk in the grass, on the day you bring your wife home." She moved ahead, mounting the stoop with her face touched by the gold and silver sunlight.

✑

"Glory Alleluia!" Bursting across the lawn came a barrel-chested man in dingy work clothes and a tricorn hat. "Mr. Hayward, you've come home at last, sir. And with guests?"

"No, Addison. This lady is my wife, and your mistress. Remember what I told you?" Hayward took Eliza's hand as she stood beside him. "Greet her properly."

Addison slapped his hat against his chest and bowed. "Welcome to River Run, mistress. I wish you and Mr. Hayward much joy."

She thanked him with a gentle smile. Then his eyes shifted to Fiona, who stood a few paces behind Eliza. "And may I ask, sir, who this lady is? My mistress's sister, perhaps?"

Eliza smiled at Fiona's giggle, but she saw Hayward glower. He did not like flattery from servants, even the sincere kind given from one to another. Surely Addison meant no affront by it, but only to make Fiona feel at ease.

"No, this is Fiona Goodall, my wife's serving woman. She will be living in the house with us."

Hayward walked on with Eliza, and as she let go of his hand and hurried ahead, she fixed her eyes on the stones of the house. They changed to deeper, more variegated colors as twilight fell. "The windows are more than I had counted in my dreams," she said over her shoulder.

In her haste, she failed to notice the slight dip before her. Her ankle turned as she stepped into it. She lost her balance and ended up on the ground. Hayward hurried forward and crouched down in front of her with his arms reaching out. "Are you hurt?"

She felt the heat of embarrassment rise in her face, and she thrust her skirts down past her exposed calves. "I do not believe so. Just a twist, I think."

Hayward looked concerned. "Here, let me help you up."

Fiona rushed forward. "Dear me. Oh, my girl."

"I am all right, Fiona. Do not worry."

Addison looked stunned. "I meant to fix that. I'm sorry, Mrs. Morgan."

"No need to apologize, Addison. I should have been more careful and watched where I was going."

"You need to unload our horses." Hayward looked at Addison with a reprimand. "Take them to the stable, rub them down, water them, and give them plenty of oats."

Addison nodded and sprinted off.

Eliza shook her head. "Oh . . . It is just like me to ruin a moment such as this."

Hayward put his arms beneath her, and she locked her fingers around his neck. "You have ruined nothing. I shall carry you the rest of the way." He lifted her into his arms.

"Ice, sir," Fiona said. "Have you any hereabouts? My girl needs a cold compress."

"I am uninjured, Fiona." To Eliza, Fiona's voice drifted afar off as she looked into her husband's face. A lock of his hair fell over his forehead, and she moved it back. He gazed into her eyes, and she felt weak and longed to be behind closed doors in his arms. He carried her up the steps onto the porch, and on to the front door. She ran her fingers over the brass plate affixed to the stone, dated 1732.

"Who built this house, my love?"

"A wealthy English adventurer, so I am told, who wished to conquer the wilderness. He died childless, with no family. So he had no one to pass the estate on to." He pushed the door in with his boot and carried her inside. Silver shafts of sunlight poured through the front windows and crossed the floor.

"Well?" He paused inside the doorway. She scanned the foyer with its pale plastered walls, broad staircase, and fireplace.

"It is beyond what I imagined." She kissed his cheek, and for a moment thought she saw a glimmer of love flash in his eyes. But it faded. Somehow, she would change all that and break through his hard exterior.

He stepped further inside, and she rested her head against his shoulder. "I can see why you wanted a wife and children to fill your house. It is too large for one living alone. The foyer is twice the size of the parlor in the vicarage. You can put me down."

"Your ankle is swollen. Let's not risk it. Here's my study." The room contained only a desk and chair, with near-empty shelves hugging the walls beside a window that faced the fields. "You will help me acquire enough books to fill my library?"

"Yes, of course, I will."

"You do know literature, I should hope?"

She gave him a playful scowl. "I do. And I am well versed in Latin and religion as well."

"Anything besides all that?"

"Yes. I am keen on poetry."

He gazed into her eyes. "Hmm. I am not surprised. Poetry is for the romantic soul."

Leaving the study, he carried her from room to room. Eliza was enjoying this. A mishap had turned into good fortune. Because of her fall, Hayward had carried her over the threshold and through the house. She kept her fingers locked behind his neck, feeling the warmth of his skin against her hands.

Fiona followed at an acceptable distance, and Hayward looked over at her. "The kitchen is the rear of the house, Fiona. We should like coffee. You will find all you need in the larder." With a quick dip, she hurried off.

Hayward took Eliza upstairs to a room bright with sunshine. "This is our room. If it does not please you, tell me. Perhaps different curtains or a change in the wall color is what you would like. You have only to ask for what you need, and I shall see to it you have it."

"I like it just the way it is. And what can we see from the window?"

"The river. Here, I will show you." He set her down, strode to a pair of French doors and opened them to a balcony. He lifted her again, and took her outside. Below and beyond, through a break in the virgin woods, the Potomac flowed in a haze of magenta light, slow and peaceful as she imagined it had for a thousand years. A warm breeze caressed her face, scented with the wet earth, forest, and field.

Gladness filled her. Praise seized her heart. "I should kiss you well, Hayward, to show my gratitude." She touched his cheek with her fingertips and guided his lips to hers. Gently and lovingly she kissed him, then moved her mouth away.

"You are beautiful, Eliza." He held her close and brought his lips near hers. But before another kiss could happen, a clamor at the door drew them apart.

"Mr. Morgan, Eliza had a terrible fall. She needs to rest her ankle." Fiona set the tray down and wrung her hands like a worried mother. She hurried to the bedside and propped pillows against the bolster. "Do you ail, my girl?"

"I am fine, Fiona. The fall was not as terrible as you think."

Hayward carried her over to the bed and set her down. "Perhaps it is best you yield to Fiona's intuition. Besides, we have had a long journey and you should rest. I have business to discuss with Addison."

He poured coffee into a cup and drank it down black. Then he stepped from the room and closed the door behind him. Eliza reached for Fiona's hands. "I shall be happy here," she said, squeezing them. "And see how attentive he is?"

Fiona wiggled her mouth and tucked a pillow beneath Eliza's swollen ankle. "Attentive as a husband should be, my girl. But I shall bless the day I see that loving glow in his eyes every time he looks at you."

11

News came downriver of the Indian massacres along the Blue Ridge Mountains that spread as far north as the Hudson River Valley. Hayward assured Eliza the Indians would not come this far east of the enclaves. Nonetheless, he taught her how to prime and shoot a musket. She had become quite good at it, and it pleased her how impressed he looked each time she hit the target, even if it was not dead center.

She worried those nights when she heard his horse and the hollow sound of hoofbeats fade as he rode off. The gentlemen in the area met in secret, and she prayed for his protection. The events that were unfolding in the Revolution occupied his mind and she felt ignored, but she understood. His life in England was over, and he considered himself to be American. Subjugation to his father had left a bitterness in his soul, a desire to live free. He had come home in the early hours of dawn, weary and spent, yet raging with patriotic zeal. She allowed him to rant, pacing like a restless panther, and then helped him off with his boots.

Eliza shuddered at the thought of war and what kind of suffering it could bring, especially to the people in towns along the coast. Boston already greatly suffered under the tight fist of tyranny. Hayward and she had only been wed such a short time, and to be separated from him was too much to consider.

One balmy night, she knelt before him, clasped her hands around one of his boots and pulled it off, then pulled off the other. "My love, you look troubled."

He leaned his head back against the chair. Beads of sweat glistened over his forehead, and a damp strand of hair clung to his throat. "I have not told you what the men in the region are discussing." He drew loose his neckcloth. "But after our meeting tonight, it is important you know."

She sat back. "It sounds serious. Tell me, won't you?"

He leaned forward and looked down into her eyes. "I have made a decision. I will take an oath to fight."

A sharp chill rushed over Eliza. She stared back into his eyes and realized nothing would change his mind. She placed her hand on his knee. "I will go with you."

"No. It would be too dangerous."

"We would be together."

"You would see death, Eliza, and wounded men, some dying in pools of their own blood. No, I want you here. Do not ask me again." He stood, stretched his hand down to her, and helped her to her feet.

"Other women will follow their husbands. Who else will do the cooking and mending, or tend to their husbands when they are sick, or care for them when they are wounded?"

"That is for the lower classes to do, not the wives of landed gentlemen like myself. I can tell you, Mrs. Washington and Mrs. Adams will not be following their husbands on the battlefields or to Philadelphia. They will be looking after their husbands' properties in their absence. You are mistress of River Run, and you will oversee it while I am gone."

She threw her hands over her hips and frowned. "To say a genteel woman cannot accompany her husband in camp is a ridiculous rule."

"Need I tell you, I am your rule and law?" he said, his tone gentle.

"No, I am reminded of it daily. Can you tell me you will not long for me—miss me? Can you not bend this time?"

"I would be compromising my principles. You will obey me and stay here at River Run."

She clenched the sides of her gown. "I will worry myself sick over you, and miss you terribly."

He drew off his waistcoat. "I will not leave you alone here without a man. Addison will stay . . . to protect you and Fiona."

Her mouth dropped open with a start. "Protect us? But you said the Indians would stay away."

He turned. "And I believe that is true. But there may be British soldiers and a few stray Indians that wander this far into the wilderness. You cannot be too cautious even when the possibility of danger is slim."

The thought of Redcoats stomping over River Run, Indians lurking in the woods nearby, and she without her husband, made Eliza frown. Despite Hayward's assurances, she imagined what the Indians would do to her and Fiona if they were to attack their home. And she feared what English officers would demand of her if they set foot on her doorstep. Yet she raised her face and said, "I am British. Surely no English soldier would harm me."

"As long as you say you sympathize with them and support the King, and show hospitality to the officer in command, they will treat you well."

Eliza bit her lower lip. How could he, knowing the risks, leave her? "I hope you are wrong and that no soldiers from either side shall come anywhere near River Run. If they do, I shall be certain to write to you and tell you of it."

"Never mind what I said. Put it out of your mind, Eliza. The fighting will stay well to the east and north of here. I should not have said anything. Now you will worry and do your best to make me feel guilty for it."

Unable to forbid angry tears from coming, they welled in her eyes, pooled, and slipped down her cheek. "I will not speak of it again, Hayward. Just promise me that you will come back."

His long sigh drew her gaze. "Where else would I go? River Run is mine. You are mine. Nothing will prevent me from returning, except death."

A moan escaped her lips, and she leaned into him. "Do not speak of death, Hayward. It frightens me, especially when there is so much for us to live for."

"There are some things worth dying for, Eliza. Liberty is one of them."

She lowered her eyes to hide her disappointment. "Perhaps you cannot promise you will come back to me, but I can promise I will be here waiting for you."

He did not look at her, but nodded. Her lips parted to speak, but the words did not come. Instead, she wrapped her arms around his waist and laid her head against his chest. She felt him breathe out. She had to put it all in the Almighty's hands and rely solely upon Him. But she could not help but yearn for the mortal closeness and protectiveness of her husband.

The next morning heat fanned across the lowlands and withered the wildflowers that grew in the fields. No breeze stirred in the trees or rippled the tall grass. The courtship song of the cicadas swept through the trees. With each passing rider or odd wagon that passed over the road above the Potomac, rusty clouds kicked beneath hoof and wheel and settled over the flora. The water in the river receded and revealed the deeper boulders and rocks scattered on the muddy bottom.

In the afternoon, when a hazy sun settled above the tree-tops, a courier upon a brown gelding galloped down the river path toward River Run. Eliza saw him from the porch and stood with her hand above her eyes to block the sun's glare as he approached. With a sweep of his hat, he dismounted in front of the house and handed Eliza a message sealed in scarlet wax.

Wrought in the most elegant hand were the words *To Mr. Hayward Morgan and Mrs. Morgan* on the front. Beneath, the slender hand inscribed in decorative scrolls *Twin Oaks, Virginia. Along the Potomac.*

Eliza, thinking Hayward would indulge her curiosity, broke the seal and unfolded the invitation, and read what she believed would be a turning point in their social life. She stepped into the sitting room, where the sunlight shone bright through the windows, and sat down across from Fiona.

"Promise not to tell Addison I am sewing him a new shirt." Fiona slipped a needle through the coarse linen fabric. "'Tis a surprise. The man has such tattered clothes, not that a laborer like him minds, but a man should have at least one good shirt to wear to church on Sundays and to social affairs—barn dances, no doubt in his case."

Smiling, Eliza picked up a length of rich apricot silk from the wicker basket beside the chair. She ran her hands over it, relishing the sleek feel of the new cloth and imagining the finished product. She only needed to add a bit of ribbon along the bodice and finish the hem. "You have a kind heart, Fiona. But beware: when a woman makes a shirt for a man, it gives him cause to fall in love with her."

Fiona hooted and waved her hand. "Oh, go on with you, Eliza. He'd never do that. We are past our years."

"You are not yet fifty. You are never too old for love. I shall keep your secret about Addison's shirt, Fiona. And you are to keep mine . . . Still, it is kind of you. I think you like him and do not want to admit it."

A wave of rose blushed Fiona's cheeks, and she wiggled in her chair. "Oh, he is a bother. Pesters me like a lad running about my feet."

Eliza laughed lightly. After a pause she said, "Hayward and I have been sent an invitation to a gathering at Twin Oaks. At last, I'll have the chance to meet our neighbors on the other side of the river."

Fiona set her sewing on her lap. "Do you feel well enough? You have seemed tired of late. It may be wise not to go."

"You are overly protective of me. I am feeling well."

"But Mr. Morgan may decline. You'll have to accept his decision."

"Oh, he will accept . . . I can finish the gown in time, if you will help me."

Fiona's eyes widened. "You cannot be serious, Eliza. A gown of that shade in summer?"

"The color is beautiful. It will be the best gown I have, and I intend to wear it."

"Women wear light colors in lustring and muslin this time of year. You will raise some eyebrows, I guarantee."

Despite Fiona's warning, Eliza pulled thread through a needle. "Why should I look like everyone else? I shall tell them it is the fashion in England."

Fiona paused, needle held high in the air. "Your good nature is due to your faith, my girl. But wherever you got your impulsive streak, I never could tell."

"Such rules are meant to be crossed when they are not praiseworthy," said Eliza. "If I had no compulsion to follow my heart, I may not have won my husband."

When she heard Hayward dismount outside, she stood and hurried out to meet him in the hallway. He drew off his hat, and she handed him the invitation. In the cool, shadowy foyer she waited while he looked it over.

"I could not resist reading it first. I knew by the handwriting it was an invitation." She pushed back a curl that brushed over her cheek. Why did Hayward have to look so serious? "I hope you are not angry."

"No, I'm not angry. It was addressed to both of us." He folded the invitation and handed it back. "Do you really want to go? There will be a lot of stuffy elites there."

"I can handle the stuffiest of persons, Hayward. What matters the most to me is the chance to attend an elegant affair with my husband. Yes, I wish to go."

"Then we shall." He walked inside the brightly lit study. There were books sparsely set upon the bookshelves now, and Eliza had moved his desk near a window so he could see out of doors and feel the breeze on a warm day.

She stood in the doorway watching him. Perhaps when he saw her decked out in her best gown, her hair dressed in the silver band of pearls he had bought her, then he would give in and say he loved her. If only he could do that now when she was plainly dressed, while her hair spilled down her back and the ends whispered over her hips.

She leaned against the doorjamb. "I'm finishing a gown for the occasion. I think you'll be pleased when you see how lovely it is."

He glanced up from the ledger he held. "I shall look forward to it. My only concern will be how many men will stare at you in it."

"I only care that your eyes admire me. Besides, the gentlemen will have their own ladies to ogle over."

"True enough, but you shall outdo them all. You'll see."

Pleased by his words, that he thought so much of her, she gazed at him, wishing he would set the ledger down and come to her. "Not for a moment do I want other men staring at me. I belong to you, and all of me is for your eyes alone."

He grinned and set the ledger down. "I am convinced it is something that cannot be helped."

A wave of happiness rushed though Eliza at his comment. But she meant what she said. To have other men admire her bothered her greatly, for too often admiration led to lust. "Perhaps I shall be of interest because I am a newcomer, and only that."

She spoke softly and shyly, glad he had no interest in what was in or out of fashion, or the etiquette of dress for ladies of her standing. Some husbands would have questioned their wives on the gown they intended to wear, or they would insist to see them in it beforehand in order to approve it.

He laughed lightly. "You underestimate the power of your beauty, Eliza."

She released a heavy sigh. "It pleases me that you see me that way, but I am not *beautiful*, Hayward. Not in a worldly sense."

He shook his head. "I do not understand you. Women are vain creatures. Why not you?"

"If God does not look on the outer appearance of anyone, then why should we? My heart is what is important, my love." She moved to him, placed her hand in his, and held it against her breast so he could feel her beating heart. "I long that you would look here, Hayward. My true self is what you shall find if you do."

With a wary look in his eyes he drew his hand away. "You are too philosophical for your own good, Eliza. God made your face and body for me, as your husband, to admire. Think on that for a while, will you?"

He pulled away from his desk, gathered her into his arms, and kissed her. Indeed she felt his desire, but what was desire without love? Perhaps that would change in time, and their marriage would grow into a lasting friendship.

He then asked her to wait for him upstairs, and as she ascended the staircase she whispered, "Who can find a virtuous woman, for her price is far above rubies." *Be that woman, Eliza. Do not falter, no matter how difficult it may be. If he never says he loves you, stay true, and know that what is in the heart is deeper than any words can describe.*

✍❦

The day Eliza had anticipated finally arrived. She came down the staircase in her new gown feeling excited and hopeful. Fiona had brushed out her hair until it gleamed in a nimbus of ebony spirals. Long strands hung over one shoulder, with the rest pulled up and fastened with a pearl band. Sunlight, warm and sultry, streamed through the open windows and spilled over her.

Hayward waited near the door, and when his eyes lifted to her as she descended the stairs, they warmed at the sight of her in the gown. How she hoped it would be enough to distract him from thoughts of war, for she had no doubt the men would engage in conversations concerning America's break with England.

At the bottom step, she turned in a complete circle for his inspection. "Do you approve, my love?" She ran her hands down the fabric. "Is it not pretty?"

His eyes ran over the lightly boned bodice, over the falls of ivory lace at the sleeves, and the lacings in the back that drew in her waist. Then he turned his eyes away. "I do not think you should wear it."

Disappointment vanquished her smile, and dashed her hopes of pleasing him. "Why not? What is wrong with it?"

"The ladies will . . ."

"Disapprove?"

"They will envy such a gown. And they will think you quite forward for wearing such a color. Do you want to be the subject of their gossip?"

"I will bear up under any scrutiny that may come my way."

She raised the hem above the heels of her satin shoes, exited the house, and made her way to the carriage. Determined she would not bend to any rules she found absurd, she sat down in the seat with her back toward Addison, who acted as coachman. She was ready to have it out then and there with Hayward if he were to order her back inside to change. But, to her surprise, he climbed inside and sat across from her without saying a word. The expression on his face, the smirk that crossed his lips, said she would get what she deserved for being so bold and defiant.

12

*T*win Oaks rivaled the finest plantations along the Potomac, encompassing one thousand sprawling acres of rich, green pastureland. The oaks that gave the estate its name could be seen atop a hill from the riverbank. The furthest point to the south and west stretched to the branch of the Shenandoah River, where it converged with the Potomac near Harpers Ferry.

It was on of the first estates in this part of Virginia, and the house, erected in 1724, had replaced the log cabin built by Thaddeus Rhendon, the grandfather of the current owner, Captain Rhendon. Abiding with him were his wife Amelia, two daughters, and his infant son, Daniel.

Hayward knew of the prosperity of Twin Oaks; Rhendon's ownership of twenty slaves, ten of which were indentured from England; and the splendid thoroughbreds that rivaled any racers in the Potomac lowlands. "One day River Run will be great," Eliza responded when he described Rhendon's good fortune with a hint of jealousy in his voice. "It will take time and hard work. Do not envy what Captain Rhendon has inherited."

Hayward lifted his hand away from his chin. "I suppose you will say it is a sin. You are your father's daughter, after all."

"It shall only bring you sorrow if you covet what is not yours. Be happy for your friend instead."

"He is not quite my *friend*. Merely an acquaintance."

"Is his wife an amiable woman?"

He laid his hand over his knee and looked out the carriage window. "I imagine so. I have not met her, but they say she is pretty, and Southern through and through, from an old Williamsburg family and one not to debate with over Southern ideologies."

"I see. That is a pity."

He glanced at her, his brow severe. "Eliza . . ."

"Never fear. I am passionate on many subjects, but for your sake I shall hold my tongue and behave. Besides, it is unseemly for a woman to debate in public."

"Humph. You would debate if you were prodded enough, I wager."

She smiled broadly. "You have gotten to know me so well, Hayward. But I promise to rein in all temptation to let loose on any subject that comes up."

Pleased to hear she would behave, Hayward fastened his eyes on his wife's youthful face. A hint of powder graced it, but nothing more. Her eyes sparkled from the flickering sunlight that danced through the trees as their carriage passed along the road.

When they crossed the bridge at the point closest to the river, Eliza leaned toward the window. He saw she had no fear as it swirled below. The quick rise and fall of her breathing caused the gold cross she wore to flash at her throat.

He wondered why he had still not fallen deeply in love with the woman behind the eyes, behind the flesh he so desired. What prevented him? What held him back from opening up his heart? The gentle curve of her mouth and the glint of her expression spoke of her kindness, her virtue, and her goodness, all things that thrived beneath the outward appearance. But her flesh meant more to him than the whole of her.

He stared, studying the inquisitive expression on her face as she admired the passing landscape. It was then he decided he had to make an effort.

A scarlet-clad footman assisted Eliza down. Eager and nervous, she gazed at the crowd of people that moved up the broad marble steps to the veranda lined with white portico columns. So much did the house resemble the Georgian manors of England that she smiled at the irony. They talked of breaking free from England, yet did not mind the architecture of Britain's most prominent aristocrats.

Greeting guests by the door stood Virginia's nobility. The Rhendons looked as regal as any blue-blooded couple Eliza had ever seen. Beside them stood a gentleman whose way of standing out in the crowd caught her immediate attention. His proud expression mirrored Hayward's—yet not so handsomely. At least that is what Eliza told herself to stave off a quick flutter of the heart.

Hayward held his arm out to her, and she coiled hers through it and laid her gloved hand over his forearm. Her wide-brimmed hat shadowed her face. The ivory-colored ribbon that held it hung loose along her throat where her necklace dangled and sparkled. The gold cross pressed against her skin, and she thought how faith had brought her to this point—faith in God, faith in herself to be strong enough to carry out His plan for her life. She sensed she would need it tonight, and decided she would always wear the necklace to remind her of where she had been and where she was going.

In unison, heads turned. Women spoke to one another in whispers. They looked her up and down, judging her over a mere color, Eliza thought. Or was it over something else? And by the glances they gave her husband behind their painted fans, she knew they found him handsome. She was proud to be his wife, and admired how fine he looked in his new suit of clothes.

The breeze rustled the wisteria that grew along the lattice of the veranda. Her nerves were taut as they made the final step. Captain Rhendon offered a friendly hand to Hayward, and they shook. Hayward bowed to Mrs. Rhendon and kissed the top of her hand. He was gracious, having not become so much of a frontiersman that he had lost the courtly manner of an English gentleman.

As Hayward brought Eliza forward to introduce her, Amelia Rhendon looked down her long Grecian nose and measured her head to toe.

Assessing me, is she? Seeing if I am properly attired in the latest fashion? Oh, Lord, how shall I ever fit in with such wealthy people?

With grace, Eliza curtsyed. Captain Rhendon reached for her hand and grasped it. "It is a pleasure, Mrs. Morgan. My, you are as pretty as a peach, if you don't mind me saying."

His tone was kind, and she liked him. "Thank you for the compliment, sir."

"You are welcome to more if your husband does not object." With a jolly laugh, he turned to his wife. "Amelia, my dear, you have at last seen the elusive Mrs. Morgan. What do you think?"

Amelia arched her fine brows high. "Mrs. Morgan is the personification of what I imagine an Englishwoman to be.

But I declare, is that the fashion in Britain these days, my dear, that a lady should wear such earthy colors this time of year? As you can see, the ladies present wear cooler shades." Amelia swept out her hand to point out the crowd of maids and matrons.

Eliza smiled lightly. "I have not yet learned the customs in America, when it comes to dress." She then looked at the ornate frame that surrounded the doorway. "Twin Oaks is beautiful, Mrs. Rhendon. It reminds me of home."

"Which is where, exactly?" Amelia asked in her finest Southern drawl.

"Well, home is River Run. But Derbyshire before that."

Amelia snapped open her fan. "As it was for our ancestors here in Virginia. But more specifically, Mrs. Morgan. Where were you born and raised? What are your family connections?"

"I am from the Hope Valley, ma'am. My father was a vicar, my mother a gentleman's daughter."

Eliza's hostess raised her slim brows again. "A vicar, you say? How interesting."

"If you please, Mrs. Rhendon, I would be grateful if you would educate me on the customs of His Majesty's Colonies. I know so little, and . . ."

Murmurs rippled through the crowd, and heads turned. The gentle pressure of Hayward's hand around Eliza's fingers signaled she should say nothing more. Mortified, she felt heat color her cheeks.

However, the good-looking gentleman who leaned against the wall nearby smiled. He looked quite amused at Eliza's comment, and fastened a pair of dark blue eyes upon her. So long did he stare that she grew agitated, all her muscles tensing.

Then she heard the words, "to Hades with King George." A swift chill raced through her. She glanced at Mrs. Rhendon.

"I . . . forgive me. I believe I have said something wrong, or may have spoken out of turn."

"Your husband will explain," said Amelia. "You will excuse me. I must attend to my other guests." With a proud lift of her chin, she sashayed away.

Hayward leaned near Eliza's ear. "You mustn't refer to the Colonies as belonging to King George. As you can tell, the majority of the company here would prefer to hang him rather than kowtow to the inane monarch."

Eliza placed her hand against her lips. How could she have made such a blunder, embarrassed him and offended her hostess? "I am sorry, Hayward. It was a mere slip of the tongue."

"Take care of what you say from now on." He turned from her, and soon they were separated. Convinced she had disappointed him, his departure grieved her.

Captain Rhendon patted her hand. "It will take some time to acquaint yourself with our ways."

She lowered her head. "Thank you, sir. Whatever my husband's politics are, I shall keep to those."

"Very wise, and a sign of true devotion, ma'am." Rhendon took her a few steps past the door and held his hand out to her. "Now come along. I wish to introduce you to someone."

13

The gentleman whose face had caught her eye earlier, stood with arms folded and turned when Captain Rhendon hailed him. Eliza could not help but notice how broad his shoulders were. His hair, the blond color of a buckskin stallion's coat, fell between his shoulder blades in a neat ponytail secured with a crepe ribbon. He wore a suit of buff linen, and riding boots. Hayward would never allow mud to remain on his boots like this man, Eliza thought.

"Halston, may I introduce Mrs. Eliza Morgan of River Run? She is newly come to our country from England and is in need of friends—she and her husband, whom you shall meet in a moment when he rejoins such a lovely wife. I believe you are close neighbors, on the other side of the river."

Halston dropped his arms and bowed. His eyes locked onto hers.

"My young cousin, ma'am," said Captain Rhendon. "Jeremy Halston. He knows more about horses than anyone I know— besides myself."

Halston reached for her hand, then kissed it. "Your servant, ma'am." Quick as she could, Eliza withdrew her fingers from his.

At that moment, Hayward returned to Eliza's side, and he and Halston were introduced. "Halston recently acquired land on your side of the river, Mr. Morgan," Captain Rhendon said, "and that fine blacksmith shop along the road. If I didn't have a good smithy of my own, I would take my horses there to be shod."

"I am familiar with Old Benjamin, sir." Hayward directed his comment to Halston. "I hope you kept him on."

Lifting his eyes away from Eliza, Halston looked over at Hayward. "He is too valuable to let go. His time of indenture has passed, but I was able to bribe him into staying with a yearly sum of fifteen pounds and an apprentice. I hope you will continue to avail yourself of Ben's skills, sir."

"Of course," Hayward nodded.

A silence followed, and Eliza saw a spark of dislike grow between the two men, as if they had raised crossed rapiers between them. How stiff and cool Hayward had become. As for Halston, a look of challenge flared in his eyes.

Hayward set her hand on his left arm and withdrew with her through the door to a cavernous foyer, where twin staircases wound to the upper story. Two footmen, sentries whose eyes never met a guest's and whose gloved hands were ready to open the door wider, flanked the ballroom doors.

Making their way amid the rustle of silks and a sea of quivering fans, Hayward brought Eliza to a chair beside a pair of open French doors. These led to a terrace that allowed the breeze to float indoors. The scent of roses from the garden reminded her of the rose vine that grew up the walls of the vicarage. She thought of her dear papa, felt the tinge of grief grip her, and forbade the careful smile that graced her lips to fade.

What would he think of her running off and marrying Hayward Morgan against his father's wishes? What would he say if he knew how Hayward had broken his mother's heart by leaving England, by wedding a girl below what she insisted he deserved? Would her papa share in her belief that her feet were set on this path by the Almighty?

Ah, but he would be proud I married for love, and be content that my needs are met by a husband of means.

Hayward left her to talk to Rhendon about *matters best left to men*. She knew what he meant—war, rebellion. Wives and husbands separated. Nevertheless, he promised to return shortly after a few pressing details were discussed that were on his mind. Feeling a bit lonely and out of place, she glanced over at Amelia and her bevy of ladies. Not a one acknowledged her. She might as well fade right into the walls. What she overheard nearby caused her to frown.

"Hayward Morgan could have had his pick of any unwedded woman in the room—in the whole of Virginia and Maryland for that matter."

"He is so handsome. I am glad he has returned, even though he brought a wife back with him."

"Yes, but was it necessary to go back to England to find a wife?"

"I saw her a moment ago on his arm. She is beautiful, and puts most of us to shame when it comes to our Southern good looks."

"Is it true he had an understanding in England, with a lady of quality?"

"Rumor has it she rejected him, and out of desperation, and no doubt to quell embarrassment, he married a vicar's daughter, not that a vicar's daughter is any less than quality. But I imagine she does not stand up to the other lady socially."

"I am not surprised he was jilted. So few upper-class Englishwomen would leave their comforts for River Run."

"Hmm. A lack of fortitude, I would say. Well, we can at least give that to the Mrs. Morgan. She does not strike me as being snobbish, as I would have imagined."

"But oh, that gown. It is not the fashion at all, and the neckline is too low."

"Ladies." Eliza heard Halston's voice clearly above the others. "Mrs. Morgan is seated near. Perhaps you should ask her for yourselves all those nagging questions that are swimming in your pretty heads?"

In unison, four young women turned their heads in her direction. Eliza stood to face them. They curtsyed, and then each made her excuses. Halston remained where he was, his hands clasped behind his back.

"You must pardon their ill manners, Mrs. Morgan. They are only curious."

"Thank you, Mr. Halston. You came to my rescue."

He bowed. "It was my pleasure. Our ways must seem judgmental to you, and I am afraid they are."

"Now that they have met me, I wonder what they are saying."

"God is the only one who knows," he said. "They are jealous, I can tell you that. Just look at them grouped together like clucking hens, their faces flushed and sweaty from the heat."

The heat suddenly made her feel faint, and she drew in a breath. "It is quite hot, sir."

"Why, you look cool to me, Mrs. Morgan." He stood next to her as she lowered herself back into the chair. "I wonder.

Did you inherit the deep color of your hair, those violet eyes, and your fine complexion from your mother?"

Eliza did not know what to say. Part of her was flattered. But the wife in her felt affronted he would be so brazen as to compliment her. "Flattery, Mr. Halston, is not becoming when a man directs it toward another man's wife."

"I agree. I shall restrict my comments to the weather and horses from now on so that we may be friends."

"Thank you. Nevertheless, I was told I took after my mother."

He creased his brow. "Told?"

"Yes. She has been long in Heaven, sir." To be reminded of her loss stung, and she lowered her head. "My father recently joined her."

"You believe in such a place?"

Surprised by his question, she looked up at him. "You do not?"

"I am not sure of anything, except the present."

"Then I am sorry for you, sir. Those who believe are not like those who do not. Without faith, one has no hope in this world."

"I recall my father saying faith is the substance of things hoped for . . ."

"The evidence of things not seen," Eliza finished.

Halston smiled. "Indeed."

"It is something to ponder, Mr. Halston."

"Perhaps you're right, and I should explore it further. If I call upon you—and your husband—we could converse on the subject."

"You would be most welcome at River Run," she said. "But are you not leaving to fight the British as are most of the men?"

"I'm unsure on that account as well."

Hoping he would not think her too bold, Eliza made him a promise. "I shall pray for you this night, sir, that you are given the direction you need so that you are certain which course to take."

He looked stunned and gazed at her with a smile that trembled over the corner of his mouth. His eyes were fixed on her, almost as if she were the only woman in the room. "You have just now helped me see the path I'll take, Mrs. Morgan. Your faith works quickly."

She shook her head. "I do not understand."

"I will not be leaving. Not for a long while. I will remain on my land, even if they call me a loyalist and a coward." He leaned down. "A man must protect the things he holds dear. He must hold his ground against all who stand in his way."

A wave of bewilderment struck Eliza. Never had a man spoken to her with such freedom, except for Hayward. She thought him audacious, but wondered if this was the way men behaved in the Colonies. Was it acceptable to speak honestly and with such flattery between the sexes here? Nonetheless, his admission that he must protect the things he prized flustered her as she realized his subtle implication. He spoke in a hushed tone and with a hint of passion.

Halston pointed out a lady on the opposite side of the room. "I am afraid I have caught the eye of Miss Lee. There, you see? She calls me over with a tilt of her fan."

She glanced over at Miss Lee, a petite young lady with cascades of blonde ringlets and too much rouge. On the final word, Halston bowed and stepped away.

From the French doors, a cool breeze tousled the hem of Eliza's gown. It felt heavenly and chased the heat away. Hayward stepped out of a side door with Captain Rhendon and several other gentlemen, two dressed in militia blue. Lifting her chin, she gathered her skirts and proceeded forward.

"Are you having a good time?" he asked, accepting her arm through his.

"I am lonely without you."

He leaned down and kissed her cheek, then drew her out onto the veranda to escape the closeness of the room.

14

A chestnut horse pounded down the lane at a brisk gallop, kicking up clods of dirt beneath its hooves. Everyone on the veranda craned their necks and looked in its direction. A dusty Express Rider on its back yanked on the reins, brought the steed skidding to a halt below the veranda stairs, leapt to the ground, and bounded up the steps. Catching his breath, he drew off his slouch hat, his brow studded with beads of sweat.

"I bring word from the North, gentlemen. Heralds of liberty are passing the news through the towns and plantations. We've had our first major fight with the British."

Captain Rhendon motioned to one of his finely dressed servants. "Samuel, bring this man a mug of water, and have Lily fix him a plate of food."

"I am grateful for that, sir. It has been a long ride. You're Captain Rhendon?"

"I am." Eliza noticed how proudly Captain Rhendon raised his head, as if he knew what was coming next.

"I have a packet for you, from Mr. Lee in Philadelphia."

"My uncle!" shouted Miss Lee and shouldered her way through the crowd to stand beside Mrs. Rhendon.

"Where and when did the fighting start, lad?" said Captain Rhendon. "Give us all the details you can."

"Boston. Breed's Hill." He gulped down water from the pewter cup handed him and wiped his sleeve across his mouth. "Our men were attacked. British soldiers stormed the hill. The order on our side—not to fire until we see the whites of their eyes."

A gasp circled around the crowd. Eliza glanced at the faces of the gentlemen. They were stiff with anger, their eyes riveted upon the messenger. She looked at Hayward and saw a muscle in his jaw flex. She squeezed his hand.

"The Patriots let loose a volley of musket fire when the Redcoats got within fifteen yards. Once our boys ran out of ammunition—with only their bayonets and stones to defend themselves—the Brits took the hill. But they lost half their force—in all over two hundred killed and eight hundred wounded."

Hayward took a step forward. "And the Patriots?"

"One hundred and forty killed, sir, including General Warren. You'll find the details written down inside the packet, Mr. Rhendon."

The news distressed Eliza, that those of her homeland had fallen along with the Americans, her new countrymen; and to sense her husband's fury rise caused her heart to ache. All doubt vanished. He'd certainly be leaving her to fight for the *Glorious Cause*.

"General Washington has taken command of the Continental Army," the messenger went on. "We have rallied seventeen thousand men."

"Then the struggle for our liberty is on!" shouted one man. Others followed, and there boiled over a great hubbub of talk.

Halston stepped to the rail of the terrace to be seen. "Gentlemen, we must be calm and not rush off without careful thought. Captain Rhendon, you understand how brutal war can be. You served under Braddock. You saw things no man should have to see. Do you not agree we should persuade our leaders to use more diplomatic measures before engaging in a bloody conflict that is sure to bring great suffering to our country?"

"What good does diplomacy do when we are up against tyranny?" Hayward said, raising his voice above the others. Eliza heard him say beneath his breath, "*coward.*"

The Express Rider set his plate of food aside and raised his arms to calm the crowd. "Gentlemen, gentlemen. Congress has sent the King a petition—an olive branch which expresses hope for reconciliation."

"One last attempt at *diplomacy?*" one mocked.

"Aye, and the King will trample it under his boot heels," said another.

"God bless our brave patriots!" went round.

Hayward broke away from Eliza and stood beside the rider. "I was born and bred in England by a father loyal to his king and country. I left to build a new life with my wife, and shudder to think of our children living under a monarch's rule. His power will overtake us unless we fight and win our independence. If it means bloodshed, then so be it. Future generations will thank us."

He continued on, speaking with such conviction that it sent chills racing up her spine. Eliza had never heard him speak with such authority, and it almost frightened her to think where his convictions might lead him, where they might leave her. *A widow in the wilderness? No, I cannot consider it to ever be so.*

The messenger squashed his hat back on. "Be assured, good men, the Delegates have no intention of staying under the power of a tyrant. They will stand their ground if the King dashes all hope of foregoing a war. God bless our *Glorious Cause.*"

With a nod, he touched the brim of his hat and bid them farewell. Shoving his boot into the stirrup, he climbed back in the saddle, spurred his horse, and raced off. With excitement surging through her, Eliza watched the cloud of rust-colored dust rise behind his horse's hooves. He was on to another village, another plantation, to spread the news. Some of the solemn crowd drifted back inside. Others lingered outside.

Eliza looked up at Hayward as he ran his hand slowly down her forearm. "This news is not good news. Let us go home."

A lady, who had earlier stared with disapproval at Eliza's gown, approached them. She slipped her hand into the crook of Hayward's arm, drawing close as if she were a moth to flame. The rice powder applied to her face creased with her smile.

"You have not danced the whole evening, Mr. Morgan. There is talk, you know. For you left your wife sitting all alone to fend off the young men of our party."

Hayward lifted his eyes from her and glanced at Eliza. "Let them gossip, Miss Stapleton. It is what women do best."

Laughing, Miss Stapleton tapped his chest lightly with the tip of her fan. "Such an insulting rogue. What do you expect?"

"For people to mind their own business."

"But what if there is something you should be warned of? Isn't that important?"

"If you have something *important* to say, then say it quickly."

Eliza struggled to find the words to disarm her husband and stop any further intrusions from Miss Stapleton. Chagrined at Hayward's rude demeanor, she attempted to draw him away. But Miss Stapleton kept step with them.

"It concerns Mr. Halston," she said. "You may not know this, but he chases women like a fox chases rabbits, and he cares not whether they are married. Mrs. Morgan, you must be careful. Halston was much too liberal with his compliments toward you."

Hayward fumed inwardly. Eliza knew this, for while Miss Stapleton spoke she felt his body stiffen beside her.

"I heard him praise the color of your hair and eyes. And once, he drew so close that he whispered in your ear. My friends and I saw you blush." Miss Stapleton wagged a finger at Eliza and giggled. "You must beware of Halston. He purports himself to be a man of high Christian morals, but his actions speak otherwise."

Not able to help herself, Eliza heaved a breath and bit down on her tongue to hold back what she wanted to say. No. She could not embarrass her husband by reprimanding *Miss Busybody*.

Miss Stapleton cocked her head to one side. "You are new to our country. It is not your fault he would be so infatuated."

Narrowing his eyes, Hayward strode across the room, through the weave of dance partners, to where Halston stood with his back turned. Eliza's heart went up into her throat. Hayward clapped his hand over Halston's shoulder. Halston turned, and their eyes locked.

"Oh, perhaps I said too much." Miss Stapleton said.

"Far too much, ma'am." Eliza went forward, her head swimming with what to do to prevent a confrontation that could result in disaster. As she drew closer, she met Halston's eyes momentarily and she made sure to scowl at him.

Halston gestured toward Eliza. "Does your wife trail behind you in most instances, sir? Why, she should be hanging on your arm. If she were mine, I'd not allow her to leave my side.

I'd be showing her off to every man in the room, inciting their envy."

Hayward flexed his fists at his side. "You have taken liberties with her that I will not stand for."

Halston's expression remained calm and reserved. "Neither by word nor deed did I say or do anything that was not honorable."

"It has widely spread that you did. I forbid you to speak to my wife again."

Halston looked him straight in the eyes. "Take care, sir. Some women welcome the attention of other men, if neglected."

With her temples pounding, Eliza reached for her husband's hand. But before she could grasp it, Hayward snatched Halston by his collar and yanked him forward. "You know nothing of my wife." Then he released him. Halston's face turned scarlet, and he set his mouth firm.

Without delay, Hayward took hold of Eliza's arm and strode with her out of the ballroom. They went down the broad stairs to their carriage. She climbed inside and leaned toward him before he shut the door. "Please do not be angry."

"I am not angry with you. But you should not have let him speak to you for so long. Everyone, it seems, noticed."

"I should have been more guarded."

"Well, I shouldn't have left you alone."

"But you had important matters to discuss with the gentlemen. And then . . ."

"Yes, word came of the fighting."

Her heart ached. "Come sit beside me." Beside her now, he put his arm around her shoulders. Her eyes filled as she absorbed this show of affection. Her prayers were answered, she hoped, that he loved her—finally. Or had it been there all along? "How will I do without you, my love?"

Sighing, Hayward drew her close. "We may be separated by war for a time. But nothing shall come between us."

In each other's arms, they sunk back against the seat, into the corner sheltered from the fading sunlight. As the carriage rolled on, a mockingbird's song echoed through the trees, and the scent of dusty leaves rose out of the forest. Eliza wondered if it was the roar of the rapids in the river she heard? Or was it the cry of her soul that had been borne on the wind?

15

$\mathcal{T}$hree days had drifted slowly by, and still Hayward had not returned home. Eliza had spent a restless night, and lay awake thinking of him, praying that the Lord would provide a way other than war to bring the Colonies freedom, and that He would soften the King's heart. She tossed and turned, and when she finally fell to sleep, the sound of the wind blowing through the elms woke her. Donning a linen robe, she slipped out of bed and went to the window. The night sky hung heavy with clouds, and the wind blew across the land like the breath of a Titan.

She listened to the wind moan and rage against the walls of her house. She thought she heard the hollow sound of horse's hooves on the road beyond. But when the wind lessened, the only sound that remained was the rain pelting the roof.

With a heavy sigh, she returned to bed, and smiled when a flutter moved across her belly. She laid her hand there, and, feeling content, slept until dawn.

The moment morning broke over the hills and spilled through the windows at River Run, Eliza bathed, dressed, and hurried downstairs, her bare feet pattering over the oak steps. Fiona met her at the landing.

"Good morn, my girl. Hope you have a hearty appetite this morning. The hens laid more eggs than expected."

Eliza pulled her long hair over one shoulder and drew her fingers through it. "I am hungry. Let us break our fast out on the porch. It is too glorious a morning to be inside."

Fiona slipped off to the kitchen, while Eliza stepped out the front door and breathed in the scent of honeysuckle. She watched a blue heron glide across the sky toward the river and listened to the faint hum of a bumblebee hovering over the wild daisies. "Weeping may endure for a night, but singing comes in the morning," she whispered as songbirds grew boisterous with the strengthening sun.

She sat down on the stoop, and shortly afterward Fiona handed her a plate of eggs and a mug of cold tea. Together they bowed their heads. Addison strode around the corner in work clothes, then paused and tipped his hat.

Eliza smiled. "Good morn, Addison. Had your breakfast?"

He smacked his lips. "Yes, ma'am. Mistress Goodall knows how to please a man with her cookery." He winked at Fiona and she huffed. "'Tis the best I've ever had, next to my dear mother's. God rest her soul."

"Aren't you going to thank Addison for the compliment, Fiona?" Eliza said as she handed over her empty plate.

Fiona pursed her lips. "Hmm. I suppose I must. I am not one to be so rude not to thank you, Addison."

"And I thank you, Mistress Goodall, for the fine shirt. I promise to keep it clean, and wear it to church, and not every day."

"I put a lot of work into it," Fiona said. "To be careful with it will please me."

Eliza could not help but notice the way Addison looked at Fiona. Twenty years dissolved from his rugged face, and his eyes glowed. Yet to proclaim any feeling for her would be a feat for him. Fiona believed herself to be his better, and his knowledge of the world set them miles apart. Eliza had not gotten to know him much through conversation, but thought him to be one who strove to live a godly life. He never complained, and worked hard from sunup to sundown.

"Have you heard any news along the river?" she asked.

"No more than what I was told weeks ago, mistress. I did meet Mr. Halston along the road yesterday. I took Nell to be shod, and he was good enough to give pause to speak to me. He asked about you, said he'd seen you the day before while you were out walking."

The happiness of the day sunk in her. Halston had seen her out strolling on her own and had said nothing? Why had he not made his presence known or greeted her in a friendly way? "For how long did he watch me, did he say?"

"I don't know, mistress. He told me I should go with you when you're out walking, when Mr. Hayward is away from home, that it isn't safe for you to be out on your own."

"I am fine. I take my pistol with me just in case. But if you want to come along, you may. And if you happen to see Mr. Halston again, tell him I do not fancy being watched. He should speak to me the next time."

Addison nodded and pulled down his tricorn hat. "I reckon Mr. Hayward will be home soon. If I don't get my work done, he'll not be happy."

Eliza lifted her eyes toward the place where their lane turned out onto the river path. "He has been gone four days."

Addison followed the direction of her eyes. "Don't fear, mistress. He'll be back soon and full of vinegar, I imagine. Talk of war seems to do that to men."

"That is true . . . Now I shall walk along the creek to the path where I can see the river."

Addison gave her a quick bow and headed toward the stable. Eliza stepped down from the porch, gathering her hair into a knot so as to feel the breeze touch the back of her neck. Sunlight sparkled through the trees, and the leaves twisted and turned. At the bank of Israel Creek, she found a patch of blue forget-me-nots. She bent down and ran her hand across the blossoms. The gallop of a horse grew louder, and she stood.

Hayward. My beloved!

Out of the dusky light, a riderless horse appeared. The reins dragged along the dirt, and the horse shook its mane and snorted. Refusing to believe what her eyes beheld, Eliza stood motionless, her breath coming in short gasps. Omega flared his nostrils, lifted his head, and stood still in the middle of the road. She ran to him, and, taking the reins in hand, she soothed the horse with gentle words and touches.

There were no signs of injury to the horse. No sign of a struggle of any kind. Hayward's saddlebag and musket were untouched. She called out to Fiona, to Addison. She led Omega back toward home, reaching the lane breathless and tearful. Addison met her at a sprint as Fiona hurried down the porch stairs.

She struggled to get the words out. "He came down the road without my husband."

"I know this trail and these woods better than any man along this river," said Addison. "I'll find Mr. Hayward. You have my word on it."

Addison mounted the stallion, turned it around, and galloped off.

16

*E*liza walked an anxious quarter mile with Fiona hasten-ing beside her. Not once had her steps slowed as she hurried down the path shaded by ancient trees. She scolded herself for not thinking to fetch her mare and follow after Addison. He hollered up the road, galloping back at breakneck speed. Rounding the bend, he jerked on the reins, and the horse halted abruptly.

"Not far . . . I found him . . ." Addison steadied the horse as it turned in a circle. "He was thrown from the saddle. Alive, thank the Lord."

Eliza's heart pounded. "Is he badly hurt?"

"Yes. He's hurt all right."

Her mind whirled with fear. "I must go to him. Give me a landmark—something to go by."

"He's under the sycamore, the one with the markings of the Shawnee, about a quarter mile down the road."

"Hurry and fetch a litter, Addison. There is no time to lose."

With his face set like flint, Addison urged the horse into motion with a swift kick of his heels. Eliza hurried, gathered her skirts to her knees, and, once she was a distance down the road, her eyes searched intently for the sycamore. Somewhere within those dim and fearsome shadows, upon the tall grass alongside the dusty way, lay her beloved.

The long trill of a cicada signaled the coming heat of the day. Eliza wiped the sweat off her forehead with her sleeve and rushed on. Fiona lagged behind. Just beyond a crop of willows stood the old tree, and upon sight of it, Eliza's heart grew in her throat, and she ran toward it.

Hayward lay with one arm beneath him, his head cradled in the crook of the other. His hair was matted with blood above his left ear. A scarlet trail of it curved down his neck and stained his stark white neckcloth.

Eliza fell to her knees beside him. Eyes closed, he made no response to the trembling sound of her voice. With deft fingers she felt his warm skin and the pulse that passed through his body. Tears fell from her eyes, and she swiped them away with the back of her hand.

"He makes no sound," she said to Fiona. "Oh, he is badly injured." She tore the hem of her chemise, the cotton cloth giving way easily to the strength of her hands. Wrapping the cloth carefully around his head, she spoke softly. She tore another and handed it to Fiona. Down the bank to the river Fiona hurried, then returned with the cloth soaked with water. Eliza touched Hayward's lips with it, and ran it gently over his face, hoping to revive him. A moment later his eyes slowly opened, and he moaned.

Eliza stroked his forehead. "Lie still, my love."

"Eliza . . ." He grimaced in pain and strove to move.

"You have had a fall and must not move."

"Horse . . . I . . ." His eyes closed again. The reality that his injury could mean his life coursed through her, as if an icy hand had grabbed hold of her and tapped frozen fingers over her skin.

"Do not take him from me, Lord. Be with him now, and show me what to do." She kissed Hayward's face as her tears dropped onto his hair.

Clouds gathered over the Potomac and made their way to River Run, up the hillsides and across the fields. The threat of a thunderstorm hung in the air, and all the birds had stilled by the time they carried Hayward to the door. He had not woken, nor had he stirred the whole time they hurried with him upon the litter, down the road and over the path to the house. Every fiber in Eliza trembled. Her hands turned white as she gripped the handles of the litter, her eyes not leaving his face, not for a moment.

She gave instructions to her servants as they lifted Hayward with great care from the litter onto the bed. "Open the windows wider, Fiona. We must allow as much fresh air in as possible . . . Bring me the quilt in the chest so I may cover him with it. Addison, do not stand there. You must ride like the wind and bring a doctor."

A quick nod, and Addison hurried out the door. She listened to his hurried footsteps run down the stairs and then Omega galloping off. A breeze filled with the scent of rain passed through the windows.

Eliza ran her hands along her husband's arms. No broken bones. But when she touched his thigh, a moan raked his throat. He tried to rise, and she moved him back.

"What should we do, dear girl?" Fiona threw her hand across her mouth and stifled a sob. "Poor Mr. Hayward."

"We need water."

She gazed at him, her vision blurred by tears. Tucking the quilt close to his body, Eliza whispered all would be well. God would see to it.

From the pitcher, Fiona filled the blue porcelain bowl on the washstand and brought it to the bedside. Eliza dipped a cloth into the water, wrung it out, and touched Hayward's brow. Blood seeped through the cloth that pressed against his wound.

Her hand trembled. "He bleeds so."

"Head wounds always do, my girl. Do not be troubled."

"How can I not be? He is gravely hurt. Pray for him, Fiona. God cannot take him from me." She turned to the woman who always comforted her in times of crisis. "He would not do that, would God, Fiona? Not now. Not when he has shown me he loves me, and that, well, I have not told you, not even Hayward, that I carry his child."

Fiona's brows shot up. "You are with child? And you helped carry your husband on that litter. I do say, Eliza, I sometimes wonder . . ."

"If I have any common sense in my head?"

Fiona shook hers from side to side. "Oh, 'tis there. But I wonder if you use it. You cannot do tasks like that when you are carrying a babe. Never mind all the reasons why. 'Tis only common sense."

Sighing, Eliza reached over and touched Fiona's hand. "You worry a great deal over me. I'll be more careful. But for now, turn your mind to my husband."

"Here, let me do that." Fiona took the cloth from Eliza's hand. "You sit beside the bed and hold his hand." And so Eliza obeyed Fiona's wisdom and sank into the chair. The breeze flowed through the window and brushed over her face, cool and comforting.

"Eliza . . ." Hayward turned his head to see her. His gaze fell on her face, but it seemed as though he did not see her.

She pressed his hand to her cheek. He wet his lips with his tongue. "Snake . . . Omega." He then drifted off.

Eliza looked over at Fiona. "A snake frightened the horse. It must have reared and thrown him off."

Hayward moaned. Eliza untied Hayward's neckcloth and slipped it away from his throat, loosened his shirt, and laid her hand on his chest to feel the beat of his heart.

"I must set my heart to prayer." Drawing in a deep breath, she closed her eyes and prayed as she had never prayed before.

Fiona lit a candle, for the room had grown dark with the thickening sky. She drew beside Eliza, knelt next to her, and folded her hands. "And Jesus saith unto him," she quoted, "I will come and heal him."

❧

Two hours passed with no sign of Addison or the doctor. Eliza stayed at her husband's bedside. He lay so still that at times terror seized her, and she would lean close to hear his breathing, in agony, not knowing whether he were still with her.

By the time the clock on the mantelpiece chimed another hour, a pair of horses galloped down the lane and halted at the door. Footsteps climbed the stairs, and Fiona hurried to open the door and go out into the hall. She returned, tugging a black-clad man by his sleeve. He brushed her off, smoothed his waistcoat, and set his bag on the foot of the bed.

Placing the back of his hand on Hayward's brow, he paused, his brown eyes attentive to the task. He lifted Hayward's wrist and timed his pulse with his pocket watch.

"There is no fever, Mrs. Morgan. But your husband may have suffered a concussion. You must keep him still, you understand." She nodded and kept her eyes intent upon the doctor's face. From it she could read more than he might want to tell her. He went on examining Hayward's wound. "You must keep this clean. Change the bandage every day."

He checked each of Hayward's limbs, examining his obviously injured leg last. Hayward cried out. "A small fracture of the femur," said the doctor, looking alarmed. "This is most serious. Again, he must be kept still. Otherwise, the bone may be bent for life. Fortunate for him, it was not a compound fracture. I will place a splint."

He looked over the rim of his spectacles. "You must keep a close eye on it. We do not want gangrene setting in. He could lose his leg if it does . . . and possibly his life."

Gangrene. Lose his leg. Possibly his life! His words sent a shock wave though her.

"As for the concussion, let us pray he wakes soon. It would be wise for you to consider what will happen if he does not."

Fighting back tears, a lump swelled in Eliza's throat and she looked worriedly into her husband's face. His head rested against the pillow. His hair fell over his neck. Such love she bore for him that she begged God to spare his life at any cost to her.

The doctor touched Eliza on the shoulder. "He should be kept quiet and cool."

"Yes."

"If he comes around, you may feed him apples boiled in milk if he is hungry."

"May I give him tea, sir?"

"If he wants it. He will need to stay in bed for several weeks. It is not necessary, however, that he should lie all that time upon his back. After the second week, have your manservant gently raise him up."

"May we seat him near the window? It is shaded in the late afternoon, and the breeze from the river is refreshing."

"Yes, that would greatly revive him. Your husband is not to exert himself in any way. It could delay healing."

She recalled that, when she was fifteen, a poor farmer, one of the members of her father's flock, had fallen from the pitch of his roof while making repairs. For days, he lingered in and out of consciousness, until at last he died. She remembered the lost stares of his eight children, and how his wife had wept to the point of exhaustion. Nothing her father said or did could console the distraught woman.

After the doctor left, Eliza fell on her knees at Hayward's bedside and grasped his hand. She put her lips to his fingers and kissed them. She prayed until she could no longer keep her eyes open, drifting to sleep near him, believing that the Father of all comfort heard her pleas.

It was not until the next evening when darkness came that Hayward opened his eyes and looked over at her. A candle set on the bedside table bathed his face in amber light, while the gibbous moon paled the room.

"Eliza . . ." he spoke her name in a sigh.

She drew closer.

"You should be here . . . beside me."

She kissed his lips. "Only if you promise to be still, my love."

"I have nowhere to go . . . for now."

"Yes, only for now." She told him what had happened, and what the fall had done to him. Tomorrow, she decided, she would tell him about their child.

Softly she climbed into bed, faced him, and eased her arm across his chest. Long into the night, she listened to his breathing, felt the beat of his heart against the palm of her hand. Finally, when the clock on the mantle tapped out two in the morning, she drifted off to sleep with the breeze flowing through the window upon them both.

17

$\mathcal{B}$right sunshine touched Eliza's eyelids. She woke at the sound of the cock's crow and rose quietly—so as not to wake Hayward. Her feet touched the cool floor, and she tiptoed over to the window, where she tied the curtains back with a broad ribbon from her sewing basket. It was already a warm day, the sky pale and cloudy. She stood there a moment to feel the breeze sweep over her face. Eyes closed, she drew in the forest scents that came down from the mountains, where hardwoods shaded fern and rhododendron.

Turning from the window, she slipped into her brown homespun gown of soft cotton. She ran her hand across her belly, the fabric slightly tauter than the week before.

Warmth prickled over her body, and she turned aside to her husband. She touched his hair with her fingertips. It was soft between her fingers, and the feel of it caused her heart to swell as she looked down into his face. He did not stir, and she prayed he would remain so a little longer.

She went to wash her face and hands, but the pitcher and basin were dry. There would be water downstairs in the kitchen, and so she stepped from the room, pitcher in hand, to fetch more. Little remained in the wooden cask, and so she picked up the bucket beside it and went out into the heat and sunshine.

The path had been swept clean by the night winds. Spheres of sunlight flickered over it. Eliza did not neglect to take in the beauty that surrounded her. Great trees shaded the way, and honeysuckle vine wove through patches of wild rose. She could have fetched water from the creek, for it was closer than the river. But when she saw the patch of blue water through the trees and a pair of cranes standing on the rocks, she set the bucket down at creek side, and headed toward it. A few moments to herself was all she needed.

She lowered herself to the shore and dipped her hand into the river. She washed her face, and allowed the water to ripple down her neck. She sat down on the bank, listened to the rapids tumble over the rocks, and watched the water swirl in deep eddies. Hayward would be all right, her heart told her. He would come down to this spot with her in a month or two and watch the sunset tint the river magenta and indigo.

She saw something indiscernible float toward her, turn in the current until it met with a rock and halted. Rapids gushed over it, and a crow fluttered above the water and landed on the rock. The crow paced close to the object, poked it with its beak, and then flew off.

Slowly Eliza stood. Realizing what her eyes beheld, she stared at the mass of gray and blue, at the Indian arrow imbedded in the dead man's back. She could not cry out, but stood frozen from the horror she saw coming toward her as the body dislodged itself. Hands, white and gnarled, stretched out to her, as if pleading with her to pull him out. A lump in her throat gave way, and a trembling breath escaped her lips. She scrambled up the embankment to the path. Fear gripped her, clutching at her heels as she ran. Could the warrior who killed the man be close by?

A horse whinnied, and she looked in its direction. She hadn't expected to see Mr. Halston riding toward her on his gray stallion. He lifted his hat to her, swung one leg over the saddle, and set his booted feet on solid ground.

"Good day to you, Mrs. Morgan. I hadn't thought to find you out walking alone, not with such dangers as we cannot imagine are possible. I heard your husband met with an accident, and I came to offer my condolences."

Eliza pushed a strand of her hair back from her eyes with a trembling hand. "There is . . . a man in the river."

Halston glanced toward the Potomac and placed his hand over the hilt of his pistol. "Did he try to harm you?"

"No. There is a body . . ."

"You're in shock. Come. I will take you home."

He placed his hands around her waist and lifted her onto his horse's back. Taking the reins, he led his mount on, over the dry earth that had hardened in the sun. Eliza looked down at him as he trudged ahead, grateful he had come along to help her. Surely Hayward would not object, but be as thankful as she.

She glanced back over her shoulder. Who was the poor soul who had been murdered? What was to be done with him? If he had not come far, she feared warriors were close enough to threaten her family.

The moment Halston helped Eliza down, Fiona bolted out the front door. "Come quick, my girl. Mr. Hayward is burning with fever. It came on him all of a sudden. He's making no sense in anything he's saying."

Eliza hurried up the stairs, then paused before going through the door. "I left the bucket at the mill. The cask is practically dry, and Hayward needs water."

She turned and started back down the stairs. Halston put his foot on the first step and stopped her. "Send your servant," he said. "I will return to the river and investigate what you have seen."

She set her hand over the railing. "Thank you, sir."

He bowed. "It is my honor."

She held his eyes a moment, then said to Fiona, "Find Addison for this gentleman. He has need of his help."

Hayward lay propped against the pillows, his leg wrapped tight in a splint. He made great effort to breathe, something Eliza knew was due to the force of the fever that raged through his veins. He looked at her through barely open, glassy eyes filled with pain. She hurried to him and touched his hands and brow. His skin was moist and hot, and tears welled in her eyes. He turned his head at her touch and spoke incoherently.

"My love, it is I, Eliza."

"Eliza—so thirsty."

Distressed, she grabbed the glass on the bedside table and put it to his lips. There was barely enough for a swallow, and he took it down. "More is coming, my love. Rest easy."

She drew back the bedclothes, stood and went to the window, where she flung the curtains back as far as she could. The breeze blew over her husband's flushed skin. Her hands hovered over him, searching for what to do, how to help him. It wasn't long before Fiona returned with water and poured it into the blue and white pitcher.

"Mr. Halston would not tell me why he and Addison were going down to the riverbank." She plunged a cloth into the washbowl and soaked it. "Only that my eyes should not see what was there." She wrung out the rag and handed it to Eliza. "What is it you saw?"

Eliza proceeded to wash Hayward's face. To tell Fiona the truth would cause her great worry. To hide it from her would be unfair. Deciding Fiona should be forewarned, Eliza bid her sit. "A man is in the river—killed by an Indian arrow. He could have come a long way downstream, so you mustn't allow your worries to rise."

Fiona's eyes grew large. "Lord, have mercy upon us. Perhaps Mr. Halston should stay a day or two to safeguard us."

"No, Hayward would not like it."

"Well, at least Addison is a good shot. And with Mr. Hayward so ill, we need the help."

"Addison knows what to do, Fiona. And remember, Mr. Hayward said there were no Indians that we need to fear this close downriver."

"I shall be more than obliged to help in any way you might need me, Mrs. Morgan." Halston stood just inside the door, his hat dangling from between his fingers. "Is Mr. Morgan very bad?"

Eliza pushed her hair back from her forehead. "I am distressed for him, sir. His fever is strong."

Halston showed no outward sign of compassion, and Eliza wondered why he had bothered to inquire in the first place. The rivalry and dislike between the two men proved evident in Halston's demeanor. And if Hayward knew that Halston stood in his doorway looking down on him with marked disdain, he would have him thrown out. But Eliza could not bring herself to ask him to leave—not after he had come to her aid.

Halston stepped back into the shadowy hall at the mention of fever. "Shall I send your man for the doctor . . . or, better yet, the minister? Fevers of this kind are known to take a person quickly."

His words caused Eliza to shiver. She stood and faced him. "I'll not allow it."

He leaned his hand against the doorjamb. "It is up to God, ma'am. Not you. You should prepare yourself for the worst."

Tears filled Eliza's eyes. "God will not allow it. He knows I love my husband and would not take him from me. Hayward is strong in body, and has a will to live."

Halston raised his brows, and his mouth curved into a quick grin. "Your trust in the Almighty is astounding, ma'am. I've seen too many people taken by fevers, so that I have little faith in miracles." He turned to leave. "By the way, there is no way of knowing who the man in the river was. He may have been a lone backwoodsman, so no one will ever know. Addison is burying the body and will mark the spot."

Eliza shut her eyes a moment, sorrowful for the unknown man. "It is not Christian to put him underground with no prayers spoken." Hayward moaned, and she drew back to him. His face was scarlet and beaded with sweat.

Eliza's brow creased with worry. "Mr. Halston, if you would send for a minister, please . . ."

"I'll have my servant ride over to the nearest parish church. I believe that is Mr. Hopewell. He is a Methodist, if that is suitable with you?"

"Of course." She bathed Hayward's face once more, stroked his cheek with the back of her hand. "It would give me ease if he would pray over the poor man's grave."

"Certainly. And no doubt it would ease your mind if he were to pray for your husband as well."

She nodded and looked over at him with misty eyes. "It would."

Halston left, and Eliza listened to his footsteps going down the stairs. The front door opened and closed. An impulse to go to the window and watch him ride away seized her, but she resisted. She loved Hayward and swore to be his alone, but realized suddenly her heart was vulnerable and needed to be guarded. Looking into her husband's face, she drove Halston from her mind.

She pressed her cheek against Hayward's hand and whispered a prayer. "Let him live, Lord. Please."

❦

By three that afternoon, the heat rose even higher. No breeze blew and the land stood still in the hazy heat. Eliza stayed at her husband's bedside, cooling his brow with water, but left him in Fiona's care when she heard the minister dismount and leave his horse at the hitching post.

Eli Hopewell and Eliza followed Addison out to the field where the backwoodsman had been laid to rest. Dressed in black and wearing the traditional white collar, Hopewell held his Bible close to his heart. His dark brown hair hung at shoulder length, touched at the temples with a bit of silver. His green eyes were sincere, and he had a kind, expressive face that was cleanly shaved.

"Mr. Halston gave me the details regarding this poor soul, Mrs. Morgan," Reverend Hopewell said. "It is good of you to provide a final resting place for him on your husband's land. Most would not." He stood over the mound of red clay and opened his prayer book.

Eliza gathered her hands together. "I only wish we knew who he was, sir." The heat grew oppressive, and she wished to feel a cool breeze blow. Standing in the shade, she looked up and noticed that the leaves on the trees had curled. Cicadas whirled, and bluebottle flies darted through the air.

Hopewell shook his head. "God knows who this man was, and that is what is important in the end. Your husband is ill,

I hear. When I have finished here, I will see him. I've also learned that this day the only doctor in these parts has left for Annapolis for good. Life in the frontier is too difficult for some people."

No doctor. This troubled Eliza. What would people do?

"There is no one else to care for the sick?"

"Most folks in these parts will make do on their own. They are of hardy stock."

After prayers were said, they walked back toward the house. There was not much he could do but pray over Eliza's husband and give her a comforting word. The grave look in his eyes when he saw Hayward, and his sudden pause in the doorway as he was leaving, disturbed her. Were her hopes too high for his recovery?

Hayward's dark eyes seemed to look past her, through her, and she knew his stupor had deepened. His breathing grew shallow as the hours passed by, causing her to fear he would slip away. She laid her head on his chest, and with her heart aching she listened to the beat of his. Her arms lay over his body in a gentle embrace. He shivered, and his muscles tightened. The heat grew excessive, and she stripped him of his clothes and washed his body to cool him.

In the predawn hours, his fever broke and he opened his eyes.

"I am hungry." His voice was weak and broken.

"I imagine so, my love. Fiona is preparing breakfast and will be upstairs with it soon. I hope you like apples and milk."

"Is that all?"

"For now."

"I would prefer a mess of eggs and bacon."

"Tomorrow," she said.

He winced in pain. "How long do I have to stay in this bed?"

"Weeks. So that your leg may heal properly."

"It will heal *properly* as long as I don't waste away here."

"I shall see to it you will not. But you must not be stubborn."

"If you would bring me work to do and books to read, that will keep my mind occupied."

A flutter crossed her belly, and she smiled. Happy, she set her hand over her stomach, shut her eyes, and prayed for the life growing inside her. "I've something important to tell you, Hayward. If you would lie still a moment and let me speak."

He looked at her, curious. "Yes, of course, Eliza. What is it?"

"Do you remember the day I told you there was so much for us to live for?"

"You have told me many things. But I do remember that."

"It was the day we received the invitation to Twin Oaks. I could have told you then, but something begged me to wait. Now that I am sure, I have to tell you . . . I am carrying a child."

She studied his face to see his reaction. It was as she hoped. Warm pleasure swam in his eyes. "A child? When?"

"Late February. Please tell me you are happy and that you love me."

He closed his hand over hers and held it. "Of course I'm happy. And you thought to ask to follow me off to war? Such foolish notions come into your pretty head, Eliza."

"Say you'll not leave until the child is born." He let go of her hand. "Please, Hayward. Surely, the army can do without you until then. Wouldn't you like to hold your baby in your arms when he takes his first breath?"

"I cannot promise anything. If I'm ordered away, then I must go."

She sighed. "I understand." She lowered her eyes and looked at her folded hands. How would she convince him to stay? Eliza hoped the love that had grown within him for her would prevail over a call to war. That nothing could be so strong as to pull him away from her or their child. Again, the babe pressed a tiny foot against her side. It caused her gladness to increase, and nothing else mattered in the world.

Sitting beside him on the bed, she leaned down and caressed his cheek. His eyes glowed as he looked into her face, and she touched her lips to his mouth. When she drew away, he wiped away the tear that escaped her eye.

"No, Eliza. I will not leave you. It would be wrong of me." He then drew her back to him and kissed her.

18

February, 1776

Hayward's recovery took time, but his temper quickened. Kept from joining his regiment in Annapolis, unable to ride, forbidden to walk without aid, the inactivity had hardened him. As Eliza's baby grew, her figure changed, and it broke her heart to see how he resented it. She saw in his eyes a cool gaze that said he longed for the once soft curves of her waist and hips, the slightness of her weight, and he told her on more than one occasion he hoped she'd return to her former beauty soon after his child was born.

More and more he withdrew affection from her, offering no embraces or even a warm kiss upon the cheek. She'd lie in bed long into the night and weep in silence. She missed the touch of his lips against hers, how he'd fill her with desire and make her feel wanted—loved. She said nothing to him about it. She needed to be patient.

His leg healed with time, but it left him with a slight limp. Determined not to allow his injury to affect his part in the fight for independence, he kept up with the correspondences that were a regular occurrence but kept the contents a secret. Once he had read them, they were tossed into the fire, and

Eliza wondered as she watched them burn what they were about. He would never share them with her.

After the harvest, farmers came to the mill, and Addison would take Hayward down to the creek to see them. Eliza would follow, and as soon as she came within earshot, the conversations among the men would stop. Although she disliked the secrecy and exclusion, she welcomed the sacks of flour they gave her, and sat beside Hayward, watching the mill wheel turn and the water splash over the rungs.

Mr. Halston had passed River Run with his blacksmith and apprentice on three occasions. He owned a substantial apple orchard and sent up to the house a barrel of the ripened fruit, a cask of cider, and several pounds of dried venison. Always his messages were directed to her, never Hayward.

> Dear Madam,
> Seeing we are neighbors, I am sending a portion of the fruit of my labor. I have heard of the impending arrival of your child and hope these gifts will sustain you in good health through the winter.
> Your humble servant,
> Jeremy Halston

At Christmas another gift arrived, a bolt of flax linen. Eliza ran her hands over the smooth fabric, elated by such a kind present, for linen of this quality was precious.

> Dear Madam,
> For your child—in hopes of a fine baptismal gown.
> Your devoted servant,
> Jeremy Halston

She had never shown Hayward the notes or mentioned the gifts. He was too preoccupied with going to war to be bothered by a barrel of apples and a bolt of fabric. In some ways, Eliza felt guilty for accepting Halston's presents. But as the notes became more frequent, she found herself anticipating them, and her heart beat more rapidly as her eyes traced his words, thinking it was only friendship she felt—nothing more than that.

A clouded sky thickened that night. A lengthy letter was placed in her hand, and at the end of the missive, Halston said he loved her. Deeply troubled by this, she stared at the ceiling and watched the shadows quiver over her head.

I must tell him not to send me any more letters. It could come to this, that he loves me—oh, but I think he does, Lord, and it is wrong. And wrong that I should feel anything for him. I must stop this at once. I mustn't accept anything from him, or see him, especially if Hayward joins the army and leaves me here alone. You must help me, Lord. Strengthen me to resist what my heart is feeling.

She drew herself up. Hayward was asleep in the chair by the fire. Bits of wood were bright red in the hearth, the ashes white. Snow stuck to the windows and heavy gales rushed across River Run. At the stroke of midnight, she felt the first pang of labor.

Shifting her legs over the side of the bed, she stood and made her way toward him. "Hayward . . . you must wake."

He sat forward and ran his hand over his face. "What is it?"

"I think you may need to wake Fiona."

He stood. "The child?"

"Yes." She gathered the bedclothes in her fists and clenched her teeth.

The fire crackled. The wind pushed against the house and deepened the chill of the room. A woolen wrap lay at the foot of the bed, and Eliza drew it over her shoulders. She shivered, and the babe turned within her.

"No, you mustn't." Hayward lifted her in his arms, carried her to the bed, and laid her in it. Afraid of what she faced, she noted the first tender gesture he'd given her in months.

"You love me, don't you, Hayward?" *Please tell me.*

"How can I not?" He drew her feet beneath the blanket. "I'll be back in a moment with Fiona. Lie quiet."

She set her hand over his arm. "I wish you would say the words. Especially now."

"It is hard for me. Besides, a man shouldn't have to say it. A wife should know."

"It is no effort for men to declare their love before marriage. Why should they stop afterwards?"

"Deeds are greater than words."

"But you've been so distant and angry since your accident . . ."

"Only because it prevented me from joining the Continentals."

She lowered her eyes and bit her lip. "You are well now, so I suppose you will leave me soon."

"Yes, but my heart is yours alone."

I do not believe you.

He touched her cheek. "Is that not enough?"

Not without you telling me you love me.

"Now I must wake Fiona. Stay in bed."

Hurt, she looked away from him to hide her feelings. Tears stung her eyes, and she forced them back with a vengeance. "You must stay out of the room until your son is born."

He paused by the door, nodded, and went out with a candle in his hand. She had done everything she could to please him, and still his feelings for her were not the swift, constant current she desired. Had she made a mistake in marrying him, in thinking he would love her as she loved him? She had to accept his ways. That was all. He showed his love through *deeds, not words*. He'd given her his name, protection, a roof over her head, and food to eat. Did that not show he loved her? She had beautiful clothes, and everything she wanted. Now she was about to bear his child. It would only deepen his feelings for her, would it not? To press him again for poetic words of love might drive him away. And after the baby, her figure would return. Surely this would please him.

Another pain gripped her, and she reached for the bedpost and pulled herself up.

Hayward returned with Fiona, who hurried to Eliza with outstretched arms. Eliza turned to her, and with her dark hair falling over her shoulders, with fear that rose to the surface as her breath was snatched from her lungs, she watched him turn aside, place his hand over the brass knob, and quietly pull the door closed.

Alone in his study, Hayward stared at the flames that licked the bricks in his hearth. Troubled, he dragged his hunting knife over a piece of kindling, caring not for the shavings that fell onto the floor. His leg ached, and he paused to rub the muscle. Then he threw the chafed wood into the fire.

Nothing could drown out Eliza's cries upstairs. Not his thoughts, not the crackle of the fire, not the rattling branches outside his window. He squeezed the arms of the high-backed chair and tried to resist the impulse to go to her. Another anguished cry caused his muscles to tighten. He could stand it no more and rushed upstairs.

As he stood in front of their bedroom door, his hand hesitated over the brass knob. He dared not go in. She had told him not to, and so he withdrew his hand and leaned his back against the wall, waited, and found himself praying for Eliza's and his baby. The door drifted open and out stepped Fiona. She took him by the arm and pulled him inside.

"I cannot get the child to cry," she whispered. "Please, sir. You must try. Rub the baby's back vigorously."

Eliza lay quiet against the pillows, the sheets wrapped around her legs. Her damp hair clung to her throat, and her eyes were closed. "Is she all right?"

Fiona nodded. "She had a time of it, but she will be fine." She handed him the newborn, wet and coated, and as pale as the fear that stole into his breast. No sooner had he taken the infant into his arms that it began to whimper and turn pink. It thrust out two fists and wailed.

"Ah, she is perfect now," cooed Fiona.

"A daughter?"

"Yes, sir. And pretty as her mother the day she was born."

Hayward felt slightly disappointed, but the glassy dark eyes that stared at him, the delicate bow mouth, and the tiny fingers conquered his heart. "Thank you, Fiona. I suppose you feel like a grandmother, having raised Eliza as you did."

Fiona wiggled her head and smiled down at the babe. "If only it could be so, sir. But I know my place. I shall serve this little girl and love her just as I have loved her mother until the day I die."

Eliza opened her eyes and stretched her arms out to Hayward. "Are you angry that I did not give you a son?"

"No. We do not determine our children, Eliza. That is God's doing."

"She is beautiful, isn't she?"

"Beautiful and healthy."

"I'd like to call her Darcy, after my grandmother. I did not know her, but my father said she was a good woman, happy in life and love, and that is what I want for our little girl."

And so, Darcy Morgan came into the world on a cold winter's night to a hopeful mother, and to a father whose duty to *The Glorious Cause* outweighed his duty to her.

19

*W*eeks passed quietly at River Run. Bitter cold settled over the valley, though blue skies let rays of sunshine through the windows of the house. Stepping down the staircase, Eliza saw that the door to Hayward's study stood open. She paused a moment and listened to him speak to Addison. His tone seemed serious and his words rehearsed.

"Nothing to worry about, sir. The cold cellar has enough venison to last through spring," she heard Addison say. "And I've cut enough firewood to last the season through."

"I doubt we shall see any harsh weather this winter," Hayward said. "You'll need to have Mrs. Morgan's mare shod. She will give you the coin."

"Old Ben does a fine job, sir. And Tom, he's a hardworking lad. When Old Ben passes on, Mr. Halston will have no problem with Tom stepping into the old fellow's shoes."

"Well, it is too bad Halston's blacksmiths are the only ones nearby. Otherwise I would take my business elsewhere."

Her husband had said nothing out of the ordinary, except for his comment about Halston. She knew he did not like him, that whenever his name was mentioned a jealous glint shone in his eyes.

Addison spoke after a pause. "If you don't mind me saying, sir, when Mr. Halston weds, a wife will tone down his forward-ness, and she'll be a good neighbor for your lady, sir."

Hayward cleared his throat. "I should find *my lady* another servant. Someone young who could help her take care of the child. There are still plenty indentured in this country, so I should have no trouble."

"Again, I beg your pardon, sir. But a lady's maid should be of the lady's choosing. At least that's how it's done in this part of the world."

"Then I'll leave it up to Mrs. Morgan. I wouldn't want her out of step with the rest of her sex."

Compelled to go into the study and speak to Hayward about this, Eliza made haste down the staircase. Addison strode out into the foyer, stopped when he saw her, and drew off his hat. He had a sorry look on his face, his eyes glancing left to right. Without a word, he squashed his hat on, bowed quickly, and left.

Eliza smoothed down the front of her gown, glad she was able to squeeze into it. The ribbons on her bodice were not pulled so tight as before, but that would change in time. She wore a day gown of dark green linsey, a kerchief of bleached linen fastened at her breast in a snug knot. Hayward had not approved of the fabric when first it arrived, saying it was for women of the lower class, but Eliza told him it was warm and practical for a lady living in the wilderness, far better than most had.

She laid her hand lightly against the door, and it drifted open. She wondered why he had not worn his working clothes that morn, his leather breeches and hunting shirt. Instead, he wore his dark navy coat, beige breeches, and black riding boots. His hair lay back in a ponytail secured with a strip of black taffeta.

"You look pretty this morning, Eliza. I will keep your image in my mind while I am gone."

Gone? She looked at him with a start and hurried to him.

"Just for the day, I hope."

"No." He placed his hands on her arms. "Eliza . . ."

She blinked back tears, knowing what he meant to tell her. He was leaving. "You must have breakfast before you start the day's business. Come, let us sit together."

"I had something before you woke."

"That had to be early."

"It was."

She lowered her eyes, dreading what she knew he'd say next. He dropped his hands and moved her to a chair. "Sit down, Eliza." Slowly she lowered herself into the chair and fixed her eyes on him, as if she had to sear his face into her memory, for the chance he'd never return haunted her.

Hayward took hold of her hands and held them gently. "It is time I join the Maryland Patriots. I know how that must make you feel, but it is my duty, and my heart and mind have convicted me day and night. America is my country now, our country, and I cannot sit idly by, doing nothing. You understand?"

"But Darcy is barely a month old and . . ."

"There is nothing to worry over, Eliza. It should not be long that I will be away, perhaps a few months, but no more than a year."

"A year?" she breathed out the words painfully and fought the tears pooling in her eyes. She laid her head against his breast, gathered the lapels of his coat in her hands, and held onto him. Beneath his waistcoat, she heard the beat of his heart and shut her eyes to take it in—to remember.

Hayward ran his hand over her hair and sighed. "I cannot bear your tears. I'll not torture you or me a moment longer." He kissed her forehead, then both her hands, and strode from the room and out the front door. With a low, desperate moan, Elisa raised to her mouth the hands he had just released and hurried after him. Cold hit her face when she stepped out onto the porch. The wind freshened, rustled through the bare limbs of the trees, and stirred the dead leaves that lay twisted and crumpled on the grass.

He is leaving me so soon, and with no warning!

She stood between the posts and watched him mount his horse. Stunned, she stood motionless, unable to find words to speak, something to say that would make him stay. "Can you not kiss your baby daughter farewell?" she finally said.

At once, he gathered the reins through his gloved hand and looked at her with pained eyes. "Kiss her for me, Eliza. Tell her every day her papa loves her. Goodbye. I shall write to you first chance when I reach Annapolis."

He turned Omega and galloped off. Her hands clasped at her breast, she whispered, "God go with you, Hayward."

Stronger blew the wind, colder and more relentless, louder and swelling in the forests, hushing the rush of the river beyond. Tears blurred her vision, and she allowed them to fall down her cheeks. Then the wind lay low, and she could make out the sound of Omega's hooves passing over the dusty river road. The sound faded and silence sunk into her lonely heart, until she heard her baby girl crying upstairs.

Part 2

I am in torment within, and in my heart I am disturbed.

Lamentations 1:20a NIV

20

Since Hayward's departure, the summers had sweltered, and every stream flowed low through the valley as dust covered leaf and vine. On a hot July night in 1776, the Declaration of Independence was read publicly, and patriots took their stands in the fields and meadows across the Thirteen, engaging not only the British, but also the Crown's Indian allies.

Winters were raw and bitter. The Potomac froze so deep that it could be walked across from one side to the other. Wolves grew bold with hunger, and turkey buzzards could be seen circling the sky, spying out carrion.

Two years he'd been gone, and Eliza, never growing accustomed to his absence, sat one gray morning in an armchair reading over a letter she had finished writing to Hayward. For a moment, she glanced down at Darcy and watched her place wooden blocks around the cloth doll she had made for her. The blocks tumbled down, and Darcy gathered her doll and cradled it close. It made Eliza smile, and she wondered at the swiftness of the years passing, how quickly Darcy was growing, how she looked so much like her father with her own tumble of brown curls and her dark eyes.

"Hayward is missing so much, Fiona. If only he could have been here to see Darcy grow. He would be proud of her, I know."

Fiona drew a needle with scarlet thread through the fabric and tugged at the thread. " 'Tis hard to believe she is two already."

"Indeed. It grieves me she does not know him."

"Well, perhaps he will come home soon, my girl."

"I pray that is so. If only he would write to me like he promised, I would not worry."

"It may be hard for soldiers to get letters back to their families. But I'm sure whatever letters you may have sent, he has been the better for them."

Eliza picked up a piece of needlework from her basket and studied it a moment before setting it on her lap. "You may not approve, but I have asked Reverend Hopewell for help."

Fiona looked askance at Eliza. "Reverend Hopewell? What can he do?"

"He told me he has connections in the army and would inquire about Hayward. I am grateful for it, for when we finally hear that he is safe and sound, I will not worry so much."

"It is good of the Reverend. Let us pray the Lord directs his inquiries into the right hands. And I've no doubt you'll receive a letter of your own from Mr. Morgan that will explain everything." Fiona smiled and leaned forward. "He'll ask for your forgiveness for being so neglectful. You'll see."

No matter how Fiona tried to assure her, Eliza could not accept any reason for her husband's lack of communication. Night after night, she prayed for his safety, that the war would be over and he would come riding down their lane with his hand raised high to her. They would start again where they had left off, and have more children to run about the house. She managed to keep the mill running, bringing enough money in to meet their needs, and kept the books in order. He'd be proud.

Mr. Hopewell's sermons had also been a source of strength for Eliza. She clung to every scripture he read, and strove to absorb the meaning in his words. Grace Church stood on a rise of ground a mile from the river, with a congregation now consisting mostly of women, old men, and children. One hundred souls were present during the warmer months, but when the frigid winds of winter blew and the snow lay deep, fewer left their hearth fires to attend a Sunday service.

As the Revolution wound on, people stayed at home when word had reached the settlements, farms, and plantations that British soldiers had been trampling through the wilderness of the Virginias and the Maryland frontiers. Fortunately for Eliza and her family at River Run, they had not seen a single Redcoat or Indian brave.

Eliza felt restless. A slate sky hung over River Run with bands of indistinct clouds in variegated hues of gray and dreary white. Trees stood motionless along the riverbank, where the current trickled beneath sheets of glassy ice. No wind blew that day, and a biting cold fell over the land and sunk into the marrow. Every hearth in the house burned bright with piles of logs. Beneath them glowed red-hot coals and powder-gray ash.

Eliza drew her cloak over her shoulders and passed from the foyer to the front door, then out onto the porch. Her breath came out in pale wisps against the frigid air. Outside, the cold touched her face in one freezing embrace. Her lips parted, and she scanned the sky. The clouds were heavy, oppressive, and threatening.

Longing for Hayward filled her, along with the sense something was about to burst loose upon the land and smother River Run in a treacherous siege.

In the dark, the candle on Eliza's bed table gently burned. The gilded flame flickered as the fire in her hearth lent gentle warmth to the room. She lay across her bed and stared at the gold-netted ripples of light moving over the ceiling. Her dreams found room between lonely hours, but tonight she found no sleep to escape into them.

She cried a little. Then she rallied her courage to drive back her emotions and wiped her face dry with a brisk sweep of her palm. Darcy slept in the room across from hers. When she heard her whimper, "Mama," Eliza rose, donned her wrap, and went to her. To gather her child in her arms, to look down into her angelic face, gave Eliza reason to go forward and faith to hold on.

"Lord, what would I do without Darcy?" At the sound of Eliza's voice, Darcy opened her eyes and through a tumble of hair looked up at her mother. Eliza kissed her cheek. "You were sent from Heaven, my sweet girl, to comfort me. Did you know that?" Darcy rubbed her eyes. "Now you must go back to sleep. Dream about your dear papa, and he will come home soon."

Eliza tucked the covers around her daughter and smoothed the crown of her head with a gentle hand. She stepped out into the hallway, and as she laid her fingers over the cold brass knob, she saw Fiona coming up the stairs with a tray.

"I heard you moving about and brought mint tea to settle you, my girl. 'Tis a cold night, and Addison says there are signs of snow coming." She followed Eliza inside, set the tray down, and handed her a mug of hot tea.

"What kind of signs?" Eliza asked, holding the mug between her hands.

Fiona shrugged. "Hmm, he says the birds are nowhere to be seen."

"I had noticed." Eliza stepped to the window. "Not a star in the sky tonight. It is so thick with clouds . . . But we've had snow before. Nothing to worry over. We've extra wood and kindling inside and plenty of venison in the cold cellar."

"And an abundance of my mint to keep off the chill. You know I found it growing wild and dried it myself. It is not as tasteful as our English tea, but it has a soothing effect." Fiona drew an extra blanket out of Eliza's cedar chest. She appeared nervous as she smoothed it out over the foot of the bed.

"What is troubling you, Fiona?" Eliza asked.

Fiona wrung her hands—hands that Eliza noticed had grown spotted and slightly gnarled with age. Her hair was so gray. "I don't know," Fiona replied. "But I feel uneasy and a little afraid."

With a sigh, Eliza set her mug down and placed her hands on her servant's shoulders. "There is naught to fear. We have each other, and God will watch over us. You were never afraid of snow before."

"I know, but tonight feels different. And with Mr. Hayward away—oh, I wish he hadn't left." She looked straight into Eliza's eyes, a pleading look that sought validation. "Mr. Halston is our nearest neighbor and the only well-bodied man who has not gone off to fight. Surely he'd come if he thought we needed help."

"I have no doubt he would. And surely he would call upon Mrs. Rhendon at Twin Oaks as well, and the other ladies who are without their men, to see how they fare."

Fiona shook her head. "Mrs. Rhendon has plenty of servants to watch after her. But we are different."

After Fiona had removed the tea tray and gone to bed, a dreadful anguish deepened inside Eliza as she thought of

Hayward. Sharp fear stabbed her, wondering if he were warm this night, wherever he was. Was he hungry? Sick?

All that night, in those moments when sleep eluded her, she shut her eyes, envisioned his face, and pretended that he lay next to her, his arms holding her close. Before she drifted off to sleep, she conversed with God about her feelings.

"Why hasn't he written to me? Please, tonight, remind him of home. Let him think of me, long for me, so much that he will send me word of his condition. The pain of missing him is hard to bear, Lord. Thank you for giving me the strength to make it through these days. Watch over Hayward and bring him home soon."

She glanced over at her bed table to an unopened letter that she had left on the pewter plate next to the candlestick. Even though she had asked Halston not to send her letters of a personal nature, he continued to do so. His missives were mild, only expressing that if she needed him at River Run for any reason she should summon him. She had replied, asking him only to send her word if he had news about Hayward. Perhaps this time he had news for her, and so she reached over, and broke the scarlet seal.

> I am lonely here, and wish to call upon you, only to inquire as to your well-being and to enjoy your company for a few precious moments, since we are good friends and neighbors. I have not received word as to Mr. Morgan, but believe I shall soon enough. I have no doubt General Greene will search him out among his ranks and reply to my letter.
>
> And having had enough time to determine where I stand in breaking with England, I have decided to set my affairs in order and join the

regiment. If it pleases you, you may now refer to me as a Patriot.

Lastly, I paid a call to Mrs. Rhendon, who has been ill these past few months, and she had reports to tell of my cousin, Mr. Rhendon, who was slightly wounded in the shoulder during the defense of Philadelphia, but has recovered. She sends her kindest regards.

Your servant,

Jeremy Halston

The mixed feelings his letter brought startled her. Hope concerning Hayward drew a sigh, and yet, the words *I am lonely, few precious moments,* and *your servant,* along with the news he'd be joining the fight, caught her breath. She laid the paper against the flame of the candle, watched the edge burn and curl, and then placed it in the dish, where it fell apart in flakes of powdery gray.

She would not reply to his letter.

Later, snow began to fall in earnest, and she woke to the crackling of icy flakes pelting the window glass. The clock on her mantle tapped out midnight. She slipped out of bed, and as soon as her feet touched the cold floor, the wind rose and shook the four walls of the house. All the shutters had been closed and latched, but the gale blew so fiercely one came loose and with a deafening whack banged against the stone.

Eliza hurried to the window, lifted the sash against the grip of the relentless wind, reached out with it lashing against her body, and pulled the shutters back with all her strength. She pushed the hook down into place to hold them closed and shut the window tight.

Never had she felt such bone-chilling cold. Snow had dampened her chemise, and she shook it before the fire. Then the wind rose again—this time sounding like it would crush down the walls and tear into every tree that surrounded them. Eliza froze with fear. The wind rushed over her, through her limbs to the tips of her fingers, leaving her cold and shivering. She hurried out the door into Darcy's room for fear the storm would frighten her child. Amazed to find Darcy had slept through the tumult, Eliza drew the blanket closer to her daughter's chin.

The fire in the corner hearth struggled against the force of air that raced down the flue. She set another log over the blaze of coals and tucked her wrap tighter about her shoulders. She sat in the chair near Darcy's bed and listened to the relentless wind batter the house. The fire could not conquer the cold and the wind that sucked at the chimney.

By two in the morning, the storm had mounted into a blizzard. Snow blew sideways across the land, whirling in an unstoppable tide of hurricane-force gales so furious the trees bent. Limbs cracked, some at a distance, others close by. They snapped off and toppled to the ground. Horrific and chilling were the breaking of the trees and the moaning gales. Eliza went down on her knees beside Darcy's bed and prayed while gripping the bedcovers tight in her fists.

A soft knock, and the door opened. Addison stood within the darkened entrance, his chest heaving, his greatcoat slathered and wet with snow. Fiona stood behind him, candlestick in hand, the amber flame showing on her face, her cap covering her hair, and a gray mantle thrown over her shoulders.

"Mistress," Addison said. "I've secured the stable as best I could, and all the doors and shutters. I must ask that you and Miss Darcy retreat downstairs. The temperature is dropping so rapidly, and the wind blowing so fierce, we'll not be able to keep the rooms warm even with fires burning in all the hearths."

As he spoke, Eliza caught the fearful expression in his eyes. He coughed and she grew worried, for she had noticed a malaise had come over him the morning before. "You are not to go out again, Addison. Stay with us downstairs. Fiona, we will need tea and provisions."

"Can't stay in the kitchen, mistress."

"Why not? It is the largest hearth in the house." She pulled the blankets from her bed and handed them to Fiona.

"True, mistress. But its size lets more wind into the flue and it'll be harder to keep the fire alight. The best is the sitting room."

Eliza agreed. Addison stepped aside, and Eliza gently woke Darcy. She slipped woolen stockings over the child's legs and put her warmest dress on her. Then they headed downstairs to their sanctuary.

In the sitting room, a fire glowed in the grate and battled the bitter chill that had laid siege on the house. Firelight shimmered across the floor and the opaque walls. A constant rush of wind deafened the ears against the crackling of the blaze. Eliza set Darcy down on the settee and laid a blanket over her. Addison banked the fire, his hands shaking with cold. Fiona returned from the kitchen with a basket full of provisions, including a tin of her tea and the copper kettle.

Eliza stepped across the used Turkish carpet Hayward had allowed her to buy from a passing peddler their first summer. Summer warmth—how she longed for it now as she shivered in the cold.

Anxious, she drew Darcy across her lap and held her close. She suddenly realized how old Addison looked. The first day she had arrived at River Run, his hair had shown no hint of silver. No longer robust as he once was, he stretched his gangly body before the fire and drew his greatcoat across him.

She'd let him sleep. And if the fire burned low, she would build it again.

"Oh, how the wind howls." Her face contorted with worry, Fiona placed her hands over her cheeks. "Never in my life have I heard such wind. It does not stop. How long will the storm last?"

"I do not know. Let us hope it ends soon." Eliza grabbed hold of Fiona's hand. A blast of wind surged. It slammed against the house, shaking the walls and rattling the windows. "We must pray for God's protection." They huddled closer. "Father in Heaven, we are afraid. Comfort us. We are cold. Keep us warm and our fire burning. Watch over us. Keep us in the shelter of Your mighty wings . . ."

Fiona squeezed Eliza's fingers. "It is written," Eliza continued, "she is not afraid of the snow for her household: for all her household are clothed with scarlet. Amen."

The tempest raged as if it were a living, breathing entity with an invisible fist raised against their faith—to test it, crush it through fear. Eliza drew her daughter into the crook of her arm. The danger all around them sunk into her core, and she cried out silently to the One who could bring them through to a safe haven. *You stilled the storm with one word, Lord, and it obeyed you. Still my heart. Calm my fear. Protect us . . .*

Harrowing cold seeped through the walls and brushed over her face. She felt Darcy's cheek. *So cold.* Gently she drew the blanket tighter over her child. And as the wind battered River Run, she feared for them all—especially Darcy.

21

$\mathcal{E}$liza drifted off to sleep and woke with a start. Between the storm's moans, she heard Nell whinny and their only cow lowing inside the barn. Their awful cries of distress pierced her heart, and she bolted from the settee and hurried to the window. The shutters were locked tight, but she peered through a space where the wind had torn away the slates. Beyond the frosted glass, the snow whirled. The wind strengthened again and muffled the forlorn wailing of the animals.

Addison hauled himself up from the floor and grabbed his coat.

"You cannot go outside," Eliza said. "Not in this. It is too dangerous."

He wrapped his scarf tight around his neck. "Best I do, before this gets any worse and you lose your horse and milking cow. The snow is not so deep I can't reach them." He shivered, Eliza thought from the cold. Catching his breath, he laid his palm near his heart.

"What is wrong?" Eliza said, alarmed. "Are you ill? Have you pain?"

"'Tis a trifling sore muscle, that's all."

The icy draft outside the sitting room door rushed inside when Addison slipped out. Eliza gripped her arms against the cold and turned back to the window. Her eyes followed the orange star in Addison's lantern and the spray of light that flickered from it across the thick haze of windswept snow. She pressed the palms of her hands against the sill for a closer look, and they grew slick. Wind whirled misty flakes across the glass, and Addison disappeared into a curtain of swirling white. He had made it into the structure, she trusted, a sign he could make it back.

She worried about her mare and the piebald heifer in the stall beside her. Darcy needed milk, and life at River Run would be difficult without a horse. As the fire in the hearth crackled, fatigue took hold of Eliza's limbs. She continued to stare through the window, one anxious minute at a time. Soon the lantern appeared and its light grew stronger. A gust of wind swept down between the barn and the house. The lantern light swayed as the next monstrous gale bent the trees and blew clouds of snow through them.

Then the light vanished.

She waited with lips parted. Her breathing hurried. She fixed her eyes on the barn door. "Dear Lord, help Addison."

Fiona rubbed her eyes. "What is it, my girl?"

"Addison. He went out to check on Nell and the cow. I told him not to go. But he said we could lose them if he did not. His lantern . . . the light has gone."

"Do not fear. Likely the wind blew it out."

Eliza pulled down the pewter lantern from off the mantle. From the fire, she set alight the wick inside it. Then she pulled on her leather boots and laced them hurriedly. "Stay with Darcy, Fiona. I will be back shortly."

She caught the flood of concern that spread over Fiona's face. Determined, she quickly moved into the hall. From the peg by the front door, she grabbed her cloak, drew it over her shoulders, fastened the cord to her hood, and tucked her heavy locks inside it. Picking up the lantern, she hurried through to the kitchen and pushed against the door until it opened enough for her to squeeze out. The cold snapped across her face and stung her eyes. Wind whipped her cloak tight around her legs.

Through the falling snow, Eliza saw dawn creep across the blanket of white. Blackened trees encrusted with blue ice, heavy with snow, bowed low. Windblown drifts banked the house to the windowsills. She glanced at the leaden sky, stunned at how rapidly it whirled in an ocean of snowflakes and clouds.

Drawing in a breath, she plunged onto the meager path Addison had carved out with his boots. Halfway to the barn she spotted him face down in the snow, the lantern toppled next to him. Calling out, Eliza hurried forward, her clothing gathering sticky snow.

She set her lantern down and managed to turn him over. "Addison!" She shook him. "Get up. You must get up." She pulled at the lapels of his coat to make him rise. He opened his eyes and blinked up at her, his lashes coated with snow.

Upon hearing a man's voice call to her, Eliza jerked her head. Through the haze a horse plowed through the snow toward her, its rider covered in a black greatcoat. She could see his eyes beneath the slouch hat he wore, above the dark scarf that covered his mouth and nose. He whipped his horse forward and drew down off the saddle. Without a word, the rider hoisted Addison as if he were weightless, flung Addison's arm across his shoulder, and trudged toward the house. Eliza hurried behind him, the snow hugging her skirts and making them heavy. Passing him, she tugged at the door until it stood open enough to allow them inside.

She led him to the sitting room, and he lowered Addison into a chair. Fiona helped Addison with his coat and boots. Darcy ran to her mother and hugged her.

"It is all right, Darcy. This gentleman is here to help us." She drew off her hood and stared into his eyes. He dragged off his hat and uncoiled his scarf. She drew in a breath when she saw it was Halston. "I thought you were a traveler seeking shelter."

He bowed his head, and his pale locks fell over his eyes. "I am, ma'am. I had business west of here, and traveling home I was caught in the storm. I saw your lantern light in the distance and made way for it."

What kind of business could have drawn him deeper into the wilderness? "I am glad you came when you did, Mr. Halston. Addison took pity on my poor mare and our cow when we heard their cries. It was too much for him."

"They were half froze, mistress," Addison said. "I put plenty of hay for bedding in their stalls and oats in their troughs."

Halston drew near the fire and looked over at Addison. "Foolish to some, but nothing short of dutiful to others. If you do not mind, Mrs. Morgan, I would like to place my horse in your barn, out of the wind and cold."

He placed his hat firmly on his head and left her standing in the middle of the room, her daughter peering at him with wondering eyes.

"The storm is weakening?" Fiona asked.

"Yes, praise God. It is almost over."

Fiona rubbed Addison's arms to warm him. "Addison is chilled to the bone. Let me get him to a room where I can get him under covers. We don't need him falling ill." Tugging, Fiona helped Addison to his feet, and he offered no protest. "The wind is low enough now. I can light a fire in the kitchen hearth."

Eliza drew a blanket off the settee and took hold of Darcy's hand. Down the chilly corridor they followed the slow-moving pair just ahead of them. Off the kitchen was a room wide enough for a single bed and a narrow table that held a candlestick and taper. They settled him in, and then Fiona lit a fire in the scullery grate. The room grew warm, as the fire's fervor permeated the wall as easily as sunlight poured through a window.

"Why did you not tell me you were feeling poorly, Addison?" Eliza sat down on the bedside and tucked the blankets beneath his bristly chin. "I would have never let you go out to the barn if I had known."

He looked at her with watery eyes. "I thought it were nothing."

"Well, it is serious." She touched his forehead. "You are feverish. Sleep all you can. Fiona and I will take care of you."

She watched his eyes drift over to Darcy. She stood in the doorway, her finger in her mouth. "Addison shall be all right, little one," Eliza told her. "Go with Fiona. She will make you something warm to eat."

Fiona took Darcy's hand. "I'll fix a hearty stew for all of us. Miss Darcy would like that, wouldn't you, child?"

Darcy smiled and blinked her eyes. "Yes, Fonna." She could not quite form Fiona's name over her tongue yet. "Mama? Papa home?"

Eliza lifted her in her arms and held her close. "I hope so, my darling. But I doubt it shall be today."

Inside the kitchen, Eliza drew near the window, and through the slats she saw that Halston had taken his horse into the barn. Darcy peered out, too, and stretched out her hand to touch the frigid window glass. A moment later Halston stepped out of the barn door, shut it tight, and strode back to the house. His stride was strong, determined, and it left Eliza feeling weak—and a little afraid.

In the corner near the hearth sat a wide bench. While Eliza kneaded bread dough and Fiona stirred the stew in the cast iron pot over the fire, Darcy sat quietly with her rag doll cradled under her arms.

"She's a pretty child, Mrs. Morgan," Halston said. He gripped the handle of the cider-filled pewter mug.

With a smile, Eliza glanced over at her child. "Indeed she is, sir."

"She takes after you. A beauty she shall be one day."

Eliza pressed the dough harder into the flour. She understood what he meant when he lifted his eyes to her face. "I agree a beauty she shall be, but Darcy looks nothing like me. She has her papa's eyes. Her hair is lighter now but will change to a rich brown in time, like Hayward's."

"It is unfortunate he is not home to see her grow. I fear this revolution shall keep many a man away—for years, if not forever in death. I have heard of the losses on the battlefields. And what is even more deplorable are the penal ships."

Eliza's heart skipped a beat. She looked over at Halston, still kneading the dough, digging her fingers deeper into it. "What may they be, Mr. Halston?" she asked in a worried tone.

"Foul jails aboard British ships, overcrowded with Sons of Liberty. Each is a disease-infested, rotting hulk."

Eliza stopped kneading her dough. "Reverend Hopewell spoke of the injustices of the prisons at church a few Sundays ago. He said prisoners have died in the thousands from disease and hunger, more than the men on the battlefields."

"What he said is true. The intense heat of summer causes them to suffocate. And in winter, with no blankets, they either freeze to death or die from pneumonia. Nothing can stop outbreaks of disease, especially yellow fever."

The women in the church had prayed fervently that Sunday, with bowed heads and hands gripped together so hard one could hear the trembling of their souls. If only they could send aid—food, clothing, medicine, and blankets. But it was not to be, for the British High Command and the prison commissaries held a stern hand against all compassion, all pleas for mercy.

Halston ran his finger over the rim of the mug. "And there are not only ships that house prisoners, but they are using churches and warehouses to hold captured Patriots."

"Churches?" She pushed the dough forward and then tossed it into the pan. "If I were a prisoner, that is where I would wish to be. What better place than the house of the Lord? But then, God is everywhere, is He not?"

"You have quite the spiritual outlook on things. I question why God allows men to suffer as they do."

"What decision one man makes affects another. If we all chose to live by the Lord's command to do to others as we would have them do to us, then there would be less suffering in the world."

Halston grinned. "I shall not debate religion with you today, ma'am. I haven't the energy for it. But I do have a desire for that stew Fiona is tending."

After eating a hearty meal, Eliza put Darcy to bed and excused Fiona to wait on Addison. She hoped Halston might tell her news to lighten the burden she carried as they sat at the kitchen table in front of the fire. But when she asked if the war would come to an end soon, and if he had heard anything of her husband, he had nothing to offer.

He then said, "If I told you that I must fulfill my duty to God and country, would you be sorry?"

She looked over at him. "I am sorry for any man who faces war. You intend to leave soon?" Unable to avoid the tinge of regret she felt when their eyes held each other's for too long, she stood from the table and gathered dishes.

Halston reached over and touched her fingertips. "If you were to ask me to stay . . . I would."

Eliza paused and then moved her hand away. "That would be wrong." Shocked that he would make such a suggestion, she set the dishes on the sideboard for washing and tried to gather herself. When she turned back, she saw the pained look in his eyes. She refused to give in, and stepped away.

"Mama." Darcy stood in the entry.

"Why are you up, darling? Has something frightened you?"

Darcy pointed to the window, and then hurried over to Eliza and nudged into her legs. "I see. Well, the storm is gone, little one."

"Eliza," Halston said, a hint of agitation that their conversation had been interrupted. "Would you at least permit me to write to you? I have no wife—no pledged sweetheart. Not even a mother or sister to write to. Letters are precious to men at war."

"It would be inappropriate."

He stood and faced her. "Why? We are friends, are we not?"

"Yes. But I belong to Hayward."

"And he would not approve."

"No, he would not."

"Surely, he cannot object to our friendship, and I am sure he would be grateful that I've come in such foul weather to lend you a hand."

Without an immediate reply, Eliza picked Darcy up and settled her on her hip. She was her shield between Halston and her, a reminder she was a devoted mother and wife. And although her gesture meant to warn him that he treaded where he should not, Halston's eyes held no penance.

"I did not mean to sound ungrateful. I do not know how I would have gotten Addison in the house if not for your help."

A swift smile came and went on Halston's face. "I should check on the horses and your mild-mannered cow."

"I must put Darcy back to bed, and we will say our prayers together for Hayward. She likes praying for him."

Darcy snuggled her head against Eliza's shoulder, her curls tumbling over her cheek. Halston nodded, gathered his hat and gloves, and drew on his greatcoat.

He paused at the door. "The snow is deep and night is falling. I will stay in Addison's cabin the night, if you have no objection." Then he strode out into the dull gray twilight.

※

"I am a Christian, Fiona. I cannot send a man out in the snow and cold at night when the river path is covered and the wolves howl with hunger. It is the right thing for me to do. Mr. Halston is our neighbor. He deserves my hospitality."

Fiona frowned. "You are right, I suppose, to be charitable. I just don't like the way he looks at you."

"You are imagining things." Eliza wrung out the cloth in the porcelain bowl and dabbed Addison's forehead. "Oh, his fever has worsened. I will stay with him. You are worn through and need sleep."

Lifting a weary hand to her eyes, Fiona stepped to the door. "You will wake me if you need me?"

"Of course. Now go."

By midnight, Addison grew worse. In addition to the fever, his breathing became more labored, and his skin took on a bluish tint. Eliza moistened his mouth and cleared away the mucus that clung to his tongue. Delirium caused him to toss his head back and forth and mumble words she could not make out. And when he opened his eyes and looked up at her, tears filled them, and a fearful look came over him.

Eliza hurried to Fiona's bedside and woke her. Together they sponged Addison's feverish body with cool water. Nothing seemed to ease his suffering. By dawn, he was speaking to his mother, happy she stood at the foot of his bed and beckoned him. An hour later, after whispering the name of his Savior, he breathed out his last breath.

Stunned to have lost him, Eliza stood and went into the kitchen. She wept for a while in front of the fire, then dried her eyes. She had to be strong. She thought of Addison in Heaven, free from all worldly woes. She could not cry in front of Halston, would not allow him to see her deep despair. He would attempt to comfort her, and if she did not steel herself against her sorrow, she knew she would welcome his arms.

Donning her cloak, she plunged through the snow toward the cabin and told him the news. She waited at the threshold while he pulled on his boots, cloak, and hat. He followed her back to the house. The clouds were moving off to the east, and the sun was pouring down from a blue sky. They wrapped the body in canvas, and Halston carried it outside. Icicles dripped along the edge of the roof. To a snow-shrouded field he took the body over the back of his horse, with Eliza trudging behind him. She insisted Fiona stay behind with Darcy. It took some effort to lay Addison to rest in the cold ground.

"When I am able to travel to Grace Church again, I will ask Reverend Hopewell to come bless this ground." She said a little prayer, and when she turned away, Halston lifted her at her waist to the back of his stallion and took her home.

22

In time the snow melted. Streams flooded, and the Potomac swelled its banks in springtime. Summer brought thunderstorms and drought. Yet Eliza's garden flourished and they did not starve. The fruits of autumn were abundant, with a bounty of apples and pumpkins. Farmers harvested their wheat, brought it to the mill, and supplied River Run with enough flour to last the winter.

On a spring day, from the edge of the hilltop that overlooked the river, Eliza gazed down at the deep, blue water. Swift currents tumbled over rocks, washed over sandbars, and swirled around the trees that lined the mossy slopes.

"I will trust in your protection, Lord, that the shadow of your mighty wing will cover my child. I am afraid of being here alone without Hayward. Please protect him." She paused, cautious of what her lips wished to confess. "I am troubled in my mind and heart, for I do not know whether he is living or dead."

Fiona called out to her while holding Darcy's hand to keep her from following her mother. "Come away, Eliza. You are too close to the edge. 'Tis dangerous."

"You can see how vast the gorge is from up here," Eliza called back. "There are signs of spring. Green and crimson buds are on the trees."

She gathered her skirts and followed the trail that led down the hill to a level plain. Fiona met her with a smile, and Eliza took Darcy's hand and led the way along the path where dogwoods and rhododendron grew. Sunlight sparkled through the branches, and she paused and thought of her husband.

A fortnight ago, she had sent two letters by post rider. "I hope your letters to Mr. Morgan will reach him soon," Fiona said. "The post rider's horse looked poorly."

"I've decided to no longer worry whether he will answer. There may be reasons why he cannot. What matters is that he should receive word from home."

"You say that, my girl, but I know better. How can you not worry?"

Eliza put her arm around Fiona's shoulders and kissed her cheek. "You understand me so well. And I love you for it."

Along the trail, purple crocus peeked through a patch of green under the shade of the elms. She paused, leaned forward, and admired them. "Are they not lovely, Darcy? Come, you may pick them if you wish." The tiny hands gripped a bloom and tore it away. "Here, let me help you, my darling."

Nature had a way of lifting Eliza's spirits. She felt closer to her Creator here, more than within any four walls made by man's hands. Her nearness to Him gave her pause to ask for Hayward's safety. She thought of the Hope Valley so far away, and how he had come to her rescue upon his horse with his boarhound striding alongside him. Visions of the vicarage where she grew up came to her as well.

"Remember how the spring wildflowers peppered the hills and meadows back home?" Fiona said. "And oh, the heather on the moors!"

"Sometimes I miss them," Eliza said.

"Yes, but it was too windy in the valley. I am glad to have come here, and I'll not pause to regret the past."

"I am remembering Papa." A tear slipped from Eliza's eye, and she brushed it away. "I cannot help it. I miss him so much."

With a sigh, Fiona looped her arm through Eliza's. "Well, let us not forget God's promise. He shall wipe away all tears from our eyes, and there will be no more death, neither sorrow, nor crying, neither shall there be any more pain. It keeps a grieving spirit sane."

As they neared the house, a buck appeared at the edge of the woods, and several does wandered out into the sunlit meadow. Eliza shaded her eyes. "I think we have enough venison to last until October. I am glad Hayward insisted I learn how to shoot his long rifle. I've never killed anything in my life, but come autumn I will need to fell a deer."

"There are turkeys in the woods too, and wild raspberries to pick."

"And we have our herb garden and chickens."

"The corn seed has sprouted in the garden along with the cabbages. Let us pray the Lord gives us enough rain this season."

Fiona took Darcy's hand and headed on. Eliza watched them walk together with the sunshine falling over their bonnets and alighting on the path. They were her responsibility, and she would not see them starve, not as long as she had breath in her body.

Upon the kitchen table sat a bowl of bright yellow apples, the last from a bountiful autumn crop kept in the cold cellar.

Setting Darcy in the ladder-back chair at the table, Eliza chose one and polished it against her apron, Darcy watching her all the while with shiny brown eyes. Against the oak cutting board, she sliced the apple into thin wedges ribboned with the golden skin. Then she gathered the pieces into her hands and arranged them on a pewter plate for her daughter.

Fiona stepped out the door, humming, the egg basket in her arm. A moment passed quietly, and the breeze blew through the open window, fluttered the muslin curtains, and trembled the wildflowers in the jar beneath it. Eliza jumped when Fiona shrieked and bounded back inside, her face white as the mob-cap she wore.

"There's a snake in the coop," Fiona cried. "I saw him in one of the nests when I opened the door. He's eating the eggs. And the poor hens for fear of him are roosting in the rafters."

Without hesitation, Eliza lifted the loaded musket from where it hung from two pegs on the wall above the hearth. "Stay with Darcy, Fiona. If I do not get him, he will eat all the eggs and then the chicks."

When she stepped inside the darkened coop, where shards of dusty sunlight poured through the cracks, she looked to see the hens perched together, staring down at her as they murmured and clucked. Her rooster paced out in the yard making a ruckus and puffing out his feathers. Eliza scrutinized the nests and backed away upon sight of the snake's sleek body slipping over the edge of the box and down to the straw-laden floor. The head she could not see, but she frowned at the sight of the egg-shaped bulge. A shiver rushed through her limbs, as her hands gripped the long rifle. She raised it to her shoulder and cocked the hammer. But before she could fire, the serpent wound its way through a crack in the boards and slipped out.

"Oh, no, you don't!" She hoisted her skirts to her knees with one hand and hurried to the back of the coop, where the snake wound its way between clumps of grass. She raised the rifle again, sucked in her breath, and took aim. Squeezing the trigger, the musket cracked. Smoke blinded her view, and she stumbled back. Fanning it away, she stepped cautiously forward and looked to see if she had gotten the dreadful intruder. Indeed she had, for the snake's flesh was torn open—red and motionless against the grass.

She smiled. *Hayward would be so proud of me.* Then her breath caught in her throat at the cry of a jay. And when a flock of sparrows sprang from the edge of the forest, a cold sweat prickled over her skin. Hayward had taught her the signs, and she made Fiona swear to hide with Darcy at the first hint of danger.

If only she had brought the powder and shot with her. She could reload and defend herself as she fled to the house. She saw an Indian glide between the trees. Fear swept over her from limb to limb. He carried a tomahawk decorated with turkey feathers, and the black mask of the wolf covered his eyes.

"Help us, God." Slowly she backed up, then turned and ran, hoping the Indian had not seen her. Fiona stood at the window. Eliza could not call out. The brave would hear her. She fixed her eyes on Fiona and made a motion with her hand for her to move back. "Indians! Hide. Hide," she mouthed the words, and saw Fiona's eyes widen. Did she understand?

The toe of Eliza's boot caught a stone, and she fell forward. She sobbed and through the strands of hair that crossed her eyes, she looked up to see Fiona gone. *Thank you, God. Protect my daughter and servant.*

Her legs scrambled and her hands pushed against the earth in her effort to get to her feet. But a pair of calloused fingers dug into her neck and hauled her up. She twisted against her attacker, kicking and clawing until the cold blade of his knife met her throat. All atremble, her legs weak and giving way, she surrendered to the power that held her.

23

*T*error raked through Eliza. She shut her eyes tight. The blade grazed her skin, and she felt a hot trickle of blood run down her throat. *I am going to die . . .*

Slowly the blade lifted away. The arm that held her relaxed and tossed her forward. When she opened her eyes, she met those of an Indian so fierce and dark that she thought her heart had stopped beating. He stared into her eyes, with hate at first, which changed to bewilderment, then pleasure as he scanned her face. Waves of nausea rose in Eliza's stomach. Her head swam, and her brimming eyes looked away, overtaken by fear.

"Please . . ." The word struggled in her throat as a whisper. "I am a mother . . . Please."

His black eyes flickered a moment. "Mother? Where your child?" he said in broken English.

Instantly, Eliza wished she had not spoken. "She is not here. I am alone."

The Indian's jaw shifted, and she knew he did not believe her. "Come, and your child will live."

Knowing she had no other choice, Eliza held out her arms when he tore a thrum from his deerskin leggings. Another

Indian bounded from the woods and approached. How many more lurked inside the cover of the trees, she feared to know. Her wrists were bound, and she was guarded while the leader went inside the house. Eliza could only imagine the fear that must be gripping Fiona and Darcy. Tears streamed from her eyes. If they were found, the horrors of what could be done to them were too much to imagine. Her weeping turned to sobbing.

God, do not let her whimper or cry. Please keep her silent. Do not let him find them.

When River Run was built, a crawl space large enough to hold four adults had been dug out beneath the kitchen, near the large stone hearth. The rest of the house had a cellar beneath it, which could be easily searched. A trapdoor, marked with a notch, could be lifted up, then set back into place. Here, Fiona lowered Darcy, then herself, into the musty darkness. At the edge of the opening she had set a kitchen knife, and she grabbed it and drew the trapdoor back into place.

"'Tis a game, sweet girl," Fiona whispered. "You mustn't make a sound. Be as quiet as a mouse. The cat is above, and we cannot let him catch us."

Darcy's trusting brown eyes looked at Fiona as the child held her doll close. Fiona caressed her curls and gathered her gently into her arms. Footsteps above caused her to hold in her breath. With her heart heavy in her chest, she stared at the planks above. Dusty light seeped through threadlike cracks, then vanished when the Indian stepped over them. Her hands grew slick with sweat and she trembled. She prayed. She pleaded.

Eliza. Oh, poor Eliza!

The sounds lessened, and soon were no more. The Indian had stepped away, and a minute later she heard a yelp come from outside that made her blood run cold.

Fiona waited and listened. Minutes turned into an hour, and Darcy fell to sleep in the cradle of Fiona's arm, her breathing quiet as an angel's, all of which Fiona thanked God for. With great caution, she set the child back, and leaned up to draw the trapdoor open. It scraped across the grooves, and she crawled out. With the knife poised in her hand, she stepped out and crept into the hall and peered into the rooms. The kitchen had been ransacked—and no doubt other rooms were as well—and her best copper kettle and carving knife were gone. Fiona narrowed her eyes and frowned.

She had to think clearly, to gather her courage for Darcy's sake. Returning to the hiding place, she lifted Darcy out. With Darcy in her arms, she peered out the window toward the coop. Eliza was nowhere to be seen. Fiona stifled the hard lump that grew in her throat and the tears that fell from her eyes. "Dear Lord, they have taken her. What should I do?"

She sighed with relief that the Indian had gone. But her heart ached that he had taken her girl captive. Would it be too dangerous to saddle Eliza's horse and go for help? It was a risk Fiona had to take. She could not remain where she was and do nothing at all.

Her gentle, motherly hands slipped Darcy's shoes on and tied the ribbon beneath her hat. "Now remember to be quiet, little one. The cat may still be about."

"What kind of cat?" Darcy whispered.

"I have not seen him, but he is fierce. We will go to the barn and saddle Nell, then take a nice ride to Mr. Halston's house. He is our closest neighbor and will come and chase the cat away. All right?"

Darcy nodded. "Where is Mama?"

"She is in the forest waiting for Mr. Halston to come and help her."

She picked Darcy up and slipped cautiously out the back door. When she reached the barn, she slipped inside and thanked the Almighty the Indians had not taken Eliza's mare. They would not have to walk to Mr. Halston's. But the milking cow had been carried off.

ℒ❧

The Indians led Eliza into the forest. This time when she passed between shadow and light it seemed all darkness, and all the beauty she admired had wilted in the summer heat. Eliza was pulled along by her captors, her thoughts ran rampant. Would they defile her, kill her? Would she become one of their slaves or the wife of the one who led her? She trusted that Fiona would go for help. Reverend Hopewell. Halston. Tom, his blacksmith—she believed they all would search for her. And God would not delay in bringing Hayward back to her. Surely he would find her, fight for her, rescue her.

Not far from River Run they came to a clearing beside a little stream that flowed down from a large outcropping of shale jutting out of the hillside. The Indian who had admired her grabbed her wrists, brought her to the stream, and pushed her down. She moved her bound hands forward and dipped them into the water, gathered some into her palm, and then brought it to her lips. She remained there, on her knees, bent forward over her thighs, with no sense of the stones and sticks beneath her. The burn of tears welled in her eyes, and large drops fell into the dark ribbon of water below her, where she could see her face reflected.

The Indian reached down and gathered her hair into his fist. She felt his hand tighten against her scalp and tried to rise. All at once, the birds of the forest ceased their chatter. A tense moment followed, and the Indian released her, swinging her around to meet him. She could not meet his stare. His eyes caused her to fear, and she tried to turn away.

Suddenly a musket fired from within the trees. The Indian made a guttural sound and fell. At first sight of the blood spreading across his chest and the lifeless eyes staring up at her, Eliza scrambled away. The other Indian rushed at her with his tomahawk raised, then yelped when a bullet plunged into his throat. Blood gushed from his mouth, his eyes widened, and he stumbled back to join his leader on the ground.

Through columns of dusty sunlight, Eliza saw Halston step forward carrying his musket. Tom, his blacksmith, hurried beside him with a long rifle. When Halston reached her, he drew his knife and cut loose her bindings. Then he reloaded his musket, grasped her hand and hurried with her through the trees. Eliza's gown caught on a branch, and she stopped to yank it free. A whimpering sound arrested them both, and Halston moved her beside Tom.

He brought his musket forward. "Come out of there."

A young woman with hair the color of an October pumpkin looked out between the leaves in the bramble, her eyes swimming with fear. She crept forward.

Halston lowered his weapon. "Come on out. No one will hurt you."

A mass of bedraggled locks fell over the young woman's shoulders and down her back, and her sunburned face was smudged with dirt and grime. Her clothes were stained and tattered and hung on a frame emaciated by hunger. Dark circles lay beneath her green eyes.

Weak from a trial Eliza could not possibly imagine anyone surviving, the unfortunate captive took a halting step forward. Her knees buckled as if a heavy weight were tied to her body.

Her eyes rolled back, and she collapsed. Halston caught her and laid her on the ground.

The girl's dress hung in shreds along her legs, where Eliza saw bruises and cuts. Her feet were bare, blackened, and bloody from walking without shoes. A deep compassion filled Eliza, and she wondered how long this poor wretch had suffered.

She brushed back the girl's hair from her eyes.

"She's been sorely abused and half starved," she said, glancing at Halston. "We must take her back with us."

Halston handed Tom his weapon and lifted the girl into his arms. "We must hurry, in case there are more of those renegades hiding in these woods."

Eliza's tawny milking cow lowed. "Oh, my cow!" she cried and hurrying to her, took hold of her halter. Realizing how close she had come to tragedy, Eliza wept a moment, leaning her head against the cow's velvety neck.

They made their way back through the forest and across a small meadow leading to the house. Fiona met them at the door, wringing her hands, her eyes misty. Standing beside her, Darcy smiled at Eliza and stretched her arms out to her.

"Mama!"

Tears could not be helped, and she lifted Darcy to hug her. "Oh, my little girl! God kept you safe, didn't he?"

"From the *cat*, Mama."

Eliza glanced at Fiona. "Indeed, from the cat, little one."

"Oh, my dear girl," Fiona wiped the tears from her eyes with the corner of her apron. "Please tell me you are unharmed. They did not hurt you, did they?" She ran her hands over Eliza's face and looked at the cut on her neck.

"Not very."

"Oh, they did hurt you."

"Believe me, it is just a scratch. You hid with Darcy?"

"Yes, and when it was safe, I went to Mr. Halston. Thank the Lord they did not take Nell. I see you brought our cow back."

A sob escaped Eliza, and she threw her arms around Fiona and embraced her. "You saved Darcy's life, your own, and mine. How brave you are!"

When Halston stepped through the door with the girl in his arms, Fiona raised her brows. "And who may this poor child be, sir? My, she is in a sorry shape, to be sure."

"The Indians had taken her captive," answered Eliza. Fiona led Halston to the little room off the kitchen. "I'll fetch water and ointment for those wounds. Dear me, I cannot imagine what she has been through. Her kin must think her dead."

Eliza bit her lip. *As I came close to being.* She stood beside Fiona as she folded down the bedding. Halston set the girl down. Still she had not opened her eyes. "Once we discover who she is," said Eliza, "we will help her reunite with her family. For now, let us allow her to rest."

When the sun set, candles were kept from the windows so as not to alert any Indians who were near. Every door and window was bolted and locked. Eliza stepped out of a bedroom door still dressed in the olive muslin gown she had donned that morning. Over her arm lay a heap of tawny homespun and a white chemise. Halston sat in the chair near the window in the hall, cleaning the barrel of his musket.

"Will you stand guard all night, sir?"

"Tom and I will take turns." He looked at her. "What is that you have?"

"Clothes for our guest. She told me her name is Sarah."

Halston continued to clean his gun. "Ah, you are thinking of 'when I was naked you clothed me. When I was hungry you fed me . . .'"

"How can I not?" She looked away when he held her eyes, and left to go downstairs. Sarah sat up against the pillows, a hunk of bread in her hand and a mug of Fiona's mint tea in the other. The dirt and grime were gone from her face, and her hair was brushed. Darcy sat across from her in a ladder-back chair.

"It is late. Darcy should be abed." Eliza laid the clothes down, picked Darcy up, and kissed her cheek. "Thank God tonight, my darling, for not allowing that cat to catch any mice."

Darcy placed her little palms against Eliza's cheeks with her eyes glowing. "I will, Mama. I heard angels' wings, me and Fonna."

Fiona took her from Eliza, and when Eliza was alone with Sarah, she drew the chair up to the bedside. "Are you feeling better?"

"Yes, thank you for the food. I'll work it off to repay you." Sarah had a pleasant lilt to her voice that hinted of the Cornish coast.

"Never mind that. You are from Cornwall?"

"I was. Mine is a long story."

"You are too weary to tell me more tonight. Perhaps later, when you are feeling up to it. Here are some clothes. I hope Fiona tossed your old ones in the fireplace."

"She told me she did. I've never looked such a fright in all my life." Sarah cast her eyes down, looking ashamed. "Thank you for these." She caressed the cloth. "Aye, but this is fine homespun."

"Fiona's handiwork."

"She's a good woman. Is she indentured?"

Eliza shook her head. "No. She has been with me since I was baby. Fiona is more like a mother to me than a servant.

When you are ready, I have paper and ink so that you may write to your family and tell them you are safe."

Sarah's smile vanished and she lowered her eyes. "I have no family."

"I am sorry."

"Please do not send me away. I was indentured to a man who was cruel. I no longer belong to him, but he would claim me out of spite."

"Do not worry." Eliza stood and drew the curtains closed over the window. "If you like, you may stay with us. I could use another pair of hands, and you will never go hungry at River Run . . . that is, if such a life is not beneath your station."

Sarah laughed softly. "My station? I am not a lady. Are you sure your husband would not mind me staying?"

"He is away fighting the British. I am certain he would not object."

"I thought the gentleman who rescued you, and carried me, was your husband. He has kind eyes, God bless him."

"He is our nearest neighbor . . . Try to sleep. Tomorrow you may tell me more about yourself." Eliza blew out the candle on the bed table and shut the door behind her. She could tell by the weary look in Sarah's eyes that her life had been hard and not one she was ready to explain. Eliza decided not to press her. But she hoped that in time Sarah would reveal who and what she was.

Darkness shrouded the house. Eliza held the candle a bit higher as she ascended the stairs. With each step, she mused over the events of the day, how courageous Fiona had been to climb out of hiding with Darcy, saddle Nell, and go for Mr. Halston. He had come to her aid without a minute to lose and saved her from captivity—or death. Grateful, she knew she owed him much. But she wished it had been Hayward instead who had saved her.

She gripped the banister. Her steps faltered from the pain that gripped her, the longing that always lingered. How much longer could she do without Hayward? How much pain would she have to endure not hearing from him? Would God answer her prayers soon by bringing him home?

When she reached the upper floor, she met Halston. He looked tired, his eyes weary in the candlelight. "I believe you are safe, Mrs. Morgan. I doubt any more Indians will come this far downriver."

"I hope you are right. You should sleep, sir." She turned to go.

"Eliza . . ." he stepped closer.

She looked away. "I am grateful for what you have done, for saving my life."

"I would risk myself a thousand times for you." He reached out and ran his hand along the curve of her jaw. She closed her eyes. His touch eased her. But when she realized what it meant, she stepped back.

"You mustn't do that. I am wedded, and no man should . . ."

He dropped his hand. "Forgive me."

Eliza headed to her room, but he stopped her the moment her hand settled over the brass knob. "We have become good friends, and it is hard for me to say goodbye. I am leaving soon to join the Continentals. You shall soon forget me."

She shook her head. "Friends do not forget each other, Mr. Halston. I wish you Godspeed."

"I have wondered if loving you is a sin," he said.

Stunned, she stared at her hand, closed tight over the knob. His confession, a flaming arrow, caused her to draw in a ragged breath, for his were words that should not be spoken, feelings that should never be felt, and as to whether or not it were a sin—that should never be questioned.

As he leaned against the wall, moonlight outlined his form. "I think we both know we feel something for each other, and anything more than that, acting upon what we feel, would be wrong in God's eyes."

"I know nothing of how you feel. I do not want to know. I love Hayward, him and him alone. My feelings for you are nothing more than gratitude and friendship. They will never be any more than that."

Halston stared at her. A frown twitched over his mouth. "God forgive me, but how can I not love you? It is not only your eyes and your beautiful face that I adore. Your spirit, your heart is so full of life, and . . ."

She raised her hand. "Say nothing more. You must forget what you feel and never speak of it again."

She opened the door to her room, shut it as soon as she slipped inside, and set her back against it. A sense that he hesitated outside it overtook her and she turned the brass key, though she knew he would not enter, knock, or speak to her through it. His footsteps passed slowly down the corridor and descended the staircase. Moments later, she heard the neigh of his horse. At the window, she peered out and saw him mount his steed and gallop off into the sultry night.

He left Tom behind. Staying would only have allowed his feelings to mount higher. She wanted him gone, hoping she would never see him again, never hear another confession of love, never be tempted again with kindness or with warm looks that spoke of his desire. But how could she discount a friendly acquaintance with a man who had saved her life?

On the table beneath the window, where the spray of moonlight was strongest, Eliza set her candle. She pulled the curtains wider, without any concern renegades might see a light in the casement. "If Hayward returns home tonight, this candle will show him the way."

Her hand trembled, and hot wax splattered over her fingers. She wiped it away with a little cry and with tears in her eyes.

It burned, but not so deep to linger.

24

$\mathcal{A}$ warm breeze stirred the curtains through the open windows. Eliza pushed her heavy hair off her neck, then braided it, and fastened a ribbon at the end. She left the house, stepped down the porch steps onto the parched lawn in her faded homespun gown, and headed down the dusty drive. She'd tucked her flintlock pistol into the band of her apron and she thought now of the last time she used it—when those scruffy robbers stopped them on the way to River Run.

Oppressive heat shimmered across the land in the late afternoon hours. The Potomac ran placid, and the leaves on the trees curled. She would have sent Sarah, but she needed to be alone—to pray, to long for Hayward in private. At the house she had to put on a brave face, and waited until nighttime when all were abed to release her pain in the sanctuary of her room. Now the river called her.

At riverside, she drew off her shoes and dipped her feet into the water. She shaded her eyes to look across the span of gray rock to the other side. With a turn of her head she saw a canoe gliding toward her. Two men were seated in it—one a dusky youth who dipped the paddle gingerly into the current, and the other the Reverend Hopewell.

A thrill seized her. *He has brought me news about Hayward!*

Hopewell raised his hat and shouted. "Ho, Mrs. Morgan. Good day to you."

She waved back, stepped out of the water, and put her shoes back on. The canoe skidded to the bank, and Hopewell, hat in hand, climbed out.

"My old horse has gone lame," he told her.

"I am sorry to hear it, sir."

"Well, the river was quicker than walking. I have an arthritic knee, you see, that would have made my journey here unpleasant." He smiled warmly, his hair lifting in the summer breeze like the down of a goose.

"And you are wise to come armed after your ordeal with the Indians, Mrs. Morgan. Praise God you and your household are safe. It will do you good to know I have heard of no other attacks in the area. The Indian warriors have gone further north to fight alongside the Redcoats."

She looped her arm through his. "I am relieved to hear it. Have you news of my husband?"

"Let us go to the house, and I shall tell you what I know."

Together they went up the embankment and strolled alongside the creek, to the lane leading to the house. Hopewell puffed out his cheeks and kept pace alongside Eliza.

"The heat is bearable today. Not like last week. How is your little girl, Mrs. Morgan?"

"Growing fast, sir. She is reading her letters already."

"Children are a blessing from the Lord. I hope and pray you have many more."

Many more. Would he have made such a statement if he had bad news to bear? "Thank you, sir. Mr. Morgan and I would like a large family."

At first Hopewell made no reply. Then he said, "I visited Mr. Halston on the way here."

Surprised at this, Eliza shook her head. "I thought he had gone to fight. He told me he intended to, and I, that is, *we* have not seen him for some time."

"He has been delayed by a deep melancholy. I did all I could in ministering to him."

"Can you tell me the cause of his depression?"

Hopewell shook his head. "I cannot. But I ask that you pray for him."

It is my fault. I allowed this to happen. Now he is in pain because of me.

She, too, had been conscious of a sadness that had lingered since the night he confessed his feelings for her. But she shoved away every thought that came to her about him, and believed all her pain and sorrow was due to missing Hayward—the worry and the fear of what he might be enduring.

When they entered the house, she untied the ribbon under her chin and hung her hat on the peg near the door. She laid the pistol on the mantle, out of Darcy's reach. Fiona stepped out from the end of the hallway. Darcy trailed behind her, dragging her doll by the arm.

"Shall I bring a cool drink for the reverend?" asked Fiona.

He gave her a slight bow. "I have no need of anything, Fiona. And is Darcy well today?"

Darcy looked at him with large eyes, then at Eliza. "Very well, are you not, my darling?" Eliza said. The child nodded and scampered over to the table near the door and picked up the bottle that held blue bachelor buttons. "Take them to Fiona. They need water."

Eliza showed Hopewell into the drawing room and closed the door. Once she was seated, he settled into the chair across from her. Her modest dress spread over the settee. Hopewell scooted forward at the edge of his seat, reached over and picked up her hands. Eliza's heart went into her throat. *Something is wrong. Oh, Lord. Please, let Hayward be safe.*

"Mrs. Morgan, as you are well aware, *The Cause* has drawn many a man away from his wife, with good reason. Patriots risk their fortunes and lives to liberate our country. Their sacrifices will affect generations to come and will not be forgotten. Your husband has fought for your freedom, for Darcy's, and for her children's children."

Disturbed by his words, Eliza creased her brow. "I fear you have come to tell me ill news, sir. Do not spare me. Speak plainly."

He moved forward and squeezed her hands. "I have received a letter in answer to the inquiry I made to General Smallwood. Unfortunately, he knew nothing of Captain Morgan's whereabouts; only that he had been separated from his attachment. The same day I received two letters from . . . are you familiar with your brother-in-law?"

"We have not met, but his wife Mari has sent me two letters since Hayward and I were married. They live in New York, and it is my understanding that the city is occupied by the British."

"Yes, and it is so difficult to pass even the smallest message through. But I have these." From his pocket he drew out two letters, one with the red wax seal still unbroken. "He would have sent your letter to you directly, but wished for me to meet with you as you read it."

She looked at him, worried. "Then it cannot be good news. He thinks I need to be comforted."

That her brother-in-law would do this meant something too dreadful for her to face on her own. She glanced at the handwriting on the front, already feeling the burn of tears welling in her eyes. "I wish this was from Hayward."

"I am sorry it is not."

With quivering fingers, she broke the seal and unfolded the page of the first letter. Her eyes scanned the opening line. "I am afraid to read it."

"Permit me." Hopewell took it from her, put on his steel spectacles, and cleared his throat.

"Dear Eliza, I pray you and your child fare well. I write with a heavy heart concerning my half brother Hayward, your husband, whom I have no doubt has loved you with all the deepest affections a man could."

Eliza stared at Hopewell, a swell of tears blurring her vision. At the words *loved you,* the tears slipped from her eyes. All warmth rushed from her face, and a dire chill rushed through her limbs to the tips of her fingers.

"My brother was imprisoned on a transport ship, the *Whitby,* anchored in Wallabout Bay. There have been reports that provisions are poor, the water putrid, and rations scant. No doctors have been allowed to attend the sick. Hundreds have died from pestilence and starvation. The sandy shore has become a graveyard."

She drew in a breath. "Hayward—imprisoned?"

His eyes grave, Hopewell nodded. "Yes. There is more. Do you wish me to continue?"

Eliza nodded and steeled herself.

"I attempted on several occasions to speak with Provost Marshal Cunningham (a man I count among the ranks of Satan for his cruelty and unjust actions toward the Patriots), but I was refused. It was only by paying a guard all the money I had in my purse was I able to learn of Hayward's fate. He was captured at the Battle of Brooklyn and secured aboard the prison ship. He survived several months, until..."

Pale and terrified, Eliza sat mute with her eyes transfixed upon Hopewell. Sunshine vanished from the room, and a low wind stirred the trees outside the window.

"In the middle of the night he and a handful of his fellow prisoners were roused from belowdecks. It pains me to imagine it was the first time his lungs breathed in Heaven's air or his eyes beheld God's stars shining in the night sky since his imprisonment. He and the men with him had attempted escape, and for want of freedom . . . they were . . . hung side by side . . . from the yardarm."

Hung! A moan crawled up Eliza's throat and became a ragged sob that shook her to the marrow. The pain gripped her as if a flaming arrow had been shot into her heart. Tears spilled faster from her eyes.

"I will regret until the day I take my last breath that I could not save him. When this war is over, my wife and I will travel to Maryland with our children and make our home there, if anything, to aid you and your child. Mari and I shall pray for you that the God of all comfort will comfort you and hold you close during your time of grieving. Your faithful brother-in-law, William Breese."

Eliza stared at the letter as Hopewell folded it closed. She gathered the fabric of her gown into her hands until he handed the letter back to her. As the letter lay in her hand, the wind returned and the forest of River Run swayed. The fields had grown parched with heat. Vines had withered. Now, shafts of sunlight vanished from the windows, and a grim silence fell over the house.

She heard the muffled patter of Darcy's feet above and Sarah's gentle reprimand not to run. The child had lost a father she had never known. But Eliza had lost her husband, the man she loved, and the agony of it cut deep, ravaging her.

"Hayward . . . is dead," she stammered and held back the desire to scream.

Hopewell looked at her, his eyes sympathetic. "He is at rest in Heaven, Mrs. Morgan. It is but a temporary separation."

Slowly Eliza stood. "Thank you, Reverend. If you do not mind, I should like to be alone."

Long she stood in the doorway after he had left. Her eyes were wide open but she saw nothing, as her mind struggled to take in the news William Breese had sent. Now she knew why Hayward had not written. He had suffered, starved, been plagued with disease, and cruelly treated. She was sorry she had ever doubted him.

Softly Fiona stepped into the room. "Reverend Hopewell told me about Mr. Morgan. I am so sorry, my girl. Is there anything I can do?"

"Yes, leave me alone for a while." Eliza accepted an embrace, and then went upstairs to her bedroom. Beneath the window sat the boots he had worn when he worked. In all this time, she had not moved them. She opened a drawer and took out one of his shirts. She crushed the linen in her hands, pressed it to her face, taking in the scent of him that remained. A wave of grief overtook her, and she wept.

She staggered to the window and leaned against the frame, her breathing hurried. A vision of a riderless horse plodding down the road came to her mind. She drew in a ragged breath and then remembered the day Hayward had mounted his horse. His eyes had held hers one last time, and then he had ridden off. She had believed she'd see him again.

Anguish coursed through her, and she hurried downstairs to the front door and pulled at the handle until it swung open. A hot breeze met her, and she went down the porch steps, lifted her skirts and ran down the lane and to the river path, her eyes blurred by tears.

When she came to the sycamore where she had found him the day his horse threw him, where he lay sick and wounded, she threw herself against the trunk, buried her face within her arms, and cried.

"He is gone," she uttered between sobs. "He is dead, and I am the last to know."

She sunk to the base of the tree and stared through the canopy of green to the blue patches of sky that flashed between the leaves. The breeze lay low, and all she could hear was the pounding of her heart and the sound of goldfinches darting about the branches of a pine.

"God knows when the sparrow falls." She hugged her knees. "God is a husband to the widow and a father to the orphan. Oh, God! I am both!"

Long she stayed in that place, weeping, praying, then falling silent at times. She listened to the gentle wind and the bird songs, to the still, small voice that tried to comfort her. The sun sunk lower, and thunderclouds crossed the sky. The leaves made a rustling noise. Her hair clung about her face and shoulders, and she wished the gales of the advancing storm would lift her from the earth and carry her off.

When she finally stood, the wind had risen from temperate to fierce, and whipped her gown about her body. She walked down the river road unaware of time or direction. Hoofprints had cut deep into the hardened ground. She followed them to where they turned at a sandy lane. Nearby stood the blacksmith shop. Smoke rose from the chimney. She heard the clang of a hammer against an anvil.

She went on, her eyes fixed ahead, until she saw Halston's house. It drew her with its empty windows and chiseled stone. She went toward it, her legs heavy with the weight of despair. Closer, then the door opened and out stepped Halston. She lifted her eyes to him and shoved back her hair. In his eyes she saw compassion.

"Eliza. I'm sorry. Reverend Hopewell told me about Hayward."

Tears brimmed in her eyes. She fought back the tremor that shook her body. She hurried to him, and he gathered her into his arms. While she wept against his shoulder, his hand glided down her hair and pressed her to him.

The wind strengthened. Thunder rolled in the distance. Rain burst from the sky and beat down the tufts of grass. Halston drew her back, away from the deluge. Then he took her inside and closed the door.

25

Northern winds drove down hard through the misty mountains and shook the walls of the house. Eliza pressed her palm against the window glass, and the moist cold gripped it. She thought of the months that had passed since she had been with Halston—since she had learned the British had hung Hayward. Her grief had turned manifold. Her husband would not return, and Halston had joined the Maryland regiment. Who could tell whether he would survive or not? Perhaps God intended her to live the rest of her life as a widow, and raise her children without the protection of a man.

Streams of airy clouds drifted across a turbulent, leaden sky on a winter's afternoon in 1780, above the currents of the Potomac. Swift as red-tail hawks that hunted above the river, the blanket of gray moved off, and a clear, cold night descended rife with stars against an inky-black heaven. Would spring ever arrive?

She lifted Darcy to the window seat to allow her to view the enchanting moonlit world outside. A draft leaked through the window frame, and she drew her wool wrap about her shoulders. Snow weighed down the trees in hues of dusky white and pale blue. Veils of silver moonlight crept over the pine needles and caused ice crystals to flicker.

The towering sugar maple in front of the house stood stripped of leaves, its lighter branches bending in the wind. Darcy's swing moved as if pushed by an unseen hand. Frost glistened all the way up the heavy ropes. Addison had climbed the tree and tied the swing to a thick limb while Darcy sat Indian-style upon the grass in the shade to watch him. In her memory Eliza could still hear the song he had whistled, could still see his broad smile.

After setting Darcy down, the child in her womb kicked, and when she ran her hand over her belly, she felt the outline of a tiny foot press hard against her. Joy battled guilt, and she felt the all-too familiar pain that came with a heart full of regret. She could not forgive herself, no matter how many times she beat her breast with her fist and cried out to her Lord for forgiveness.

"'Tis a cold night, my darling, and a wonder we all do not freeze. Now you must go to sleep. I know you are accustomed to having the run of the house, but not tonight. Mama needs quiet." She fastened the ribbon at the top of Darcy's nightgown. "Keep your wool stockings on."

Darcy wrinkled her nose and glanced down at the leggings that covered her feet and calves. "Mus' I? They itch."

Eliza opened the top drawer to the dresser and took out a pair of stockings Darcy wore on Sundays, made of a blend of wool and silk. "Here, my sweetheart. These are much softer." She sat Darcy on the bedside and drew the old stockings off, then put on the newer ones. "Is that better?"

"Yes, Mama . . . Why you need quiet?" Darcy whispered.

"Quiet soothes the soul, little one." She drew down the bedcovers and tucked Darcy's legs beneath them.

At the window, a candle flame was reflected in the glass. Darcy yawned and lay back against the pillow. "The moon, Mama." She pointed at the silver spray that crossed the room.

Eliza allowed a gentle smile to tug the corners of her mouth. "Yes. See how it washes over the walls?"

"Angels brought it." Again Darcy spoke in a whisper. She touched Eliza's cheek. A tear slipped from her eye, and she kissed her little girl's palm.

Darcy frowned. "Why you sad, Mama?"

"I have tender feelings at times, Darcy."

Darcy screwed up her face. "Why?"

"Because there are things I wish were another way that cannot be changed." She kissed the top of Darcy's head and blew out the candle. "Go to sleep." Before she pulled the door shut, she looked over at Darcy. Her eyes had closed, and Eliza wished Hayward could see her. His absence these years had not grown any easier. Her hand gripped the brass knob and she pulled the door to.

Craving a hot cup of tea and not wishing to bother Fiona with a trivial task, Eliza descended the staircase and headed toward the kitchen. A thump of footsteps crossed the porch outside. She reached for the pistol kept on the mantle, and waited with her breath heaving. A loud knock, then another—until a voice called to her from beyond the door.

"Mrs. Morgan. I've been sent to River Run. I must speak to you, ma'am."

"Who are you?" she called back. Fiona and Sarah drew up behind her.

"My name is Ezra Lyndall, ma'am. I know Captain Morgan. Please, ma'am. It's mighty cold out here."

Eliza held the pistol at shoulder height. "Sarah, open the door."

"Are you sure I should? He could be dangerous and not at all who he says he is."

"Yes. But if he speaks the truth, we have nothing to fear. How would he know my husband's name if he did not know him?" Eliza cocked the hammer of her pistol and steadied it. "But it is wise to be cautious."

Sarah's fingers moved over the iron bolt, drew it back, and a man in worn buckskins, a tricorn hat, and moccasin boots stepped back. He was beardless and his eyes were youthful and bright, but his face was ravaged with the hardships he had endured in war.

Once he dragged his hat from his head, he bowed short. "Captain Morgan, your husband, told me if ever I needed a good meal and a warm bed of hay, I'd find it at River Run, and that his lady would welcome me."

"How do you know my husband?"

"I served with him, ma'am. I'm about starved and weary to the bone." His eyes begged her for entrance. Could he answer the many questions that turned in her head? Could he describe for her Hayward's bravery in battle, his fortitude against the adversities he faced? Did he speak of her?

Pricked with compassion, Eliza lowered the pistol. "Come inside, Ezra Lyndall."

Ezra's eyes glanced over at Sarah and Fiona. "Thank you, Mrs. Morgan. I cannot tell you how grateful I am."

Eliza turned and he followed her to the kitchen. She bid him sit with a gesture of her hand. From the cupboard, she took out the largest pewter plate she owned and piled it with venison and a hunk of bread. Ezra's eyes lit up, and he dove into his meal.

Eliza sat across from him and poured apple cider into a pewter mug. Sarah and Fiona stood by, one curious about the newcomer, the other protective.

"You knew my husband? What have you to tell me about him?" Eliza asked.

"Yes, ma'am, I knew him." Lyndall skewered the venison with the two-pronged fork, shoved it into his mouth, and swallowed. "He's been through a time of it, I can tell you that. Wounded at Brooklyn Heights, was he. The Maryland Patriots fought bravely. Their stand kept most of the army from being captured. Washington quietly retreated us all to Manhattan without losing a single man. But we were driven out of New York eventually. The worst of it was at Monmouth Courthouse last June. I cannot speak of it to women."

A bit confused as to why he spoke of Hayward in the present tense, Eliza said, "I am glad you knew him, and I thank you for telling me how brave he was."

"You're welcome, Mrs. Morgan." He lifted his eyes to hers. "He spoke of you, saying he had a pretty wife that took care of things back home. I can see he was right."

Eliza's heart swelled. "What else can you tell me?"

"His leg pained him something awful, but he never let it hold him back. He was sick with yellow fever too. But on the mend when I left. We have one of the best field doctors God ever created."

Lyndall's list of events as compared to her own confused Eliza, and she stumbled over her words. "Hayward was alive when you left him? That must have been a long time ago."

"Not long. Two weeks, in camp when I left."

Shocked, Eliza stood. "That cannot be. I received word he had been captured at the Battle of Brooklyn Heights and that the British hung him from the prison ship. But you say he was in camp when you left?"

Lyndall set his fork down and stood so quickly he knocked his chair back. "Hung? Oh, no, Mrs. Morgan. Why, Captain Morgan is as alive as I stand here before you. I swear I spoke with him the day I left just two weeks ago. He understood when some would have called me a coward. Some would have wanted me shot, but my wound prevents me from handling a rifle. I can't lift it to my shoulder, let alone fire it. And my wife is alone in our cabin with our twin boys. It took months for me to get her letter and . . ."

The air in Eliza's lungs was suddenly snatched away. Tearful, she laid her hand across the swell of her belly. Lyndall's eyes followed her gesture, and she could see what he thought. Fiona and Sarah helped her to a chair.

"Speak plain, man," said Fiona. "Are you saying Captain Hayward Morgan is alive?"

"I am."

"That he sent you?"

"Aye. I'll put my hand on the Bible and swear it. And I almost forgot I have a note here to Mrs. Morgan that he asked me to deliver."

He handed her a folded paper tied with a coarse string. The worn brown paper, one single page by its size and weight in her hand, must have been difficult to come by. Her hands shook violently as she stared at it.

His expression strained, Lyndall picked up his hat. "I wish you and Captain Morgan happiness when he returns. We men know times have been hard on our womenfolk. I know mine has been terrible lonely. I've been gone a long time."

Eliza understood his meaning. "Thank you, Ezra. Our barn has a good amount of hay in it for sleeping."

Lyndall stepped away from the table and promptly left through the kitchen door. Eliza laid the letter in front of her on the table.

"Perhaps the man is mistaken and that is an old letter," Fiona said. "And dear me, we must be more careful with people coming to the door, though so few do. I suppose the wind and the crackling of the fire drowned the sound of his horse out."

"I heard him before he knocked." Eliza felt the blood rush from her head. "The handwriting . . . it reminds me of Hayward's." She pressed it to her breast. Tears stung her eyes. She drove them back, swallowed down the lump in her throat. She felt her baby turn, and her emotions grew stronger. "It is from . . . Hayward."

Sarah took up Eliza's hand in hers and held it tight. "If it is true that Captain Morgan is alive, it is a gift. I wish there were some way to bring back the man I loved."

Knowing Sarah had suffered for loss, that her husband had drowned in the sea, Eliza looked at her with compassion. Then she loosened the string and allowed it to fall free. She unrolled the page and read it with mounting hunger. Her eyes absorbed each letter. But upon reaching the date at the end, the paper dropped from Eliza's hand. She looked into the faces of her dearest companions. Her body shook. Joy and fear mingled in one raging emotion that coursed through her like the rapids in the river.

Though she covered her mouth with her hands, a strangled cry burst from her. Fiona snatched up the letter and glanced over it. She threw her arms around Eliza and drew her against her shoulder.

"It is true?" Sarah said.

Fiona's eyes were full of worry. "It is from Captain Morgan. Dated this year."

"Then he lives."

"'Tis true he was wounded at Brooklyn Heights and taken prisoner. He escaped, though his wound was severe. He dared not go to his half brother. It would have put William and his wife and children in danger. He rejoined his regiment and says he will bear it out until the end of the war."

Eliza dashed the tears from her face. "My soul rejoices that he is alive. But I will bring him shame."

Since the day when she first realized she carried the child, she had lived in fear. She believed that her soul was condemned, and her mind reeled with images of heat and fire, suffering and pain, and eternal separation from God. Convinced that no amount of penance would change her destiny, that the prayers she uttered to her Creator were never good enough to reach His throne, she had cried for days, and had drawn comfort from Fiona and sympathy from Sarah after she revealed her secret. Halston left days after their night together—to fight in the Revolution—with a promise he would return and marry her. He left instructions with Tom to look after her and the women, and sent over a provision of food for the cold cellar.

To Eliza's dismay, in the months that followed, rumor had it Halston's property would be sold. It was then she believed she would see him no more.

Not once in nine months had she stepped outside the boundaries of River Run. She resigned herself to being confined in the house, and spent her days sewing by the light that came through the windows. At night, she read by candlelight.

Month after month, she agonized in prayer. How she hated herself for giving in to her grief and loneliness for want of tenderness. What wretched thing had possessed her to the point she could have feelings for another man? How hurt her husband would be, how he would despise and reject her, if he knew of her disgusting betrayal.

"Oh, Fiona. He may come any day. What shall I do? I cannot send the child away."

"Be at ease," Fiona said. "It is unlikely he will return anytime soon. The war will go on for some time."

"I want him home with all my heart. Yet at the same time I dread it. I have repented more times over than I can count."

"The Almighty has forgiven you. Of this you should have no doubt."

"I hope it is as you say. But how will I gain Hayward's forgiveness? He could walk through the door at any moment."

"If that were to happen, then we will face him together. But it is unlikely."

"I will not allow you and Sarah to suffer for what I have done."

"No suffering, my girl. But if you think I will stand by and see you abused or thrown out, you are sadly mistaken."

Eliza turned into Fiona's arms. "How can he pardon such a betrayal as mine?"

Sarah touched Eliza's arm. "He will have no need to. Captain Morgan will never know."

Eliza shook her head. "What do you mean?"

"When he returns home, Fiona and I will remain silent about you and Mr. Halston. Allow me to say the child is mine."

Stunned by such a suggestion, Eliza hastened out of Fiona's arms. "No. That would be deceit."

"Maybe. But it will save your marriage," Fiona said.

"But Hayward will accept the child and forgive me. I cannot do it. I must be truthful with him."

Fiona set her hands on Eliza's shoulders. "If you tell him the truth, you will be exposed to a life of shame. How will you explain the child to Reverend Hopewell, his wife, the congregation, and your neighbors? You have done well so far concealing being with child. But it has raised questions. They ask at Sabbath services where you are, if you are ill, and why you have not attended. They have visited and I've had to turn them away. You must look at everything involved, my girl."

"I am trying, Fiona. If Hayward forgives me, then it will not matter what wagging tongues say. Let them judge me. He'll stand up for his wife."

"Listen to me, Eliza. He may not. What will you do then, when he sends you away saying you have humiliated him?"

Eliza covered her face with her hands and sobbed. "I do not know."

"Could you stand being separated from Darcy?"

A tremor of heartache filled Eliza at the mere thought. "I could not."

"Then you must think of her too," Sarah said.

"How can I deceive my husband? How can the three of us conspire against him?"

Able to bear it no longer, Fiona dabbed her eyes with her apron. "My girl, if it were Darcy when grown, wouldn't you do all you could to protect her from being made an outcast?"

Blinking back her tears, Eliza paused and thought about what Fiona said. She would lay her life down for Darcy. She'd do anything and everything to protect her from harm. She looked at Fiona. "I understand now."

"Good."

"But I shall have my way of doing this. If he looks surprised and troubled, I will know to say it is Sarah's child. If he shows compassion and questions me kindly, if I see in his eyes understanding, then I shall speak the truth."

"All right, my girl. But no matter what happens, Sarah and I will stand by you."

Later that night, the first pangs seized her, and Eliza sunk to her knees. "Father in heaven, forgive me. Take my life if you must, Lord, but have mercy upon this child."

Part 3

Look upon mine affliction and my pain; and forgive all my sins.

Psalm 25:18

26

$\mathcal{O}$n a warm spring afternoon in 1782, Hayward made his way along the river path toward home. The familiar hills of Maryland deepened in the light—leafy walls of shale cast cool shadows over the Potomac.

As he urged his horse to a gallop, he imagined that Eliza's pretty face had not altered, and that her hair would be longer. For a brief moment, he thought about the hardships and loneliness she must have suffered during his long absence. For the good of *The Glorious Cause*, there was nothing either he, or his fellow compatriots could have done except hope for the best for the families they had left behind, and pray that the Almighty would watch over them.

He shook off the feelings he had come to know in war, the hardened heart of a warrior that had possessed him for too long. Now it was time for married life again. Tonight he'd sleep with her in their bed, between soft cotton sheets, with her silky skin against his. He ached for her as the weary miles lessened, which caused him to smack the sides of his horse to quicken the animal's pace along the shadowy road above the Potomac.

He left the woodland path and rode alongside fields thick with corn and knee-deep wheat. There would be a good harvest, and the mill would bring him money.

A half-mile later, under the shade of a limestone bluff, he dismounted and dragged the reins over his horse's head. Stiff from the long ride, he stretched his limbs and led his horse down to the riverbank to drink. Far in the distance, on the opposite side of the river, he watched a blue heron spear its beak into the water.

He cupped his hand, dipped it into the water, and drank. He saw his reflection in the quiet pool and noticed the lines around his eyes. How would Eliza react to his changed appearance? He looked down at his hands, plunged them back into the water, and rubbed them together. He hoped to wash away the stains—reminders of the British blood he had spilled in the fight for freedom.

Refreshed, he stood and pulled his horse back to the path to remount. He rode on and reached a point where the river grew narrower. Green-headed mallards and their mates skirted along the bank, followed by troops of ducklings. He urged his horse to a trot, and it stepped forward and raised one leg higher than the other. After he drew rein, he jumped down from the saddle and examined the hoof. No stone—just a loose shoe.

The blacksmith shop stood close by. He walked the horse toward it. A young man pounded an iron hinge with a hammer against a black anvil. Sweat soaked his shirt, for he stood close to the fire in the forge. He was dressed in ragged canvas breeches and leather-buckled shoes. Upon sight of Hayward, the smith paused in his work and wiped the sweat from his face.

"You there. Where is Old Ben?"

"Old Ben's in Heaven, sir." The corners of his eyes creased.

Hardened by the sights and sounds of death, Hayward threw the reins over a post. "The last time I saw him, he was in fine fettle. When did this happen?"

"Five years ago, sir. Can I be of service to you?"

"If you are skilled at shoeing a horse, yes."

"Old Ben taught me everything he knew. I can do the work."

Hayward moved inside. Stacks of firewood and iron, along with a barrel of water, cluttered the opening. "My mount has a loose shoe. I shall pay you good silver to make it right, and to do it quick."

The smith shook his head. "No silver, sir. A few copper pennies for one shoe is all." Stepping away from the oppressive heat of the forge, he moved outside, where he lifted the gelding's hooves to inspect them. "The others are in good shape, sir. But he cannot go any further with this shoe. I can make it right."

Hayward leaned against a post. "What's your name?"

"Thomas, sir."

"Well, I pray you be quick with my horse. I am in a hurry to get home."

"Is home far, sir?" Tom reached for a pair of pliers.

"Not very. I hope to be there right before the light fades." Hayward picked up a piece of iron and examined it. "I've been away at war and am eager to get home to my wife and daughter. Do you know River Run?"

The tool slipped in Tom's hand. "I know of it, yes. You're Captain Morgan?"

"Yes. Perhaps you have shod my wife Eliza's horse. We always brought our horses to Ben when he was alive. I left a brown mare with her. Surely she's come here."

Tom kept his eyes on his work. "I've shod so many horses, sir, I could not say."

Hayward drew out his watch and checked the time. "You would remember her if she had. She has a look not easy for a man to forget."

Tom yanked the nails free from the shoe. "Long time ago, maybe."

"Eliza might like a new kettle or something like it. Can you make those?"

Tom nodded, and hammered a new shoe on his anvil. "I can make anything you require, sir." He plunged it into the water. Steam rose and seethed. As he tacked the shoe into the horse's hoof, it sidestepped slightly. Tom steadied Hayward's horse with a firm grip as he kept the horse's leg between his knees.

Hayward tucked his watch back into his waistcoat. "It is good to see a man concentrating on his work as hard as you do. You are true to your craft."

Tom tossed the old shoe onto a pile of rusty iron and glanced over at Hayward. "Thank you, sir." Again he drew the rag over his sweaty brow.

"Were you in the struggle for our independence?"

"No, sir. I stayed right here, and worked for Mr. Halston."

"That is regrettable . . . for a man, that you missed out on the fighting."

Tom shrugged. "I did my part. I made shoes for the officers' horses, sent some upriver to Fort Frederick. I hear your time away was not so fortunate."

"Really? What did you hear?"

"That you were on a prison ship. Folks thought you were dead. Mr. Halston said your half brother wrote to Mrs. Morgan, said you attempted to escape, and the British hung you. It came as quite a surprise to everyone in these parts when we heard you were alive."

A smile crossed Hayward's face. "Before heading home, I wrote to my half brother. No doubt he'll be astonished to learn he was told wrongly about me."

"Aye. And Mrs. Morgan believed it for a long time, until she got the good news. Reverend Hopewell said a special prayer of thanksgiving at the church, and the whole congregation joined in praising God that you had been spared."

"Except for Mr. Halston, I imagine."

"Mr. Halston left before then. He was good to your wife and child."

"What do you mean *he was good to them?*" Hayward's muscles grew taut. He did not like the idea Halston had known anything about Will's letter to Eliza, or that he had given Eliza comfort, whatever that meant. Had she been faithful to him?

"Well, the Good Book does say to take care of the widows and the orphans. He made sure she had enough provisions to last the winter months. There was a fierce blizzard and an Indian attack. He . . ."

Despite hearing of the dangers his family had faced, Hayward raised his hand. He knew if he did not stop Tom, he'd hear the praises of Halston's valor. Part of him was thankful Halston had been there for Eliza in his absence. But jealousy ran deep within him and overtook gratitude. "There is no need to tell me anything more," he said. "I'll want to hear it from my wife."

He took the reins from Tom, mounted his horse, and paid the fee. "Whatever happened to Mr. Halston? Is he at home like some of the other cowardly Tories?"

"Mr. Halston was no Tory, sir. Like I said, he left a long time ago to join the army and never returned—he was killed at Yorktown. His land was bought up."

"By whom?"

"I don't know, sir. But I hear tell the new owner intends to lease the land and house."

Hayward looked up the lane leading from the blacksmith shop and fixed his eyes on the house. It would be a suitable dwelling for the Breese family. "I will write my half brother of it. He has a growing family and this would be a suitable home for them. Thank you, Tom."

Drawing his horse back, Hayward tipped his hat, and made his way toward home. The clop of hooves echoed through the trees, and with eagerness, he pushed his horse to a gallop through the dappled sunshine. Before him waited his beloved, and the daughter he had left as an infant.

❦

The sky shone as blue as the broken robins' eggs Darcy held in her hand and showed to Eliza. "I found the nest by the tree, Mama. Sarah said the wind blown it down."

Eliza took in the excited glow within her daughter's eyes. "I've no doubt Sarah is right, my darling. Here, put your treasures in this." Eliza handed Darcy the basket she used to collect herbs from her garden. "Show them to Ilene."

Darcy, barefoot and dressed in a white cotton shift, set the eggs carefully inside the wicker cradle, then dashed away to kneel beside Ilene. Having been parted from him at such a young age, she would not remember her papa's face, but she had told Eliza she imagined his gentle voice. She asked Eliza when he would come home, what war and revolution meant, something that in her young innocence Darcy could not comprehend, and no one, not even Eliza, tried to explain. Word had spread through the villages and hovels along the rivers that General Washington had won a victory at Yorktown and the war was over. Menfolk would be returning to cabin and manor. But not Mr. Halston.

Would Hayward come riding home today, tomorrow, to rescue her out of her loneliness? Or would weeks pass by, and rack her nerves with worry? Her face had not changed—not a spot or wrinkle to mar it. On this score, she was not worried he would be disappointed. No, the years had not changed her in appearance. However, events and circumstances had caused her to age internally.

The house had been readied, the pantry stocked with his favorites, the barrel in the kitchen filled with ale, his long-stemmed pipe set on the table beside his chair.

"Look, Ilene. Are they not pretty?" Darcy gently picked up one egg, and it toppled into her palm.

Ilene toddled forward, placed her hands on the grass, and on her knees leaned over to look at the little treasures. "Pretty!"

"Come sit here, Mama." Darcy looked back over her shoulder. "The grass is cool."

"I'll spoil my dress, my darling girl." Eliza took a step down from the porch but remained above the lawn. "I pray someday you shall have finer clothes than I."

"I'd rather have a kerchief like Sarah's, Mama."

Eliza glanced over at Sarah. With strong arms she carried the wash in a large wicker hamper on her hip, dry now from hanging outside, and folded neatly. She wore a faded blue dress, with a red kerchief tied around her throat.

"There is a difference between what a lady should wear and a servant's garb, Darcy." Eliza brushed her hand over her daughter's head of curls. "That is but a rag Sarah wears to wipe the sweat from her brow. It is not suitable for a lady."

"If it were mine, I'd make believe it was a string of rubies or red rose petals," said Darcy. She tumbled back with a giggle, and Eliza smiled. Her gaze drifted over to Ilene. Between her delicate fingers, the child gathered one of the eggs and balanced it in her cupped palm. Her hair, the color of ground nutmeg, tumbled over her forehead in tight ringlets that caught the sunlight. Ilene lifted her brown eyes and smiled at Eliza. Guilt stirred her heart, coupled with love.

Ilene called to Sarah, "Mama, see?"

On the brink of wishing that word had been spoken to her, Eliza shut her eyes. *I cannot mother her. I cannot, though my heart breaks, and I long to cradle her in my arms, soothe her when she cries, comfort her when she is afraid, tuck her in at night, and kiss her little face. It is my own fault, my own sin that has caused my pain.*

Sorrow and regret stabbed her as she watched Sarah bend down and look at the egg in Ilene's hand. "Be gentle, Ilene," Sarah said. "Robin eggs can break easy."

From a distance came the sound of hoofbeats growing stronger. Eliza lifted her hand above her eyes. Out of a copper cloud, man and horse appeared in the distance. The familiar set of shoulders under a blue regimental uniform, the handsome face shaded by a tricorn hat, caused her heart to run riot. But as he drew closer, and she saw him more clearly, her heart ached to see how lean he had become. Barely could her legs support her as her breath halted and she gasped. *Hayward!* Her pulse pounded in rhythm with the thump of his horse's hooves.

The door behind her opened, and Fiona hurried beside her. "It is Mr. Hayward come home!"

Sarah stood and gathered Ilene up in her arms. Eliza held her hand out to Darcy, and she skipped up the steps beside her.

"Look, it is your papa, Darcy," Eliza said. "He has come back to us. Is he not fine upon his horse?" She looked down at her daughter and saw her eyes grow wide. "He will be so glad to see how you have grown."

Hayward jerked the reins and his horse halted, shook its mane, and pawed the soft ground. He threw off his hat and slid from the saddle. Eliza hurried down the steps and across the lawn to meet him. He gathered her in his arms, swung her around, and laughed. He kissed her face, her eyelids, her lips, and gathered her close. Every inch of Eliza soared. She grew faint, the same way she had felt the first time he kissed her. She tossed her head back and gazed up into his careworn face. His eyes were the same. A sigh slipped from her lips, and she pulled him to her, kissed him, and pressed her cheek against his.

"I had prepared words, but they fail me." Hayward moved her back and placed his hands around her face. "You are as beautiful as the day I left."

Yes, but so changed.

Tears burned in her eyes, and she let them fall. "I prayed God would watch over you and bring you back to me. Is it true, the war has ended and there is peace?"

"Yes, peace, Eliza." He embraced her. His wool uniform brushed her skin. The scent of him was not as before. He smelled of woodlands and campfires, sweat and struggle.

Eliza turned out of his arms. "Darcy, come greet your papa. Ah, you have stained your knees in the grass. Never mind. Papa will not care."

"On my soul, this is Darcy?" He crouched down and took her hands in his. "You were a little mite when I left, Darcy. How pretty you are, just like your mother."

Darcy touched one of the buttons on Hayward's coat. "What's your horse's name?"

"Gareth. He is somewhat worn for war, but strong. Do you like him?"

Eyes bright, Darcy nodded. "Yes, Papa."

"What happened to Omega, Hayward? He was your favorite." Eliza ran her hand over the horse's sleek nose. Gareth blew out his nostrils.

"He was shot out from under me. I do not wish to talk about it."

Darcy tugged on Hayward's coat. "Can Ilene and I sit on your horse's back, Papa?"

Eliza touched Darcy's shoulder. "Your Papa is tired, no doubt, and cannot be bothered with such things."

She followed the direction of Hayward's eyes. Sarah cradled Ilene on her hip. A nimbus of russet hair tumbled about Sarah's face and shoulders, and down her back in sleek spirals that caught the shimmer of sunlight.

"Who is this?" Hayward asked, his smile a touch lighter.

Eliza held out her hand. "This is Sarah. She was taken by the Indians, and after she escaped she found us."

Ilene tucked her head into the curve of Sarah's neck to hide her face.

"She has a child, Eliza."

She stroked the sleeve of his regimental jacket. "Yes. Ilene."

He glanced about the yard. "The father? Where is he?"

Sarah lowered her eyes. "I have no husband, sir."

Hayward paused with a frown. "I will not ask why," he finally said. "Have you worked hard at River Run?"

"Yes, sir. I love it here. I beg that you will allow it to remain my home—mine and Ilene's." Sarah ran her hand down Ilene's back to soothe her when she whimpered. A cloud drifted over the sun, and the light faded and turned the color of the trees to a dull green.

"As long as you pull your weight, yes." He handed Gareth's reins over to her. "Can you stable my horse? Do you know how?"

Sarah nodded, and with Ilene in one arm she led the horse away. Hayward squinted and watched her. "She has an impediment, Eliza."

"Yes, but she has a strong will, and it does not hinder her."

Hayward slipped his arm around Eliza once more. Relieved that he had accepted Ilene as Sarah's, and that he would be kind to her, she leaned against him.

Fiona stood near the door in the shade, her eyes full and warm.

"You look well, Fiona," said Hayward. "Not a year has been added to your face. Is your cooking as good as the day I left?"

Fiona chuckled. "Better, Mr. Hayward. You'll see. I'll whip you up a homecoming you shall never forget. I still know how to roast a chicken the way you like. It'll put flesh back on your lean bones before you know it."

He smiled. "What little meat I have had these troublesome years has been as tough as boot leather. Prison food, if one should call it that, was not fit for pigs. So I welcome all the dishes you can provide."

"I shall begin at once, sir." With a skip, she turned back inside the house and headed toward the kitchen.

After she looped her arm through her husband's, Eliza took in a slow breath. He spoke of the house, how well she had cared for it. And he inquired as to the prosperity of the mill. She nuzzled her face against his shoulder and assured him all was well. "I have missed you for so long. I cannot say it was easy taking care of River Run. It was exceedingly difficult. But you're back now . . ."

"And for good." Hayward took hold of her hand and moved with her inside, his gaze warm with desire. "I am starved for Fiona's cooking . . . and for you, Eliza."

She leaned her head back, drew him further inside the foyer, and looked at Darcy standing in the glare of the doorway. Then she reached up and touched his face.

"Tears, Eliza?"

"Will sent me a letter. He told me about the prison ship, but said you had died. I have grieved all this time over you—until I received your last letter. And now to have you back, to see the face of my beloved, which I never thought to behold again, has overwhelmed me with joy." Her smile widened, and she laughed through her tears.

"I intend to write to Will and let him know I am now at home, with you and Darcy."

"Yes, you must right away . . . he said he intends to bring his family to Maryland, and this news will . . ."

He nudged her chin. "Eliza. I know. I understand."

Releasing her hand, Hayward reached down and lifted his daughter into his arms. Eliza smiled and wiped away her tears. Surely Hayward would never believe any child other than Darcy could be hers.

27

The heat of the day sucked at the air in Hayward's study. He loosened his neckcloth, strode to the open window, and leaned his hands on the sill. He'd been home for weeks now and not a single thunderstorm had brought relief to the thirsty fields and wilting forests. Israel Creek was running low. But the Potomac flowed deep from the rains that had fallen at the headwaters.

The days had been sweltering, the nights warm with a breath of a breeze. The moonlight that glazed Eliza's skin as she lay beside him upon the white cotton sheets, the way her dark hair clung about her throat, the way she twisted the sheets around her as she slept beckoned him. Since he'd been home, their love seemed like new love, she told him. He felt they had begun where they had left off, he still unable to tell her he loved her.

In the distance, thunderheads rimmed in gold threatened. Along the horizon the sky looked dark as slate. His eyes shifted to Eliza as she walked across the field. A basket hung from her arm, and a wide straw hat shaded her face from the merciless sun. Darcy, barefooted, skipped ahead, and Sarah trailed behind with Ilene on her hip.

They must have been out in the woods picking blackberries. He watched Eliza place one finger into her mouth. The way she soothed the wound captured his eyes, and a surge of desire welled up within him. He did not turn away, but found himself basking in the feeling that grew stronger with each step she took, with each movement, and with the way the breeze lifted her dark hair and gathered her skirts into graceful folds. The sun bathed the brown fabric with a golden hue. He could see her limbs faintly through it, could see that her thighs were shapely and firm, her calves well formed, and her ankles slim.

Sarah set Ilene down when she squirmed. The child looked as tawny as the wing of a sparrow, and small and slight. Darcy's hair was a deeper shade than Ilene's, with long shimmering spirals that framed a sweet oval face. Her eyes were of the same shape and size. But the color of Ilene's eyes was like Eliza's. Ilene rubbed them with a balled fist and cried. Sarah paused to pick the child back up, but Eliza stayed her with her hand, then bent down and soothed the child with a touch.

Hayward dragged his hand over his face and drew away from the window. He'd speak to Eliza. She needed to show less affection for the child and not step in where Sarah should. Darcy should be her focus, never the daughter of a servant. And the more he thought of the color of Ilene's eyes, the more disturbed he grew at the close resemblance to Eliza's.

By four that evening, thunder shook the walls of the house and rattled the windowpanes. To ease her child, Eliza drew Darcy close while they sat side by side on the cushioned settee. She read to her, and her daughter's head settled onto her shoulder as she drifted off to sleep. The patter of rain had a soothing effect, and she longed for Hayward to come into the room and sit beside her with his arm around her.

Fiona rolled a ball of yarn. "Miss Darcy never seems afraid of much. Not even the thunder can wake her."

Eliza looked at Darcy and set the book aside. "I wonder, Fiona, if that is a good thing."

"Hmm. A brave soul is what will get her through life. She inherited it from you."

Eliza's lips parted at those words. "Please do not say that again. Darcy cannot grow up to be anything like me. I am weak, Fiona. I am a sinner and a liar. I have kept secrets from my husband, and I will reap what I have sown one day."

Fiona set the yarn on her lap. "You cannot curse yourself like that. What is done is done, and God is merciful to the repentant. As for me, I'll go to my grave with what I know."

The door to the sitting room swung open and spread a shadow across the floor. Sarah stepped inside and struggled to catch her breath. The pallor of her skin shone white as the chemise that peeked from beneath her bodice. Her eyes were wide and fearful. Muddy along the hem, her dress was soaked through and clung to her frame, and a puddle of water was forming around her feet.

Eliza looked up to see her shiver. "Sarah? What is it?"

Sarah's hands shook as she pushed her fingers against her scalp. "Ilene . . ."

A chill rippled through Eliza. She set Darcy back and stood. "What do you mean? Where is Ilene?"

All atremble, Sarah clutched the tattered folds of her dress. "Ilene was with me in the cabin. I fell asleep with her beside me. When I woke, she was gone. The cabin door was open. Is she in the house?"

Eliza took Sarah by the arm. "She's probably in Darcy's room. Go and see. I will look down here." Fiona went with Sarah, and Eliza could hear their steps moving upstairs. She searched the kitchen, the small bedroom adjacent to it, everywhere except Hayward's study. He'd shut his door and asked not to be disturbed, as he was to write letters that night.

When Eliza met Sarah and Fiona at the foot of the stairs, Sarah threw her hands against her eyes and sobbed. "Where could she be, mistress?" She dropped her hands and looked at Eliza, shadowed by fear. "I never thought she could reach the latch and open the door on her own."

A lump, deep and painful, welled in Eliza's throat. A moan poured through her lips. The palms of her hands turned icy cold. *Ilene! She is alone out in the storm!*

"Hayward!" She hurried to his door and opened it. "Come quickly. Ilene is missing."

"How can that be?" He stood and came around his desk.

"We've searched both the cabin and the house. She's out in the storm . . ."

She hurried away with Sarah beside her. Heedless of the mud in the yard that soaked through her shoes and splashed her hem, she searched the misty stretch of land before her. She ran toward the cabin.

"Eliza, come back. You'll catch your death!" Hayward caught up with her and grabbed her by the arm. Breathless, he swung her around. The rain soaked his face and dripped from the ends of his hair.

Taking quick gasps, she struggled to find her breath. She looked up at him, the rain on the tips of her lashes, her wet hair clinging to her throat and cheeks. "We must help Sarah find her."

She whirled out of his grasp and hurried off, with him following. The barn looked gray in the rain, shadowed by an enormous elm. The branches bowed with the weight of the storm, the bark appearing as black as the crows that gathered along the limbs.

At the base of the tree, Ilene lay curled up and shivering. Eliza and Sarah ran to her and fell on their knees. Eliza brushed back the wet hair that covered Ilene's eyes. Sarah gathered her in her arms, but Hayward moved her aside and lifted the child into his own.

"We must bring her to the house," Eliza said.

His scowl darkened. "Her place is in the cabin, Eliza. I will take her in." The sternness in his voice arrested her. "I swear, if this child dies . . ."

Widening her eyes, Eliza pressed her hand against his lips. "Do not speak it!" she cried. "Bring her to the house, please."

She pulled him by his sleeve, and, with Hayward relenting, they hurried back.

✍

Hayward stared into the child's face. For a moment, he again saw a resemblance to Darcy, the same shape of eyes, jaw, and lips. Eliza spoke softly to Ilene, brushed back the child's hair, and caressed her cheek.

Eliza's hands were quick to remove the wet clothing that clung to the child's skin. "Fiona, bring hot water. Sarah, fetch one of Darcy's nightshifts."

Hayward stopped Sarah and frowned at Eliza. "You'll put one of our daughter's nightshifts on the child of a servant?"

Eliza gently pulled the soaked and tattered dress over Ilene's head. "The child's clothes are soaked through, and she will catch her death of cold, if she has not already."

"Oh, pray God it not be so." Sarah's face, marked with worry, paled and tears slipped down her cheeks.

Hayward stepped up to her. "How could you be so negligent?"

Sarah looked at Hayward, her eyes pleading. "I had shut the door, and . . ."

"I do not wish to hear your excuses. You should have been a better mother, like Eliza. She would never have let her child slip out without noticing, unlike you."

Sarah shivered and looked at him, terrified. Eliza glanced over at them, stood, and faced Hayward. "You mustn't blame Sarah. It was an accident. She is a good mother, and has a kind heart."

Sarah lowered her eyes, and although Hayward could see the pain she was in and the guilt that overwhelmed her, his disdain did not lessen. "Go do as your mistress bids." His expression was severe as he stepped over to the window and stared outside as Sarah hastened away.

"I should go see what damage the storm has done, Eliza. I will be back in an hour." Without a glance at the worried countenance of his wife, he walked out. He pressed his hat down hard on his head. The path that ran through his land curved along the line of trees. Droplets of rain fell from the leaves and splashed against his hat and onto his shoulders. He lifted his eyes and scanned the horizon.

With his heart troubled, he snatched up a broken branch from off the ground and smacked the tall weeds with the frustration he felt. He walked on, digging his heels into the soaked earth. His heart convicted him. He should have expressed more concern for a life than his land. Perhaps he had. He thought about his wife and the compassion she showed for Ilene. He shook his head. *No . . . not compassion. She showed intense fear . . . as if the child were . . .*

His jaw stiffened, and he threw the branch into the trees, chastising himself for thinking so irrationally.

It seemed like he had gone miles by the time he returned. His boots were covered with mud, his face drawn into a frown that he felt to his core. With a sluggish hand, he drew off his hat and tossed it aside. Then he looked into the sitting room, where a puddle of rainwater had stained the wood floor. He whirled around on the heels of his boots and strode down the hall to the small room where he'd been told Addison Crawley had died and where Sarah had recovered. Now a babe lay sick and helpless.

He drew up to the door and pushed it in. Sarah was kneeling beside the bed, her head cradled in her arms. Eliza sat beside her, her hand over Sarah's shoulder. He watched how intently she gazed into Ilene's face, how she lifted a weary hand and brushed her hair away from her cheek. His chest tightened, and he gripped the doorframe. A frown stiffened the muscles in his face as he looked at the child's fevered brow, saw how it glistened, how soaked the curls of her hair were.

He spoke to Eliza and thought he heard her whisper a reply while her attention was steadfast upon the child. Feeling ignored, he dug his fingers into the doorjamb. Fiona wrung out a cloth and dabbed the child's face with it. He glanced away and for the first time observed the humbleness of the room. His hand touched a crude table beside the door. A handful of wildflowers drooped in an old bottle half full with water.

Hayward moved his eyes to the cross on the wall above the bed. A simple grapevine twisted into two unequal spears hung above the suffering girl's body. Ilene shivered from the force of the fever. Hayward drew closer to study his wife's attentiveness. *It is overly zealous. Why?*

"Lord, do not take her," he heard Eliza whisper.

He laid his hand on his wife's shoulder. "Let Sarah and Fiona tend to the child. Come away." She lifted her eyes, and when he caught the sorrow that flooded them, he drew his hand away.

"Sarah is afraid, my love. It is best I stay." Her gaze shifted back to the bundle lying under the blankets.

"And what about Darcy?"

"Darcy is in her room. She knows nothing about this."

"It's just as well. I do not want her frightened. Go look in on her. Your place is with her."

"I must not leave. Ilene is very sick."

"You have done enough. Sarah will care for her child." He turned to Fiona. "You should prepare supper. Or will that be neglected too?"

"No, sir." Fiona pressed her lips together, lifted her head, and went out into the kitchen.

Eliza's hands fell over Hayward's arms. "My love, as mistress of River Run, it is my duty to be here."

"Your duty is to obey your husband. My word is law."

"You would begrudge me this?"

"Have you been by to look in on your own daughter?"

"Yes." She looked at him. "Darcy is well."

Unable to believe her, he rushed out the door and up the stairs. He found Darcy stretched out on the floor with a picture book. He slid his arms under her body and gathered her up. Troubled, he sat with her in the chair, her head muzzled into the crook of his shoulder, her curls caressing his rough cheek.

As Darcy clung to him, he pampered her with all the words a father could. Later, when night had fallen, he set her in her bed, gathered a blanket around her, placed her doll in her arms, and kissed her forehead.

Eliza looked at the beams in the ceiling, and shook off her slumber. She turned her head to see Fiona asleep in a chair and Sarah awake and staring down at Ilene with careworn eyes. She moved into the hall, went upstairs, and found Darcy sound asleep, her bow mouth slightly parted, her chest moving in an easy rhythm. Her heart swelled, and she reached over to touch her daughter's hair.

"How careless I have been," Eliza whispered. "I am sorry, my darling girl. You must forgive your mama."

She reached for her day dress, slipped it over her head, and pulled tight the drawstrings along the bodice. Out in the hall, she met Hayward as he came up the stairs. These days were like the days when her heart would skip like a young doe's whenever she would think of him. He picked up her hands. She loved how warm and strong they felt, how small hers were within his. Hayward would protect her and Darcy—and certainly Ilene. How could she believe otherwise?

"You should not be up." His eyes held hers, as if he were seeking more from her. "You look tired."

"I am." She sighed and pushed back a lock of hair. "I just looked in on Darcy. She is sleeping peacefully."

She turned to leave him, but he touched her elbow and prevented her from going any farther.

"You need to rest, and not worry about Ilene. She is, after all, Sarah's child."

The troubled look that glazed his eyes caused worry to rise in her. She had no choice but to obey him once he slipped his arm around her waist and guided her up the staircase. "Stay with Darcy," he told her.

"You will call me if . . ."

"I will call you if there is a reason. But you have nothing to worry over." He kissed her cheek and then left the room. She stared at the door as it closed behind him. *How cold is his kiss.*

Fiona met Hayward at the bottom of the stairs. The wrinkles beside her eyes deepened, her mouth parted, and she bit her lower lip.

"You wish to tell me something, Fiona?"

"Yes, sir. Sometimes women grow sick in body. But sometimes they grow sick in their hearts. It's what ails Eliza."

He stared at her a moment. "I have done nothing to cause my wife's heart to be ill, Fiona. You know that."

He went past her into the darkness of the hallway that led to his study. He glanced at the clock on the mantle and saw it was nearly nine. The gray sky outside had deepened to pitch. Five minutes later, he heard Sarah crying. Then the door swung open and Fiona stepped inside, her face contorted with sorrow, her eyes moist with tears.

Ilene was gone.

28

Two days later, Hayward walked his horse along a bridle path where hedgerows grew and the trees made a canopy overhead. Reaching the end where it lead to a field, he saw Eliza, a few yards off, sitting on the grass staring at a little mound of red clay. He drew closer, and she finally looked up to see him.

His breath heaved, and his heart seized as if an unseen fist had struck him in the chest. For a moment, it grieved him to see her eyes a torrent of sorrow. Her appearance disturbed him, and he wondered how she could display such emotion for a child not her own flesh, born to a servant and a truant father—unless his suspicions were correct.

A sickening feeling rose in his belly, and he swallowed down the bitter taste in his throat. He slid off the saddle and put out his hand for her to take. She stared at it a moment, then looked away.

"You've been gone all morning, Eliza. It is time you come home."

"A moment more."

"Come now." He lifted her up, and she bent her head against the breast of his coat. He drew her back, his hands gripping her shoulders. "What is it about this child that makes you grieve so deeply?"

"Ilene was so young. Now she is with God."

He released her. "I suppose she is."

"Do you believe in Heaven that souls are divided into classes?"

His mouth twitched, and his nerves grew taut. He did not like talking about God or Heaven when it came to this. He'd seen men do their worst in battle. Young and old were butchered before his eyes, and to think of Heaven seemed futile to him now. The eyes of the young British soldiers he had killed would never leave him, nor would the horrors of the prison ship. How could a loving God allow so much suffering? How could He take a child from her mother?

"You have no answer?"

"No."

Eliza gazed at the tilled ground near her feet. "Ilene *is* in Heaven. So are Addison, and my father and mother. Their rewards shall no doubt be greater than ours."

"Why? Because they were young, pious, poor, or good?" He clenched his hands into tight fists. "And I suppose he will punish masters, is that what you are saying? You forget how kind I've been, Eliza. I have fed and clothed our servants, provided for them, treated them fairly and with mercy. I allowed you to bring Fiona to Maryland. And I could have sent Sarah away, back to whomever she belongs to."

Shaking her head, Eliza walked slowly toward the hill. Hayward followed her. He was agitated, and his temples pounded. "Your grief over this child must end now."

She stood stark still and looked as though what he had said had hurt her. "Have you no feelings at all?"

"Yes, Eliza, I do. But you have forgotten Darcy, your own flesh and blood."

She turned to meet him. "That is not true. I love Darcy."

"Then show it. She's been asking for you, and you were nowhere to be found. I ride out here and find you pining away, instead of being at home where you belong. Thank God, no one in the county has seen your behavior."

At his words, Eliza bowed her head. "You do not understand."

His jaw clenched. "Is there something you need to tell me?"

"Why can you not accept that as a woman, I have a heart?"

"I do not doubt whether you have a heart. It is your conduct I cannot accept."

"Is it so wrong to show sorrow for a child I watched grow from an infant, that I fed and clothed the years you were away?"

"It was your duty to clothe and feed her as long as Sarah remained here."

"Food and clothing are not always enough. Sarah has been abused, treated cruelly by others in her young life. And now this happens to her . . . It pains me to see others suffer."

He laughed bitterly. "You think we should put our needs above those beneath us?"

"We are admonished to do so . . . feed the hungry, clothe the naked, give drink to the thirsty . . . visit those in captivity. It is your choice to do none of these, just as it is your choice to close your heart to a child and refuse to shed one single tear over her death."

Blood rushed to his face, the burn going deep. He went to his horse, thrust his boot into the stirrup, and hauled himself in the saddle. "Will you ride home with me?"

"I will walk," she said.

Drawing the reins through his hands, he turned Gareth back toward the hill. His hands shook as he gripped the reins; such was the surge of fury that coursed through him, that urged him to settle this once and for all.

He spurred his horse with his heels, clenched his teeth, and looked up at the sun. How he wished it would blind him from seeing the truth.

❧

When Eliza reached the house, she paused to watch her daughter spin on the swing Addison had made for her.

"Mama, where have you been?"

"Out walking, my darling."

"Did you go to that place?" Darcy slipped from the seat of the swing.

Eliza smiled lightly and came toward her. "Where, my darling?"

"That place—where Papa put Ilene."

"I walked there, yes."

"Will you take me? I can pick wildflowers. Ilene likes them."

"Not today, Darcy. I am weary."

Darcy ran to Eliza. She took her hand, entwined soft, delicate fingers within hers, and looked up at Eliza with sparkling eyes. "It's all right, Mama. I'll take you inside."

Shadows lengthened, and the house grew cool. Eliza could not stop thinking about what Hayward had said. She gathered Darcy in her arms and stayed with her until the sun fell behind the mountains and the stars brightened in the night sky. Once Darcy was asleep, Eliza tucked her into bed with her rag doll cradled in her arms. After closing the door, she stepped down the hallway to her room. Despair gripped her nerves, and she sat on the bedside twisting a ribbon between her hands. Hayward had not come to her. She had not seen him since he rode off in a fury. She leaned her head back against a pillow and shut her eyes.

"Lord, how can I keep this a secret any longer?"

She listened to his footsteps mount the staircase and sat up. The door swung open, and he stood in a shaft of candlelight. His eyes were dark and wild, his face flushed. A muscle in his cheek jerked, and her heart sunk.

She could not recall a moment when his eyes were filled with such unrestrained resentment. Her heart ached with knowing, and she gathered her courage to answer.

He moved his hand behind him and pushed the door closed. Rain rippled down the windowpanes. At first, it murmured. Then it rushed, and forced its way through the tangle of branches alongside the house. The air drummed with it, whipped up the scent of mud and decay. The rain invaded her, chilled her, snatched warmth from her, from the room, from Hayward. He remained where he was, his stare cutting into her.

"You have not eaten dinner. I will have Fiona bring something upstairs, and we can sit here together." She lowered herself in front of him. "Let me take off your boots."

He did not move, and when she glanced up at him, she saw a heated anguish in his eyes. She stood and slipped her arms around his waist. His hands grazed her arms and tightened around her wrists.

"God help me, Eliza, if you were not born to plague my heart." He stepped away.

Eliza bent her head. "I would never do that. I am your wife, and I love you."

"Yes, you are *my wife*." He clenched his teeth together hard as he spat out the words.

"Yours as long as I have breath in my body. Nothing will change that."

He let out a bitter laugh. "Nothing, you say? Do you know what you've done? You have been lying to me all this time." He then began to pace the floor. "I want the truth. I demand the truth." He forced her down into the chair near the cold hearth. "Now tell me yourself, or I shall find a way to get it out of Fiona and Sarah."

She lifted teary eyes and trembled. "I cannot live a lie any longer. You are right, I have hidden the truth from you."

He narrowed his eyes. "You best tell me now, before I lose my mind, Eliza." She waited a moment and looked into his eyes with her soul quaking. Her whole body shook. What would he do to her, say to her?

"Sarah is not Ilene's mother. Forgive me, my love."

"Forgive you?" he breathed out painfully. "Then Ilene was your child."

She stretched her arms out to him. "I never meant for it to happen. I never wanted to hurt you. I love you."

"Your love was not enough to keep you from . . . I cannot say it."

Eliza stood and threw her arms around him, buried her head against his chest, and sobbed. "I made a terrible mistake. But it is over. We can begin again as if it never happened."

He grabbed her wrists and pried her away. "That is not possible."

"Hayward . . . please . . . I thought you were dead. I told you all about it, how it broke my heart. I still have the letter." She rushed to the dresser, opened the top drawer, and took out the letter from William Breese. Her hand shook when she handed it to him.

"William told me you had died on a prison ship—remember?"

He took it from her hand and opened it.

"I was crushed, my pain unbearable. Out of my mind with grief, I went out and wandered the road until I came to Halston's house."

Hayward swept his arm across her dressing table, topping her perfume bottle, powder box, and mirror to the floor. Eliza backed up in fear that he might strike her.

"Halston? That's the man? If he were alive, I would kill him!"

She wept. "Neither of us ever meant for anything to happen. But I was weak, broken. I wanted to die." She collapsed into the chair and covered her face in her arms.

Hayward moaned, and the depth of his pain pierced through her. "If you loved me, you would have never given in." Dropping his hands, he stared at her. "What kind of woman falls into the arms of another man as soon as she hears her husband has died? You are an insult and a shame to me."

"I know, and I have lived with that shame every minute of every hour. I confess my sin and beg for your forgiveness."

"God punished you. *You* are the reason that child died."

At his words, Eliza's heart shattered. She stared up at her husband as if he had plunged a knife into her breast. Tears fell from her eyes. Her sobs choked her. Panicked she had lost him, she fell to her knees, and threw her arms around his legs. She clung to him, begged, and pleaded.

"Please, Hayward, forgive me."

"Never."

"Please. I do not want to lose you. I cannot lose you. We are bound to one another, you and I. You must forgive me . . . love me again . . ."

He flung her from him. "You disgust me. You are not fit to be my wife. I am the one who made the mistake in marrying you. I should have known better." Glowering, he walked toward the door. She scrambled to stand and follow him.

"Please, do not go, my love."

"You betrayed me. You lied. You concealed the truth. You drew our servants into your secret. You have ruined everything."

When she crumbled against him, he stood stiff as stone, his arms at his sides.

"I do not want to see you anymore tonight. Stay in your room. I've already told Fiona and Sarah they are not to see you. I should send them both packing, but I cannot blame them totally. Women are more loyal to their mistresses in these cases. I think they meant to protect us both."

Her breathing convulsed. "Darcy. I want to see Darcy."

"No," he said, and stepped out of the room.

She could no longer cry or speak. A cruel silence seized her while she listened to the floorboards outside her door creak under his footsteps. In despair, she curled up in her bed and hugged his pillow. In tears, she resigned to obey him in hopes of keeping him.

Downstairs Hayward shut the door to his study. He raked his hands through his hair. She had killed all feeling he had had for her, and he struggled with the idea of ever forgiving her.

He slumped into a chair and stared at the empty hearth. Crushed, he pounded his fist into his palm. At that moment he wondered what kind of man he had become—hard, bitter, and as much a sinner as the next. He had picked up the first stone and flung it at the adulteress. But he was justified, he thought. It was his right to seek revenge, wasn't it? How could he turn the other cheek?

By the striking of the hour, he fell asleep in the chair, a wine glass empty in his hand. At dawn, the chirping of birds outside the window woke him. The orange glow of morning shone through the glass. Fiona was in the kitchen knocking pots about, as she prepared breakfast. The scent of coffee filled the room, and he wished for some, but his mood kept him away. Instead, he went out to the stable, where he saddled his horse and brought it out to the front. Looping the reins through the iron ring, he hesitated, then went back inside and up the stairs.

Curled up with her doll, Darcy rubbed the sleep from her eyes. "My darling, you must get up," Hayward told her. "It is a beautiful morning and I'm going to take you for a ride. You like my horse, don't you?"

She nodded and pushed herself up on her elbows. "Yes, Papa. But can I have something to eat first?"

"I will take you to the inn down the road, and we shall eat there."

He pulled clothes from the wardrobe, unsure which were right, but decided what he had would do for now.

The door down the hallway opened. Eliza came and stood in the doorway. Her eyes were swollen and red, and she looked as if she had not slept. She looked at her daughter and smiled weakly. "You are awake, Darcy. Here, let Mama help you dress."

Hayward flung out his arm and moved her back. "Do not touch her."

Eliza looked startled. "I must help," she said, her eyes filling.

"No," Hayward said.

Eliza glanced at the pile of clothes on the bed. "What are you doing?"

"I'm taking her away—away from you."

She grabbed his arm. "No, Hayward."

"You have no say in it."

She began to weep. "But why?"

"You are unfit. I will not have her raised by you."

Frantic, she pulled at him. "You mustn't. Darcy is mine."

"Mama, what's wrong?" Darcy said, her eyes wide.

Hayward pushed Eliza away, and she tumbled to the floor. Darcy let out a cry. At that moment, Fiona rushed inside, and Eliza reached up to her. Fiona drew Eliza into her arms and stared angrily at Hayward.

"Put Darcy's clothes in my saddlebag," Hayward said. "Do as I say, Fiona."

"No, Hayward!" Eliza cried. "I beg you. Do not take her from me!"

"You do not deserve to be her mother."

"She is my child."

"Not anymore."

"You cannot do this. Please, Hayward . . ."

Hayward lifted his daughter into his arms to carry her out.

"Darcy! Darcy!"

"Mama!"

Eliza scrambled to her feet and reached out to grab her daughter. Hayward pushed her back, and she fell against the wall. The panic and the noise caused Darcy to cry, as her hands too reached out to take Eliza's.

Hayward hurried down the stairs to the front door. He flung it open, and it smacked the wall with a loud thud. Fiona followed behind him with an armload of clothes. Then she paused and tossed them down. "I cannot do it."

"You are to obey me, woman." Then he saw Sarah peer around the edge of the door. "You. Get out here, and pick up these clothes and put them in my saddlebag. If you do not, I will take my whip to you, girl."

Sarah stepped outside, lifted her head, and narrowed her eyes. "Why must you be so cruel, sir?" She bent down and gathered up Darcy's clothing. "Can you not see you are hurting your own child by how you treat her mother?"

"Silence your tongue, Sarah. Or I will silence it for you." He set Darcy astride his horse, then climbed up behind her. Sarah stepped back and looked up at him with a mix of pity and scorn. Hayward leaned down to her and said, "I have plans for you as well."

Sarah folded her arms and turned back to the house. Eliza twisted out of Fiona's arms and rushed down the steps past her. "No, Hayward. Do not leave me. Do not take her away."

He moved his horse so she could not reach the child. "I will be overnight at the inn. Then in the morning, I will . . ." he could not finish.

She stood shaking in her despair, pale and ashen, shivering in her snowy white chemise and bare feet. He kicked his horse's sides, and it trotted down the long tree-lined lane. With her servants close beside her, Eliza watched Hayward and Darcy disappear into the morning fog.

29

An inn stood alongside the river road, where a good woman lived with her children and her innkeeper husband. Hayward put Darcy in her charge, while he drowned his sorrow—over pints of ale—for two days.

He sat in a corner of the room, sunlight warming his flesh but not his soul. If only he could strike something, to expel the pain. The first time he had seen Eliza after his return to Havendale, she had stole his heart and soul. He could finally admit it. He'd resisted her, shunned her, and driven his feelings deep. But her willingness to give up everything for him caused his love for her to grow. He had given up his inheritance for her, had left England to begin a new life with her in the Colonies. When war had separated them, he had been in agony, but strong enough to keep her from knowing it.

They had been swept away by love, vowed to live and die for it. Never in his widest imaginings had he ever thought anything like this could happen. He wished he had seen the possibility when he saw the way Halston looked at his wife.

Though he still loved her, he could not shake the hatred he now felt. How could he forgive and forget, and move on without looking back? Rage flooded his being, and he steeled himself. He wrestled with God all that day and into the night. *He that is without sin let him cast the first stone. Forgive and you will be forgiven.*

"How can I forgive her?" He buried his head in his hands.

Later, when all were abed, the innkeeper knocked upon Hayward's door and handed him a letter. His hands shook as he opened it; there he saw his wife's name, and stains from her teardrops. She said she loved him, begged his forgiveness, and pleaded for him to return with Darcy. If he did not come home, she promised her broken heart would be the death of her.

"A woman waits outside on the porch, Mr. Morgan," said the innkeeper. "I expect she needs an answer from you."

Hayward nodded and went to pull on his boots. He looked over at his daughter as she slept soundly beneath the window. He convinced himself he was in the right for separating her from Eliza. What had Darcy done to deserve such a mother? How could he allow Eliza near her again, and risk her growing up tainted by her mother's immorality?

Outside, he found Fiona sitting on the top step with her chin cupped in her hand and her foot tapping away on the wood plank. She looked up at him, and her aging eyes caught the light from the lamp that hung near the door. His shadow fell over her, and she stood.

"You were not afraid to travel the road at night, I see."

"Only when the owls hooted at me and I saw their eyes within the trees. The moon is strong and the road well marked. I had to come. It was my duty."

He shrugged. "To me or to Eliza?"

"To my girl, of course. It is urgent I speak with you."

"You should have sent Sarah."

"No. I am closest to Eliza, and you need to hear this from me."

"Go home. Tell her no amount of begging will change my mind." He turned to leave.

"She's been crying since you left. Refuses to eat or drink."

Arrested by the urgency in Fiona's voice, he hesitated. "I imagine so, but that is to be expected. Still, it won't change what has happened."

Fiona dared to touch his sleeve with her fingertips. "She loves you, and her heart is crushed. I saw how broken she was the day Reverend Hopewell came to River Run with news you were dead. She was out of her mind with grief. If anyone is to blame, it is the man who told your half brother you had been hung. Such a lie forged out of greed for a few coins and hate for the Patriots has caused many to suffer. And then there is Darcy. You cannot take Darcy away from her mother. You must consider how much that will hurt the child, and what it may do to her future."

Hayward felt his jaw tighten, along with his fists. "I can do as I wish. It is not your place to give me your opinion on anything."

Instantly, Fiona set her mouth and put her hands firmly on her hips. "Is that so?"

"Yes that is so, and you will mind your tongue, woman."

She shot him a fiery glare. "I will, but you know what is in my mind to say. You just don't want to hear it because it convicts you." She lifted her chin and swung away from him. "She will be dead in a day or so, then you will be rid of her like you want." She walked down the steps to the mare.

Hayward followed her. Gritting his teeth, he turned her around to meet him. "Do you believe that? Most likely it is all a pretense to bring me back."

"When a woman's heart has been broken, it can lead to her end. Will you forgive her?" A cloud passed over the moon, and the night deepened. The wind rose and thrashed through the trees, causing Fiona to shiver.

Hayward stood firm, unmoved by her entreaty. "Do not ask that of me again."

Fiona's eyes filled. "Have compassion. Come back to River Run. You know it is the right thing to do. She would never have fallen into such temptation if she had known you were alive."

He turned away and stood in silence, thinking of what to do. In his breast pocket was Eliza's letter. He laid his palm over it, as an idea formed in his mind, along with the steps he needed to take.

"All right. I will come back, and I will bring Darcy with me. River Run is mine. I do not know what I was thinking to take Darcy away from her home. Go inside and wake her, put on her shoes and gather her things."

A smile sprung onto Fiona's face, and she hurried inside the inn. Darcy rubbed her eyes when she woke her. Hastily, Fiona slipped on her small leather shoes and fastened the buckles.

"I'll tell Mama about the hoot owl that was outside the window, Papa. It called and called, and I thought it was telling me to go home."

Hayward strode to the door. He waited for her to scamper to him, take his hand, and walk out with him to his horse. He lifted her into the saddle, and decided to walk alongside while Fiona rode the mare.

No words were spoken the entire way.

Reaching the house a half hour later, Hayward halted his horse and brought Darcy down. He glanced up at the window that belonged to his bedchamber. The curtains were open, and a single candle glimmered in the broad casement.

Before he mounted the steps, Sarah hurried out the front door, her face drawn and haggard with worry. Her dress was torn and the hem muddy. He had no time to question why. In silence, Hayward passed her and carried Darcy inside. He set her down, pulled off his coat and hat, and yanked off his gloves.

His house had changed. It seemed somber and dim. No streams of moonlight flowed through the windows as before. The house smelled old, and a musty odor hung in the air.

At the foot of the staircase he paused, then took Darcy's hand and proceeded upstairs. Ahead of him, Fiona opened the door, and he stepped over the threshold. He tugged at his neckcloth to ease the knot in his throat. A grim pall lay over his wife's face, which he knew would haunt him the remainder of his life.

The embroidered coverlet over her hadn't a single crease upon it. A stump of a candle burned on the table beside the bed, the tiny flame shimmering over a glass bottle of water and a drinking glass. On the dressing table were her brush, comb, and powder box, the lid of the box cracked. He had done that—in a moment of rage. He should not have dashed them to the floor the way he did, but he justified his action. Anger and pain had driven him to do it—it was Eliza's fault.

She lay dressed in a white chemise, the bedclothes tucked about her body. The lids of her eyes were motionless, and her face looked as pale as the sheets on which she lay. His heart tightened in his chest to see her in such a state. Deep within, the love he had for her forced its way through steel and stone. The thought of losing her caused a deeper wound to open. But it twisted shut when he thought of Eliza's betrayal, and his bitterness beat back any tender feelings.

Darcy peeked around his leg. He looked down at her, saw how her eyes widened. She whimpered at the sight of her mother. Fiona turned her away, but Hayward insisted she stay.

"Come. Look upon your mother, Darcy." He moved her gently forward.

"Wake up, Mama," Darcy whispered.

Hayward set his hand on his daughter's shoulder. "She cannot."

Darcy shuddered and looked up at him. "Why, Papa?"

"She's going away."

"To Heaven to be with the Ilene?"

"I do not believe so, Darcy. You've heard of Hell, have you not? Well, that is where your mama will be. You see, if you are a bad person and sin—that is where you will go. That is where your mother is going . . . forever."

Aghast, Fiona threw her arm around Darcy and moved her back. "Mr. Morgan! That is a cruel thing to tell the child."

"Why should I withhold the truth from her?"

"It is not right to put such things in her head and cause her to fear."

He felt the heat rise in his face. "I will not have you instruct me." He reached for Darcy, grabbed her hands, and yanked her against him. Darcy took in a quick breath. Tears fell from her eyes, down her cheeks, and over her trembling lips. She snatched her hands away from her father's rough ones and stood back with balled fists.

"Mama won't be there, Papa. Mama will go to Heaven."

"You have to know the truth, Darcy. Bad people do not go to Heaven."

She shook her head. "No, Papa. Mama will be in Heaven with Ilene. Mama is good."

Jerking away, Darcy hurried to her mother's bedside. She climbed into the bed and put her hands upon Eliza's cheeks. "Wake, Mama! Wake!"

❧

The warm touch of her child's hands against her cheeks caused Eliza to open her eyes. When she saw Darcy's troubled face, she wrapped her arms around her and held her close. She looked over to see Hayward standing nearby. "Hayward. You have come back."

He said nothing at first. "I am leaving in the morning on business. I may be gone several days. Are you well enough to care for Darcy?"

Weakly she smiled. "Yes." She caressed the curls falling down Darcy's back. "I will recover now that she is with me."

"Then it is just what I thought. Pretense." He turned away and walked out. The bang of the door sounded deliberate as he passed through it. Eliza's heart sunk. She read in his movements, in the tone of his voice, that he had not forgiven her, that she had not won back his heart.

Before the scarlet dawn broke, the candle on her bedside table died. Darcy curled up beside her and set her hand in Eliza's. Fiona sat in the chair across from her, with Sarah nearby on the window seat.

"Go to bed, Fiona, Sarah," she said.

Fiona rose and shuffled toward the door. Eliza smiled over at her when she looked back and pulled the door closed. But Sarah stayed. "I won't leave you until I know you are sleeping well," she said, then turned back to the window and the moonlight coming through it.

As the sun rose, Eliza listened to footfalls going down the stairs. A moment, and the front door opened and slammed shut. Outside, Gareth whinnied and the hollow sound of hoofbeats retreated down the lane.

Hayward. Come back to me. Forgive me, my love.

She closed her eyes and prayed God would make a way where there seemed to be no way.

30

$\mathcal{L}$ess than a week later, Hayward returned to River Run. Though Eliza had no idea what day he'd step through the door, she had prepared herself for his homecoming. She gave special attention to her hair, washing it with an egg mixture and rinsing it with rainwater from the barrel outside. She bathed and powdered her body, and scented her clothes with lavender.

She was standing out on the porch when he rode up and dismounted. A gentle smile graced her lips, and he looked at her, somewhat pleased at her appearance. Still, she wondered where he had gone.

"You are looking well, Eliza. Feeling better?"

"I am. Even more, now that you are home." She lingered where she stood, even though the desire to hurry into his arms overwhelmed her. She waited, her palms slick and her heart yearning, as he dusted off his tricorn hat against his thigh and proceeded to the door.

He paused in front of her and looked down into her face. "I've had a long ride and am worn out. But I wish to speak with you."

Swallowing her worry, she followed him inside. He pulled her by the arm into his study, then shut the door and locked it. "I do not want anyone disturbing us. Open the windows, if you would."

The sashes went up easily for Eliza, and she breathed in the fresh air. Feeling hopeful, she turned back to Hayward, set her hand on his arm, leaned up, and kissed his cheek. He did not draw her to him as he used to. But he was tired, she thought. She must give him time to recover from his journey.

"Sit down, Eliza," he told her in a level voice, absent of anger.

He sat across from her and leaned forward. Then he told her his plan—things she had not expected. But what good was it to argue? He was her husband, her head, and her law.

"Now, you must listen to me carefully," he began. "I will have no opposition from you. My word is my will, and you must accept it. Remember wives are to obey their husbands in all things. Do you understand?"

A small spark of hope still lived within her. Perhaps his plan would somehow heal their marriage, and bring about the forgiveness she longed for. With her head low, she nodded. "Yes, I understand."

"Good. Be silent as I speak." He took a breath and proceeded. "I had this time away to think about our situation. I can forgive the fact you went to Halston thinking I was dead, that you were grieving and in despair, thus making you vulnerable. I can believe this was the first and only time you were alone with him. But I have no doubt he courted your friendship in order to weaken you to him. Everything you have told me, his aid during the snows and when the Indians attacked, gave him opportunity to win your affection. You were here alone, without me, and your loneliness was his mark. I cannot deny I am grateful he came to your aid, especially in regards to your capture. I have seen with my own eyes what the Indians can do to a woman. We can praise God you were spared."

Eyes warm, she looked up at him. "Then you understand?"

"In some things I do."

She touched his hand with gentle fingertips. "Then you are willing to begin again?"

Withdrawing, he settled back against the chair. "Yes, but not in the way you may be thinking."

Disappointed, she felt her eyes flicker with tears. She fought them, steeling herself for the blow. "What do you mean, Hayward?"

"Your reputation has changed, Eliza. Did you not notice the way the women at Sabbath services snubbed you? How the men glowered. How Reverend Hopewell looked at you with a strange pity. They all know."

"I am sorry, my love," she said, her emotions rising.

"I know you are. But for both our sakes, and for Darcy, you must do the following if you are willing to save our marriage and safeguard our daughter."

Determined to keep him, she answered, "I would do anything."

"I am glad to hear it, because what I require you to do will cause you pain. But you must bear it. With God's help you will."

Her heart stood still and her blood ran cold. "Sometimes pain is necessary to heal a wound. Tell me, Hayward, what it is you want me to do."

Shifting in his chair, he hesitated. Then he stood. "You and I are going to Annapolis. We leave tomorrow."

A smile graced her lips, warmed her heart. Time away. Time to renew their love and commitment to one another. It seemed the perfect plan. "Annapolis? Yes, it will be good for us to go away for a little while, to get to know each other again, love again . . ."

Displeasure glinted in his eyes. He raised his hand to stop her from going any further. "No, Eliza. Say nothing more. Just listen to me." His gruff tone arrested her, and caused her hopes to plunge.

"I received word that my father has passed away—a heart ailment of some kind, or more likely a blood vessel ruptured when he was in a rage. It has caused a malaise to overtake my mother. She is gravely ill. I met with Will on his way to set-tling in a house not far from here. His wife is too frail to leave his side . . ."

Eliza's sadness lifted. "Your half brother, his wife and chil-dren? They are settling here after all?"

"Must you interrupt me?"

She lowered her eyes. "I am sorry. I did not mean to. It's just that this is very good news."

"It has little to do with what my plans are for us. In Annapolis, you will board a ship, where you are to go back to England . . . You are to help my mother recover."

Fear pulsed through her, and she stood. "No."

"You will obey me in this, Eliza."

"Hayward, please. Oh, God . . ."

"You are to stay at Havendale until she is well."

"It could be months, perhaps a year or more. And Darcy is too young to be without me. And why can we not all go to England together? Why must you send me alone?"

"I have already explained why. I shouldn't have to repeat myself."

Tears drifted down her cheeks. "Can I not take Darcy with me?"

"Not when my mother is so ill."

Bewildered, she shook her head. "Why should we separate and give up our life because of a few gossips? In time, they will forget. I know that is the true reason you want to send me away. You are worried about your good name, which you say I have blackened. Our love is more important than what people think."

"Stop the tears, Eliza. I won't be swayed by them."

She swiped the tears off her face and sat down. Indifference shone on Hayward's face. Sunlight came through the window, blanching her face, and she gazed up at him. If words could not plead her case, her look could. "Do not send me away. Please. I cannot be without Darcy or you. Do not separate us."

The silence that came over Hayward said it all. Eliza knew she could not reason with him, or change his mind. Her remorse deepened. Her sin had damaged all those she loved. Even River Run suffered in the heat, in the flame that consumed all their hopes and dreams for a good life and a lasting legacy. No longer would this be the blessed land Hayward had fought for. She had shattered both his heart and his dreams.

He took her hands in his and gently held them. "Eliza, my love, I know this is hard, but you must trust me. Besides, as my wife, you have a duty to make sure my mother is cared for as she should be. You want to make things better, do you not? Then do as I say."

Long she stared into his eyes. Perhaps by obeying him there would be redemption. Perhaps this step was a way of binding their wounds. But to go away alone, without him, without Darcy, to care for his ill mother, a woman she hardly knew? Indeed, he told her right. His plan would cause her a great deal of pain. She gazed into his eyes. "It is a difficult thing you require of me."

"Here, read her letter. It should convince you I am right. She specifically asks for you. How can you deny her or me?"

It taxed her emotions—his mother's pleas, her expressions of discomfort and pain, her regret she had not known Eliza, that they had left England without a word to her. Her illness grew worse as the dull days dragged on. *If Eliza could come to me, only for a time, I would find comfort in her company.*

Folding the letter closed, Eliza set it aside, and pulled in a ragged breath. "You are my husband. If this is what you want, I will do as you say."

Pleased, he kissed her hands, then stood and pulled her up to him. "Go upstairs and pack. I will explain to Darcy."

Eliza wondered how her daughter would ever understand. She prayed and cried that night as she fell in and out of sleep. Agonizing over leaving River Run—and the daughter she loved—brought her renewed sorrow. In the morning, she came down the staircase one last time. She had fixed her hair, and along one side it fell over her shoulder in thick ringlets. To dress her finest she hoped would plague Hayward's heart. She wanted him to look at her with desire in his eyes. She wanted his heart to ache with missing her, not after she was gone, but long before.

As she came down the stairs and saw him turn to her, and his eyes take her in, she momentarily felt guilty for wanting him to feel this way—for wanting to punish him for what he asked of her.

The plum-colored gown graced her form with a white cotton underdress, delicate lace cuffs, and matching striped ribbon sash. Over her arm she carried her favorite cloak of burgundy wool to cover her during the journey.

The front door stood open. A pair of horses, saddled and waiting, swished their tails. When Hayward placed his hat on his head and walked out the door, Fiona threw her arms around Eliza and kissed her cheek.

"Worry not, my girl. I will look after Darcy while you're away. And in time, we will all be back together. Mr. Hayward said so." She dabbed her wet eyes with her apron. "But 'tis cruel he will not let me go with you," she whispered through her sobs.

Sarah met Eliza at the door. She stopped suddenly inside the door frame, where the sunlight fell over her hair. Sadness shone in her eyes.

"God bless you, Eliza," she cried out.

Eliza embraced her. "You have been my dear friend, Sarah. I pray that you find the love you seek."

Sarah turned and struggled down the steps. Eliza gazed after her, saw her walk out into the meadow limping, her hands clenched and her head low.

"Mama," came a small voice behind Eliza.

Turning swiftly, Eliza went down on her knees and gathered Darcy into her arms. She clung to her child, kissed her cheeks, and soothed her with all the words a mother could. "Just for a little while, my darling."

Darcy's quiet sobs were more than Eliza could bear. She held her daughter closer. "Oh, how my heart breaks to leave you. Remember I love you so. Never forget, Darcy. Never . . ."

Hayward's hand fell over her shoulder, and he pulled her away. Grieved, she felt her body shake beneath the folds of her gown. She heard Darcy whimper. She halted. A cry tightened in her throat, and she battled it back, shutting her eyes to keep the tears from coming. Then she moved on without a glance back.

Lord God. Watch over my darling girl.

L

From the river road, they traveled on horseback up the gentle sloping hills down into the valley to Fredericktown, a village of German and English settlers nestled along the foothills of the Catoctin Mountains. On the edge of town, Hayward boarded the horses at a stable and hired a coach to take them the rest of the way. After he helped Eliza down from the saddle, she waited patiently outside, running her gloved hand down her mare's velvety nose.

When she saw the coach and driver draw up, pulled by four dappled-gray horses, an indiscreet smile edged across her well-formed lips. Hayward had gone to such extravagance to hire a private coach, as opposed to a stage wagon that would be crowded with people.

"We will have plenty of room to stretch our legs," he said, noting her smile. "Who wants to travel in a packed coach with strangers?"

"It must have cost you much." She admired the brightly painted green doors.

"Not really. I have the money. Besides it gives us time to ourselves." He took her bag and led her past the horses. "You will be away for some time, and this will do us good, don't you think?"

She agreed with a nod, the hood of her cloak slipping back to reveal her dark hair. He sat opposite her, his back to the driver, took off his hat, and set it beside him on the seat. For several miles, they looked out at forest and field, only quiet comments passing between them.

Dust rose behind the wheels and sank over thistle and milk-weed, as well as the hedgerows that lined the road. Feeling the air grow warmer, Eliza removed her cloak and smoothed out the folds of her dress. She adjusted the lace on her sleeves and combed her fingers through her hair. Her hands trembled as she did so, even when she repeated the gestures several times.

Not long after their departure, Hayward put his boots up on the seat, folded his arms over his chest, and fell asleep. *He acts so indifferent to me leaving. I still have not won back his heart. I only pray he longs for me as much as I longed for him when he was away.*

She wondered would he be lonely without her? Would the days drag on in a slow cadence and would the house seem empty with her gone? She found her reticule tucked into the fold of her gown, pulled on its strings to open it, and took out a lock of Darcy's hair. She would show this to her mother-in-law, let her see the fine color of her granddaughter's locks. *She will no doubt regret she did not ask for Darcy as well.*

Already Eliza missed her child, and the thought of being so far from her, and the many days she'd have to live without her, caused her heart to ache.

After an hour of bumpy roads, she moved across to her husband and laid her head against his shoulder. He did not stir, remaining as he was, arms crossed, head back. She glanced up to look at his closed eyelids and hoped he'd put his arm around her. Her affection was not enough to bring him closer. Still, she pressed into him and listened to his heartbeat.

When they reached Annapolis, and the banks of the Chesapeake Bay, the sun was setting. The coach slowed and pulled up to the docks—the same ones they had come to years before. Worn from the relentless roll and pitch of the coach, Eliza gazed out the window. Seagulls banked in the wind, hovered above the bay, dove and squawked among pelicans and sandpipers. Fishing boats heaved gently in the tide. Tall ships lay in the harbor, their bells clanging while lanterns brightened.

"Come, Eliza," Hayward said. "We've arrived, and in good time, I'd say."

He opened the coach door and stepped out. Then he extended his hand to her. She took it, and he helped her down. The wind of the bay blew cool, and she drew her cloak over her shoulders.

"You there." Hayward called to a seaman. "Are you a crew member on *The Beacon?*"

The sailor dragged off his cap. "Aye, I am, sir. Who wants to know?"

"Mr. Hayward Morgan of River Run. This is my wife, Eliza Morgan. She is to be one of the passengers aboard your ship."

The cap between his hands, the sailor bowed short. "Our skiff waits for you and the others. Captain says he wants to set sail before sundown."

Eliza glanced at Hayward. "So soon? I thought it would be days before we would . . . I would leave."

Hayward said nothing in response, showing no disappointment or surprise. It seemed he knew in advance that this was how it would be. She clutched her cloak at her throat. She gasped when he looked at her.

"Do not worry, Eliza. These men will take care of you. And the captain is a good man, I hear. Time will go by fast. You'll see. As soon as my mother is well, come home to me. I'll be waiting."

He leaned down, kissed her forehead, and their eyes met. Desperate to read his feelings, his thoughts, she looked deeply into his eyes. He turned away and instructed the seaman to carry Eliza's bag. "Take care that you help her into the skiff. Tell Captain Payne I am counting on him to get my wife safely to England."

At the sight of this young sailor taking her belongings in hand and heading down the wharf to the boat, fear washed over her. It gripped her with such force that she grew faint. A tremor passed through her body. "Hayward. Can we not stay in town a few days together? This is too soon."

"You heard the sailor. The ship is to sail."

"But there are other ships."

"I'm afraid not. It would be weeks to wait for another."

She stared into his eyes and knew he was lying. "Come with me. Perhaps if you did, your mother would recover much faster, and then we could come home sooner than if it were just I. Perhaps with you there, she would be willing to return to River Run with us, instead of living alone so far from you and Will."

"We have been over this before, Eliza."

"I know, but I am afraid."

"Do not embarrass yourself or me. If I can settle my affairs . . ."

"What affairs?"

He sighed. "Things that concern River Run. The harvest; the mill—plans for the future . . ."

"Can you not hire someone to do that?"

"No. I cannot. Now, if I can settle things in less time, and I will endeavor to do so, then I will not send word to you to return home. I will come and fetch you myself."

There was some hope. "You promise you will?"

"You mustn't doubt anything I say." He kissed her cheek and walked with her to the waiting vessel. Three others were ahead of Eliza, and each in turn stepped down. An oarsman took her by the waist, swung her down into the boat, and instructed her to sit. Once seated, she pulled her cloak over her knees. Hayward stood on the wharf, hat in hand, watching her.

As the oarsmen pulled on the oars and the skiff slid away, Eliza sat silent and still, her eyes brimming and fixed on

Hayward. A moment, and he moved away, back to the coach. She saw him climb in and latch the door. She wanted to dive into the waves, swim back to him, stop him. But his words echoed over and over: *If you want to save our marriage, you will do as I say.*

With a snap of the reins, the horses pranced forward and the coach rolled away. The reality that he had gone, and that she would not see him again for a long time, grew overwhelming as she sat in a boat with people she did not know, going to a ship that would take her across the sea to England.

As the boat drew up to *The Beacon*, she watched the Maryland shoreline turn misty blue and indistinct. The massive hull of the ship cast a deep shadow over her, cold and foreboding. Once aboard, and shown to the cramped quarters that would be hers for the duration of the voyage, she stared at the small cot with the ticking pillow, the wool blanket, the chamber pot, and the washing pitcher.

Mortified, she shut the door and collapsed to her knees. There, upon the planks, she poured out her heart and soul to her God, like the violent sweep of waves that buffeted the blackened timbers and crashed back into the sea.

Part 4

But with you there is forgiveness;
therefore you are feared.

Psalm 130:4 NIV

31

*E*liza put on her best gown, one of three she had packed for her journey. The rest of her clothes she had left at River Run, believing they would somehow assure her return. The garment, made of soft muslin, draped her body in loose folds. The bodice no longer hugged her waist, nor the three-quarter-length sleeves her arms. Its only flattering feature was its deep plum color, which enhanced her eyes.

During the voyage, to eat even the smallest morsel of food had proved tedious. In her tight quarters, she had stared at the pewter bowl before her, a ladleful of bland gruel growing cold within it. How could food mean anything to her? Hayward had sent her away, without Darcy, Fiona, or even Sarah. Now, she shoved the soupy gruel around with her spoon and groaned.

She stood and looked at her face reflected in the tin mirror that was nailed to a post in the wall. How pale her skin looked, and her cheeks, once rosy and round, were sunken and void of color. Loneliness settled deep into Eliza's being, showing in the dark circles beneath her eyes. Seeking solace, she read from her Bible and prayed by candlelight as the ship rose and fell in the ocean swells. God would be her sustenance through her trial, and she clung to the hope that He would forgive her. Fiona told her that the Lord had done so, but she needed to be convinced. She wrote a verse from Psalms upon a strip of paper and kept it tucked inside her dress.

Be merciful to me, O God. Be merciful to me! For my soul trusts in You. And in the shadow of Your wings I will make my refuge, until these calamities have passed by.

When she came up on deck, the salty breeze struck her face. She looked up at the gray sky that peeked through the shrouds and sails. On the horizon, mist covered the land, drifting over the shore, and along the blackened cliffs that brooded above, casting long shadows on the rocks below. England. Would it be welcoming to her, like a mother she had left?

Oarsmen helped her down into the skiff. Their strong arms pulled the oars against a choppy sea and brought the boat into shore, where it skidded across the stones that covered the beach. The village bustled with people, and she stopped a merchant and asked him where she could catch the overland coach. On the road above, he told her.

She opened her bag. Yes, Hayward's letter was safely tucked away. But would they accept his words—accept her? Would they badger her with questions?

She picked up her bag and proceeded on. The captain called to her, bid her wait, and she turned back to him as he leapt from the side of another skiff and strode up to her.

"Mr. Morgan asked me to give you this upon your arrival, ma'am." He handed over a packet wrapped in brown paper, tied with string, her name inscribed on it in Hayward's hand.

"Thank you, Captain." She looked back at him. "A man told me I may catch the coach at the top of the hill. Do you know if that is so?"

"To my knowledge, yes. Good luck to you." With a courteous smile, he touched the brim of his hat and stepped away through the menagerie of people.

"Instructions? A love letter?" whispered Eliza. She decided not to open it until she was inside the coach, where she could read his missive without disruption.

She gathered her dress above the heels of her shoes, well away from the muddy street. Gathering her resolve, she headed up a path to the brink of the hills. At the top, a windy road rutted by carriage wheels stretched northwards.

A short distance away stood a carriage inn that faced the bluffs and the sea. The stone exterior reminded Eliza of the dark shale cliffs that overlooked the Potomac gorge, and she grew lonesome for Hayward and Darcy, and grieved for Ilene.

She drew in a long and troubled breath and noted the mullioned windows and how it appeared that no one lived at the inn. Just then, the blare of a coachman's horn startled her, and a stage pulled by four chestnut horses rounded a bend in the road at a furious gallop, heading toward the shabby and weatherworn inn.

Drawn in, the horses pawed the ground. Eliza caught up with coach and spoke to the driver. "I am in need of transport north, sir, to a place called Havendale in Derbyshire. Can you take me?" She hoped she did not look like a gypsy, for the wind blew strong and tossed her dark hair.

The driver, shrouded in a gray greatcoat, looked down from his perch. "I'm heading north to Manchester. I can take you as far as Congleton."

"You have my thanks, sir."

"Pay your fare, and after the horses have been changed over, we will be on our way," the driver said, jumping down.

Eliza handed him the fare, and once all was ready, she climbed inside the empty coach. If only the sun would break through the clouds, the place would not look so grim, she thought.

With a snap of the driver's whip, the horses moved on. The coach creaked and groaned over the road, and as it swayed, Eliza, overcome by fatigue, drifted off, and woke hours later as daylight faded. How she had ever slept with all the rocking and dipping she could not explain.

She gazed out the window at the vast expanse of land. Field and moor, farmhouses miles apart met her eye—a desolate, lonely land that seemed alien to her. As she peered out the window, she wondered how long it would take her to reach Havendale. She would look worn through, and hoped they would understand the long journey she had endured.

She took from her bag the letter given to her by the captain and held it in her hand. Now seemed a good time to open it. Anxious, she slipped free the string and broke the seal.

"Congleton," cried the driver. The coach slowed to a halt, and her door opened. "This is as far as we go."

She climbed out, and he handed her down her bag. Then he snapped the reins and drove off. Eliza stood alone at the roadside, bag in one hand, the unopened letter in the other. She walked on a few paces, feeling a bit stunned that she had to make the rest of the way on her own, hoping some kind-hearted person driving a wagon would offer her a ride. She knew that with the way she looked the gentry in their carriages would avoid her.

A lone tree stood behind her, and she leaned against it. She unfolded the letter, and when she saw the letterhead, her knees buckled. She sank to the ground. "It cannot be. He promised . . ."

Tears burned in her eyes. He told her she had no rights to her child, and she would not be able to find Darcy if she made an attempt. She was considered deceased to him. She was never to return. He explained that his mother had not been ill, but that it was true his father had passed away. The idea that Madeline had asked for her was a sham to lure her into doing as he wished. And if she were to return, he swore he'd see to it she would face charges of adultery and be imprisoned.

I am returning you where I found you. And there you shall stay.

She cried out, then wept. Panicked, she crumbled the letter in her hands and bent over in agony. "Oh, Hayward. What have you done?" she whispered through her sobs. "Why could you not forgive me?"

Long she stared at his words, her tears dropping onto the paper, smearing the ink. The desire to tear it into pieces and toss it away, to let the wind carry it off, filled her. She stood with an effort and braced her hand against the tree. A chill rushed through her body, and she could barely stand. Her fingertips held the paper. Weak now, she let it go, and the wind blew it across the road, where it caught in the stems of a thistle. For a moment, she stared at it.

Go! Go!

But then it dawned her that perhaps she should keep it. It was what Hayward wanted. He had lied to her, and now she was an unknown without a husband, a child, and a home. Yes, she had to keep it as a constant reminder of how cold his heart had become.

Breathless, she hurried across the road and snatched the paper free from the needles that held it. With her thoughts reeling, she folded it up and shoved it into the bottom of her bag. And before her eyes lay the letter addressed to Hayward's mother. She lifted it and stared at the words *Madeline Morgan, Havendale*.

She could not go there now. What would she say to her? That her son had cast her off? How would she explain the reasons? The door would surely be slammed in her face.

A moan slipped from between her teeth. She had to see for herself what he had written. She broke the seal with fury racing through her, and spread the letter open. Her eyes widened at the page before her. A single word appeared. *Adulteress.* He had deliberately planned to humiliate her. It said more than a hundred words could.

Down the road she walked, then out into the fields, where she roamed until the sun slipped behind the hills and the low clouds gathered. Broken, Eliza staggered forward, her limbs heavy weights that dragged her toward the ground. Her mind sunk into an abyss of despair. Rain fell in a gentle mist. Her hair, wild and loose about her, dampened. Her cloak covered her, but her body shook from the cold the rain had brought.

Eyes half-opened, she whispered, "Darcy. God, help her. What will he tell her?"

The wind swept across her, blew her hair over her eyes, which blinded her to how far she had traveled. With all hope gone, she wept no tears. They had been spent.

Too weary to go on, she laid her head down upon the cold, drenched earth. "I am now no one. I am without anyone. I am a tainted soul. Where will I go? Lord, let me die. Take me, please."

Then through the sigh of wind and the whisper of rain, she heard a gentle voice speak into her heart. *I will never leave you, or forsake you.*

She drew her knees up close and stared up at the whirling sky over her, until she fell halfway between sleep and wakefulness. Faint though they were, she heard footsteps draw near. Hands slipped beneath her and lifted her into arms strong and warm. The lapel of a man's coat rubbed against her cheek, and she pressed into it.

Had an angel come to take her to Heaven? She struggled to open her eyes. But the stupor conquered her. The one who held her in his arms hurried across the fields, the stones, the dips and rises without pausing.

Soon she heard a door knock against a wall and a masculine voice call for aid. She felt the heat of a fire and smelled burning cedar. She was lowered to a couch, and a blanket folded over her. It smelled of lavender.

Her lids fluttered open. Shapes moved about her, indistinct and colorless. Voices soothed her, and her fears weakened. The brim of a tin cup touched her lips, and she sipped the hot broth within it.

Hands clasped hers, strong hands larger than hers that rubbed them together. She lifted her eyes and saw his face. The eyes were bright blue, his hair black like hers but streaked with gray and curled on the ends. Crimson scars crossed his jaw and curved down the left side of his throat.

She was not afraid of him, for his eyes were kind. He was not handsome like Hayward, but his face looked strong and noble in the firelight—like Gabriel or Michael, and older than she.

"Feeling better?" he asked.

"A little." She watched a faint smile creep across his mouth.

"Drink more of this. It will give you strength." Again he held the cup to her lips. She wrapped her hands over it. But they trembled so that he closed one hand over them to steady them.

"I found you out on the moor, unconscious. What is your name?"

"I am no one." She could not meet his eyes. But when he touched her hand to gain her attention, then withdrew his hand, she looked back at him and saw compassion and understanding in his expression.

"Everyone has a name. But if you do not wish to tell me, perhaps you will later. At least you are safe, and inside out of this foul weather. Can I send word to a friend, or a relative, perhaps your husband?"

"There is no one."

"No one at all?" He looked at her, surprised. "You mean you have no home to go to? By the look of your clothes you are not poor."

"I had a home once," she said. "But I cannot go back there."

Rain tapped against the windows. Eliza glanced at the darkness outside, thankful this kind man had rescued her from a night that promised numbing cold and even death.

☙

A stout woman of middle years entered the room. A white cap covered her hair, but small wisps poked out along her forehead. Her large gray eyes fell over Eliza's face, and she shook her head and clicked her tongue.

"You must allow me to get her upstairs," the man said. "Dry clothes and a warm bed is what she needs."

Eliza looked over at the man and tried to get up. "No. No. Mrs. Hart will help you. Again, you have nothing to fear here."

A pair of plump arms helped Eliza rise, and led her out of the room and up the staircase. The man followed. She could hear his boots fall over the steps behind her. But one glance back from Mrs. Hart said "You need not follow. I can take care of the young woman."

"Care for her well, Mrs. Hart. And whatever she needs, I shall provide," he said.

"Yes, sir. But let us hope she is not a gypsy that will rob us. You should be more cautious."

"I cannot help it. She seems a lost soul who has been through much."

When Eliza came around the top of the stairs to a long hallway, she glanced over the railing to see him standing downstairs. He looked up at her, concerned. Their eyes met. He hesitated a moment and then stepped away.

✐❧

Sunlight poured through filmy curtains and alighted on Eliza's face. The warmth, the sensation of light, woke her. Mrs. Hart sat in a spindle chair near the fire. Her hands were busy with a pair of knitting needles, and she paused in her work to look over at Eliza.

"Well, you are awake at last."

"How long have I slept?"

"Two days. You were bone weary when you came to us. It's a miracle Mr. Brennan found you, else you would have caught your death of cold and died out there. We had a biting rain, you see, and the wind had been howling all day. Not fit for man or beast. But Mr. Brennan takes his daily walk in all kinds of weather. I can't say how surprised I was when he rushed through the front door with you in his arms, dripping wet and looking like a vagabond."

She went on knitting. Eliza tried to absorb all she had said. "Whose house is this?"

"Mr. Brennan's, of course. Don't you know Fairview?"

Eliza shook her head. "No."

"It belonged to his cousin, George Brennan, whom I served for many years. He passed on, God rest his soul, and Mr. Brennan inherited the estate. And a good thing, too, having had no real home of his own."

A moment, and she set the needles and wool on her lap. "He has suffered much in his life, and has had losses no one should. But I shall not tell you of them. If he wants you to know, then he'll tell you all about it. I will say that Fairview has been a haven for him. It has been a house that draws the wayward, the lost, and the brokenhearted. Like you, miss. You were lost, and now you're found."

Mrs. Hart wiggled her head, as if to indicate she had seen many a stranger come and go. The door opened, and in stepped Mr. Brennan. "Leave us, Mrs. Hart, if you please."

After Mrs. Hart had gathered her knitting basket and shut the door, Mr. Brennan took hold of the chair and drew it up to the bedside. Eliza pulled the covers up closer to her chin.

"I take it the rest you've had has improved you." He cleared his throat. "If you wish to tell me your story, I will listen. I am not judge or jury. I only wish to help you, if you will let me."

His kindness warmed her. The expression in his eyes was unlike Hayward's. His were stern, aloof, and often stoic, whereas this man had a light within his eyes that came from his soul, an unearthly brightness that burned deep, not for her as a woman, but for her as a fellow human being. It seemed to Eliza that Brennan looked upon, or rather sought her heart— her true self.

"Someone has hurt you," he said. "I can tell your pain is great. That is why you ran away. Am I right?"

"My pain is my own, sir. I will not burden you or anyone else with it."

"Well, I'll have Mrs. Hart bring you up a tray. You must be very hungry." He stood to leave.

"Please, do not go. I take back what I said. Let me talk to you now. And when I am finished, if you wish me gone, I shall go immediately. But first call your wife, so I may speak to her first."

Sorrow suddenly flinched over his face. "I have no wife—not now. It's been many years ago. She died."

"I am sorry. I should not have asked . . ."

"A fire took her, one night three years ago. We had a fierce storm. Lightning struck the roof and ignited it. I tried to save her and our little girl, but I failed. My son and I are what is left of our little family."

"How terrible. I know how it feels to lose someone, but not in that way. Is that the reason for your . . . ?"

He nodded. "Scars? Ugly, are they not? They have been my cross to bear and a constant reminder of that awful night every time I look in the mirror or see my reflection in a window. As for Emily, I know she waits for me in Heaven. God has given me a great deal of comfort in that knowledge."

Eliza regarded Mr. Brennan. Indeed, his life had been tragic. To lose the one you love and a child in such a way would have caused her to go out of her mind. She wondered how he had survived such excruciating pain. Barely was she able to carry the grief of losing Ilene, and then her separation from Darcy.

He sat still and looked down at his clasped hands. She noticed he still wore his wedding band.

"You speak of Heaven. I wish you had left me to die. My parents and my child are there."

Brennan frowned and lifted her away from the pillows by her shoulders. "Do not ever wish for that, even when you miss them. Life is a gift, no matter what you have been through.

And think of the others who would be hurt by your death. Wishing for it is a selfish thing."

She gazed into his troubled eyes, saw the gentle nature of the man as well as the pain he lived with. Her eyes filled, and she gasped. "I am just so . . . alone." She fell against his shoulder, and he allowed her to cry. When she realized a stranger held her, she pulled away and briskly wiped her face dry.

"You must tell me who you are. You understand, don't you?" He stood and went to the door. "I will be downstairs in my study."

After the latch on the door had clicked shut and his footfalls had faded away, she climbed from the bed and dressed. Yes. She would tell him. She had to tell someone.

32

$\mathcal{T}$he door to Mr. Brennan's study stood open a few inches, enough for Eliza to see him at his desk working and to know she was welcomed. He wore spectacles, and when he sensed her presence, he looked up from the books before him, pulled off his glasses, and stood.

"Please. Come inside." He stepped away from his desk. "You might find it a bit austere in here, but I haven't had . . . there is no . . ."

"I understand," Eliza said. "But it is pleasant room. You have a magnificent view." She crossed the room to a large bay window. Beyond it she admired the green fields dotted with sheep, and the line of thick forest in the distance. The sunlit blue sky hung cloudless.

"Indeed." He joined her. Then he turned to her, and she to him. "Now, tell me who you are. I must call you by some name."

She sat down in the window seat, her hands clasped. "My name is Eliza."

He bowed short. "A lovely name. I had an aunt named Eliza. And what brought you to the fields near my house?"

"I was sent here." She went on to explain. Eliza hung her head. "I had no idea my husband would do such a thing."

"So you are abandoned here. You cannot go to his mother, for no doubt she will have nothing to do with you. But if you wish it, I shall write to her."

"I am afraid that would do no good. But I thank you." She looked at him as he stood in the light of the window. "Part of me wants to conceal my story. But if I could tell someone, it might help." Though he was a stranger, she felt she could trust Mr. Brennan and that he would aid her in any way he could.

He sat in the chair across from her. "Where does your mother-in-law live?"

"Havendale."

Instantly he lifted his hand away from his chin. "Havendale? I am familiar with that estate. I ministered there, at Saint Anthony's."

Shocked, Eliza felt her mouth drop open, and she gasped. "Then you are the clergyman who took my father's place. He was Matthias Bloome."

Equally surprised, Brennan scooted to the edge of his chair. "Yes. I came there after his passing. You were gone by then. I can hardly believe it."

"And you, your wife, and five children came to live there with you. This is quite amazing, Mr. Brennan." *Oh, his loss. Again he has been reminded. But where are the other four children?*

"You were told wrong, Eliza. Emily and I arrived with two children—I left with one—my son. The vicarage was destroyed in the fire. We stayed briefly with a few kind parishioners, but then I received word that my cousin, George Brennan, had left his estate to me. I am raising my son here and God willing shall see him fully-grown. Although I have no pulpit to preach from, and have retired from the church, I am able to devote myself to my studies and to give aid to those in need—like you."

Eliza shook her head. "I am so amazed I can hardly speak, sir."

"It is a miracle, I would say."

Eliza clenched her hands. He, a retired clergyman, should not have a person like her in his house. "I shall leave once you have heard my story."

"You are free to go if you wish it. But I insist you stay until you are strong enough. Now, tell me about your life, dear girl. What brought you so much sorrow, and why did your husband cast you aside?"

She bent her head and stood silent. While she rallied her courage, Brennan stared at her intently. She then poured out the course of her life, from meeting Hayward on the moor; to her journey and life at River Run; about her dear Darcy, Ilene, Fiona, and Sarah; and then Halston and her *fall from grace*.

Before he could prevent her, she collapsed back onto the window seat near where she had stood, and laid her head in her folded arms. Her whole frame trembled, and her tears were silent. He bade her rise, but she could not.

A few minutes went by, and then Eliza sat up and wiped her face with the back of her hand. Brennan stood at an arm's distance, his face etched sharply with concern. "You need have no fear of being cast from this house. I shall pray the Lord gives you the peace you need."

"I am sorry, Mr. Brennan. I did not mean to cry."

"You miss those you love. It is understandable."

"God has a right to punish me for what I have done."

"And He has the right to forgive all of our sins, no matter how great or how small. Do you believe this?"

No one had asked her that before. "Yes . . . I think for the first time I do."

"Then you must forgive yourself. I believe God has led you to Fairview for a purpose. Do not answer me now, but would you be willing to be a governess to my son? I had thought of sending him away to school, but I cannot bear the idea of him gone. I will pay you, of course, not much, but a bit for you to put by. And you will have food and lodging. And then . . . if we find a way whereby you may be with your daughter, you will have all you need to accomplish that."

Brennan leaned toward her. "Ah, I see you are contemplating the offer. Perhaps you should meet my son." The door drifted open, and a boy with straight brown hair poked his head around the corner. "Come in, Ethan. Meet our guest."

Eliza thought him a handsome lad. His dark brown eyes looked straight into hers as he walked inside and stood near his father. He held out his hand and shook Eliza's.

"This is my son, Ethan." Brennan laid his hand on the boy's shoulder.

"How do you do, Ethan? You have a firm grip for a boy your age."

"Thank you, Miss Eliza," he said. "You were lost, and father found you?"

A quick glance at Mr. Brennan, and she smiled for the first time in many days. "It is true, Ethan. I had lost my way. But I think I may have found it again."

33

*D*ays turned into weeks, weeks into months. But the anguish of Hayward's rejection and her separation from Darcy stayed with Eliza with every sweep of the clock's hands. At night, with her head upon the pillow and her eyes fixed on the ceiling above her, she prayed fervently for them both—and for Fiona and Sarah. When dawn broke and light streamed through the window, she'd wake with an aching heart. But Ethan gave her solace, and she poured herself into her new role. Mr. Brennan promised to pay her fifteen pounds annum, which was all he could afford, along with a roof above her head for the rest of her natural life if she desired it.

Winter days were short. In the evenings, she joined Mr. Brennan and Ethan at the dinner table, and read to them by the fire afterwards until it was time for Ethan to go to bed. Then she would leave Mr. Brennan alone with his thoughts and memories. A deep friendship had formed between them, and soon she would sit with him for an hour or more and they would talk of various things.

A hint of spring's promised arrival soon lingered in the air, and the fields that surrounded Fairview were lush green and scented with scythed grass. On one such day, Eliza sat in a sunlit room penning another letter to Hayward. She knew it would take months to reach him, but she had written two other letters before and never received a word in reply. She hoped he would have read the letters she enclosed to Darcy. Darcy had to know she still loved her and missed her with all her heart, that her mother had not abandoned her.

In her first missive to him, she wrote rapidly and with emotion, asking him why he had deceived her. No matter what had happened, they were man and wife in God's eyes, and should be together until death would part them. She wrote the second with more constraint, but begged him again to send Fiona with Darcy to her, that a girl needed her mother, and to send Sarah as well if she desired a new life. She had discussed this ardent request with Mr. Brennan first, and he had agreed.

So now, the third letter lay before her, and she held the pen above the paper, searching for words that would persuade him. What more could she say to Hayward that would soften his stony heart? A seed of bitterness had rooted deep within him.

A fox out in the field barked and caused her to look up. From the window, she watched it run toward the woods and disappear within them. Then her eyes shifted to the end of the lane. A woman, carrying a hefty carpetbag and wearing a gray cloak and wide-brimmed hat, walked with hurried steps toward the house.

Perhaps she has an appointment with Mr. Brennan and thinks she is late. But he is away. Then it must be a friend of Mrs. Hart's. She looked down at her letter, then back up again. *She reminds me of Fiona.*

"Most likely she is in need of work, Roscoe. I hope Mrs. Hart has something for her to do. She is only here part of the time." She stroked the ears of the orange cat that sat on the edge of the desk. Roscoe blinked his green eyes and licked a paw.

On the carpet, Ethan had spread out his father's atlas and stretched out to study it. "I cannot find the Potomac, Miss Eliza. I see the Hudson, though."

"Look further down the map, Ethan, to Maryland. You will see the Chesapeake." She kept her eyes fixed on the cloaked woman.

Ethan chirped. "There is the bay, and here is the *Po . . . to . . . mac*. I think I should like to see that river someday when I am grown. Do they have horses there?"

"Of course."

"And do they have farms for breeding?"

"Yes."

"I read that George Washington had a grand horse named Blue Stockings. I do not think King George had a warhorse like the president's. I prefer the American quarter horses and Arabians. I would like to own an American quarter horse someday."

Eliza continued to stare at the woman, who paused a moment, set her bag down and looked as though she had stopped to catch her breath. She lifted her bag again with a heave-ho attitude and walked a bit quicker. Then, with a start, Eliza dropped her pen. The cat leapt from the desk almost toppling the inkwell. Eliza stood. The realization of who the woman was hit her. Surprise pulsed through her, and she moved around the desk, closer to the open window.

By now the woman had reached the house, and Eliza looked down at the top of her hat. "Fiona?" she called out, giddy with joy. "Fiona, is that you?"

The woman stretched her neck back and looked up at the window. A broad smile swept across her face and her eyes brightened. She dropped her bag and cried out, "Eliza, my girl! I've come. He sent me. Couldn't stand me a minute longer."

With hurried breath, Eliza charged from the window, out the door, and down the staircase. She pulled open the front door and ran out into Fiona's arms. They embraced, laughed, and wept tears of joy.

"Mr. Hayward said he no longer needed me, that he couldn't stand my nagging ways," Fiona said, speaking rapidly. "I badgered him day in and day out about you, when you were coming home, when he was going to sail to England and bring you back. He would not answer, so I hounded him until he told me it was I who had to go to England, not him."

Eliza squeezed Fiona's hand. "I begged him to send you. I have missed you so much. But how did you know where to find me?"

"Your letters said you were at Fairview. Mr. Hayward knows of it and shoved the directions in my hand as I was going out the door."

Fiona paused and looked into Eliza's eyes. Then she gently placed her hands on Eliza's face. "I know what he did, my girl. He told me. I cannot tell you how long I stayed on my knees praying for you. But all shall be well, won't it?"

Eliza looked past Fiona to the lane as if she thought Darcy would suddenly appear. "Darcy? He would not let you bring her?"

Fiona's smile faded. "He would not. He has sent her to live with William and Mari Breese. He said it is best, for Darcy has five cousins, all girls."

"Is she healthy and happy?" asked Eliza.

"Healthy as can be. Happy too. But she asks for you all the time."

"She is young. You know, Fiona, in time she will forget me. Come inside."

"Whose house is this?"

"My employer's."

Fiona gasped. "You are a maid?"

"No, a governess."

Saddened over Darcy but happy to have Fiona, Eliza put her arm across the woman's shoulder and drew her inside the house. Ethan stood in the foyer staring, and when Eliza introduced Fiona and explained who she was, the boy welcomed her to Fairview.

"He's quite the little gentleman," Fiona said.

"Indeed he is. His papa, Mr. Brennan, is out taking his daily walk and will not be back for an hour. I'll see you settled in the room next to mine, and when he returns we shall speak with him."

"He may not let me stay, Eliza. You must be prepared for that. I can find work nearby. As long as I can see you, that is all that matters."

Ethan turned to Eliza. "May I go down to the creek, Miss Eliza?" He held up a jar. "I want to catch minnows for Roscoe."

"Yes, but be back within the hour."

Despite Fiona's concerns, Eliza lifted the hem of her gown and led her upstairs. Her quarters were at the far end of a long corridor, and there were several empty rooms in the great old house. They talked for the next hour about all that had happened.

Fiona sat on the edge of the bed and folded her hands in her lap. "Mr. Hayward is so changed. He is not the man you wedded but has grown coarse and sullen. And he has given in to drink. I have to say, I am glad to be far away from him. He became cruel toward Sarah, working her to the bone. I would have brought her with me, but she left River Run. She did not say where she was going, only that she was called away. I wished Mr. Hayward had allowed me to bring Darcy. But he would have none of it, and insisted she was better off where she was."

Distraught, but endeavoring to be strong, Eliza looked at Fiona. "Do you believe she is?"

Fiona pressed her lips together. "Hmm. I do, considering the circumstances. Believe me when I say she is happy with the Breese family. I went to see her before I left and saw her romping in the yard with the girls, giggling and rolling on the ground like happy angels. And Mr. Breese and his wife are very kind to her and treat her as if she were their own."

"But she is not their own. She is my child." Eliza gripped her arms as if she were cold. But sunshine warmed the room. "I should go back. I can speak to the Breeses—surely they will return Darcy to me."

"And you would go where, my girl? You have no home there. You would be destitute, have to find work in a town. Darcy could suffer, don't you see?"

"I could bring her back here."

"I wish you could. But Mr. Hayward would stop you, and you could face prison for the attempt. It would cause more harm than good. I know you love Darcy with all your heart, and that you put her well-being above your own. Give this to God to work out. Somehow, it will."

"As much as it grieves me, as much as it breaks my heart, I will heed your advice, Fiona. But I promise, I shall not die until I have seen my daughter again."

"Oh, my poor girl." Exhausted from her journey, Fiona pressed her hand against her forehead and sighed.

"Poor Fiona, I should say." Eliza kissed her old guardian's cheek. "You rest now. I love you as dearly as if you were my own mother."

Fiona settled back, and Eliza drew a quilt over her.

Later, when Mr. Brennan returned, Eliza brought Fiona downstairs. Lightly she knocked on the door. Told to enter, she drew Fiona in beside her. Mr. Brennan looked up and took off his spectacles.

"Who is this?"

"Fiona, sir. Remember, I told you about her, the woman who helped raise me." With her hand in Fiona's she urgd Fiona forward. Fiona gave him a little curtsy, which was as much as her knees would allow.

Brows raised, Brennan stood. Eliza glanced at Fiona and saw a stunned look in her eyes and a blush on her cheeks. Perhaps his burn scars alarmed her, or his age. At forty and nine most men had grown sons. By this time, Eliza had grown accustomed to his appearance.

"As you see, sir, Fiona has come all the way from Maryland—to remain with me, if you would allow it." She went on to tell him all the news Fiona had brought. "If she cannot stay, perhaps you can refer her to another household in the area so that she may work nearby?"

He held up his hand. "Eliza."

Eliza stopped talking and pressed her lips together.

"I fired Mrs. Hart."

"You did?"

"Yes, this morning. She was slack in her duties, and I caught her stealing from the larder. I'll not tolerate thieving, especially when there is no cause. Her husband makes a good wage, and they have plenty. She had no remorse, offered no apology when I caught her red-handed with a sack of flour in her arms after she had left the house and was heading home. So I am in need of a housekeeper." His eyes shifted to Fiona. "Do you accept the position?"

A bright smile burst onto Fiona's face. "I do, sir. Thank you."

"Eliza, you may settle Fiona in any of the upstairs rooms near yours. Afterwards you may show her around the house."

Eliza turned to Fiona, and even though it may have shocked Mr. Brennan to see someone of Eliza's rank embrace a servant, she did so.

She looked over at Brennan. A quick smile lifted his mouth, and his eyes glowed warm while he gazed at her. At that moment, it became clear. Mr. Brennan loved her.

34

$\mathcal{W}$ith the sober winter past and spring a triumphant mistress over frost and cold, May Day had come to England. A local fair was announced, and Mr. Brennan informed his son's governess that he should like her and Fiona to accompany him.

"I'm counting on buying Ethan a riding pony and would value your opinion," he had told her the evening before while she read to him by the fire.

She looked up from her book. "But I know little of horses. Perhaps one of your neighbors could be of help."

"An excuse on my part. You and Fiona could use a day's outing. You have not left the boundaries of Fairview since you came here."

"Fairview has been a sanctuary for me, sir. I have found peace here."

"Yes, but do not make it a prison. You must get out in the world. Besides, Ethan will be greatly disappointed if you do not come with us. You have set a bit of money aside, have you not? You should buy something special for yourself. There will be a lacemaker and a milliner there. Perhaps a new hat?"

"Perhaps." She set the book on the table next to her. "I am worried, Mr. Brennan, that with so many people gathering there someone might recognize me. Then I'd be questioned, and what am I to say? That my husband tricked me into returning to England?" She hung her head. "I would hate to speak of it."

"The possibility of you meeting anyone from your past is remote."

"I know, but what if I do?"

"You owe no man or woman an explanation. What has happened to you is between you and God. You have nothing to fear."

Impressed by his sensitivity as well as his power of persuasion, Eliza smiled. She could not turn him down, especially when he spoke to her with such wisdom and looked at her with his eyes full of anticipation.

As she listened to him speak, she envied his courage. If only she could be more like him, full of faith and vigor, not afraid to show his face in public. He refused to hide his scars. She wore hers on her sleeve.

"You are not ashamed to be seen with me?"

Surprised, he raised his brows. "Are you ashamed to be seen with a man so grossly disfigured?"

Eliza shook her head. "I do not see you in that way at all."

"Then, there you have it." And he stood and walked out of the room smiling.

❧

The morning of the fair, Eliza tried to ease her worries of meeting anyone from her past. The years away would have made people forget her face. The possibility of anyone recognizing her was slim at best.

Nevertheless, she wore a wide-brimmed hat to shadow her face from curious eyes. She wore her hair up, allowing a few dark spirals to hang over her shoulder. Dressed in fawn linsey, without lace or ribbon, she took on the appearance of modesty and simplicity, which she believed Mr. Brennan would approve of.

They traveled into the meadows not more than a mile from Fairview. The road was cluttered with people from the farms and hamlets, some on foot, others in carts and wagons, with a few gentry riding in carriages. Sunshine beamed down through the trees from a cloudless blue sky, and Eliza tilted her head up to feel it pour over her. Then she looked over at Mr. Brennan and Ethan beside her. Indeed, they were a Godsend, but neither could abate the loneliness she felt for Darcy and the grief for Ilene—nor the anguish over losing Hayward.

Scattered throughout the field, artisans pitched awnings and set up their wares. Farmers stalled cows, sheep, pigs, chickens, and geese for sale. The breeze blew fragrant with the scents of freshly baked goods and bundles of lavender and sage.

As Eliza walked with Fiona, behind Mr. Brennan and son, she paused each time someone spoke to him, hanging back, until he'd turn and introduce her as his son's governess, in case any rumors had begun to circulate after Mrs. Hart's dismissal. She would curtsy short or nod, the brim of her hat shading her face and her violet eyes down. So far, so good, she thought. Not a single person even showed a hint of recognition.

Mr. Brennan went with Ethan to look at horses, while Eliza and Fiona chatted with the village lacemaker, who was proud to show off her latest collars. Next, they spoke with a potter over a display of porridge bowls. She looked through the crowd for Brennan. On a rise of ground several yards away, he stood next to a stall of fine chestnut ponies and was speaking with the seller. Ethan weaved in and out beneath the rope that held the horses back, and Fiona let out a moan.

"They will step on him, I just know it." And she hurried up the slope, calling out to him to take heed of the horses. Eliza watched Fiona take Ethan by the hand and in her gentle way lead him from danger. *She treats him in the same loving way she treated Darcy. I wonder if she realizes how deeply I miss my girl.*

The sun heated up the balmy day, and Eliza, a bit faint from the warmth, stepped away to stand beneath the shade of an oak tree. Children played and rolled on the grass. She watched them with an aching heart and thought of Darcy doing the same with her cousins so far away. *Darcy*—Eliza remembered her smile, her bright eyes, and how musically the word *Mama* tripped over her tongue. No one could see that she prayed in silence for her little girl, prayed that God would reunite them someday.

She wondered what Hayward had told Darcy. Her memory drifted back to that awful day when she lay sick and longing for death, when she heard him say she was going to pay for her sins, and that if Darcy did the same as her mother, she too would perish in the same manner.

It caused tears to rise, and she blinked them back. Had he told Darcy her mother would never return? She had hoped he would be kind enough to read out her letters to Darcy, but she believed Fiona when she told her he discarded each and every one. *I will ask her and insist she not spare my feelings, Lord. And if Hayward has been so cruel as to tell Darcy these things, shield her somehow from his bitter words.*

When she gathered her skirts and stepped away, someone grasped her wrist from behind. She twisted back and came face to face with Langbourne. All the blood suddenly rushed from her face and she felt pale and chilled when their eyes met. Shocked, she lowered her head to keep him from seeing her face. He did not move, and she heard him draw in a long and labored breath.

"Eliza?" His grip loosened and he let her go.

"Let me pass, sir. I must join my party." She proceeded past him. But he moved in front of her.

"Look at me." When she did not comply, he placed his riding crop beneath her chin and lifted her face. "It is true. I wasn't sure when I first saw you. But now to look into your eyes again after so many years, I know it is you, Eliza."

Her pulse raced and she trembled while forced to look at him. He had grown older, the lines on his face deeper, a hint of gray at his temples. Yet his expression held the same mix of pain and pleasure at beholding her.

She smacked the riding crop away. "You are mistaken."

"I would know you anywhere, having burned your image into my mind. I did not expect to ever see you again."

Persistent, he stepped closer, and she moved back. "I am amazed. I must say, for all these years you have not grown older. You are still as beautiful as the last time I saw you." Then he laughed. "But what courage you must have learned living in the wilderness."

"You mock me, sir."

"Do I? You do not see it as a form of flattery?"

"I do not."

"I would say you should."

"I suppose you have learned everything, and that by now I am considered an outcast. So why should you even speak to me?"

He looked through the crowd. "So where is Hayward?"

"He did not write to his mother?"

"Not that I know of. Where is he? Did his dream in America fail?"

"He is not here."

Looking surprised, Langbourne gasped. "Why not?" She did not answer. "Ah, I see. He sent you back without him. I knew it would not last."

"I do not wish to speak of it. I must go."

She took a step, and he stopped her again. "I strove to rid myself of every memory of you, Eliza. But I never could. Would that not be the ultimate revenge: to win you, to marry you, and let Hayward know of it?"

She bit her lower lip. "I cannot listen to you. Let me go. Or I shall call out."

He looked in the direction of her eyes. "To Mr. Brennan?"

"I am his son's governess."

"Indeed? What a dull life it must be. Hayward separates from you, and you come back here and live as a servant? Are you not in the least ashamed?"

She shook her head. "Mr. Brennan kindly offered me a position, and I took it. I cannot starve."

"If you had wedded me instead of Hayward, you would not be in danger of ever starving." Langbourne's smug expression vanished. "Allow me to end all this, Eliza. My offer still stands. You are married still, but you can come and live with me."

"As your mistress!" She snatched her hand away when he reached for it. "You think I would accept such an offer?"

"I think you will as you have time to think about it. You can find me at Havendale. It is mine, you know. The old gentleman passed, and as he promised, he left all his estate to me. I'm a wealthy man. Think on it, Eliza."

"I will not give it a moment's thought."

"You are not considering an affair with Brennan, are you? He is much too old, ugly, and, as I hear, committed to Christ morally. He'd throw you out if you made an attempt to tempt him."

"He is all you say. A good man, unlike you. Mr. Brennan is more a father to me than anything."

"Then I'm sure he would appreciate my offer to you."

He gave her an arrogant bow, held her eyes a moment, and stepped away. A group of women had gathered nearby and fixed their eyes on her. Mrs. Hart stood among them, her stare sour. What had her gossipy tongue reported to them? Had they heard the conversation between Eliza and Langbourne? Or had they stood there observing this unexpected meeting?

She glanced away, then walked from beneath the tree and out into the sunshine. Just then, someone called out, "Strumpet! Letch!" Then a wad of mud struck her in the face.

Cold and wet, the mire trickled down her bruised cheek to her throat and onto the edge of her bodice. Stunned and hurt, Eliza lifted her hand and wiped the mud away. Tears pooled in her eyes, and through her blurred vision, she saw Mr. Brennan and Fiona hurry toward her. When they reached her, Brennan put his arm around her, not as a lover would, but as would a shepherd, guarding his sheep.

"Such a disgrace, the lot of you. You dare pick up the first stone and throw it at her? Are you so righteous you have no sin of your own to prevent you?" The women looked at him, shamefaced. But Mrs. Hart raised her chin in defiance.

Brennan set Eliza behind him. "You there, Mrs. Brown, cast the next one. And what about you, Mrs. Garforth? Go on, all of you, pick up more mud and throw it at her, and at me as well. I am not without blame or sin."

"You have done wrong, Mr. Brennan," one woman cried. "That woman is married, cast off by her husband, and you have her under your roof teaching your son."

"You know nothing about her," he said.

"We've all heard why she's come here. Isn't that right, Mrs. Hart?" Mrs. Brown turned to the expelled housekeeper.

Brennan drew himself up. "If it were a sin on my part to bring her in out of the cold, to give her food and warmth, to show kindness for one whose heart is broken, then so be it. But mind what you say, for it may come back on you sevenfold."

A man of considerable stature stepped beside the women and glared. Then he looked over at Brennan and his charges. "Good day to you, Mr. Brennan."

"Good day to you, Mr. Hart."

"'Tis fine material, this is, for a sermon, I'd say. And you could include it with a lecture on *thou shalt not steal*." Hart—a hardworking carpenter and a man of good reputation— scowled down at his wife. His heavy, dark brows compressed above his sharp brown eyes as he placed his hands on his wife's petite shoulders.

Mrs. Hart went red in the face. "You take their side?"

"I do, woman. You've no right throwing mud at that lady or speaking so low to Mr. Brennan. If you do it again, you'll be down in it. Now go home."

Soon the crowd dispersed. Brennan handed Eliza his hand-kerchief, and she patted it over her soiled cheek. "It is all over, Eliza," he said. "Let us, too, go home."

He took her by the hand and led her to the wagon, where he helped her and Fiona up alongside Ethan. He had bought a small brown pony for Ethan, and had hitched him to the rear so as to lead him home.

Ethan tugged on his father's sleeve. "Can't I ride him home, Papa?"

"Not without a saddle, my son. It is important to be secure in all things."

Fiona rattled away about "those women getting their just deserts, the meddling no-goods." But it was Hayward's words that came back to haunt Eliza. *Your reputation has preceded you.*

35

*W*hen they arrived back at Fairview, the windows stood open to a dusky sunset and the curtains stirred in a bittersweet breeze. Upon entering the foyer, with all the shades and hues of a day that was drawing swiftly to a close, she excused herself to Mr. Brennan, went up the staircase to her room, shut the door, and turned the brass key in the lock.

She tugged on the ribbon beneath her chin, pulled it loose, removed her hat, and tossed it onto the chair. In the looking glass, she saw the red-clay stain on her gown and the streaks on her cheek and throat.

The pitcher on the table had enough water left to wash off the dirt and the stains, and she poured it into the blue and white china bowl. She dipped a cloth into the water, wrung it, and ran it over her skin. Her hands shook with each stroke. If only she could wash away the stains on her soul, especially the ones others knew about, and be someone else.

On her bed, she curled up and wept in the cradle of her arms. A dam of emotion broke and poured out of her—all her pain, the dashed hopes, mistakes, loss, and fears. There was no going back to change the course of things. Even though she had found a sanctuary and people kind enough to accept her despite her past.

An hour later, there was a rap on the door. "Eliza. Open the door, my girl. Let me in. I need to speak to you . . . Please."

Eliza rose up from the soft coverlet she lay upon, pushed the heavy spirals of her hair from off her forehead, and went to the door. Fiona stepped inside and set her candle down on the table. She looked over at the carpetbag and the heap of clothes sitting on the bed.

"What are you doing, my girl?" An urgency marked Fiona's voice and expression.

"I cannot stay here." Eliza shoved a dress into the bag.

"You are leaving because of those women? Ignore them."

"Perhaps what they called me is true."

"No. It was cruel. Do not leave on their account. I could not bear it. Think of Mr. Brennan and young Ethan."

"I am thinking of you and them," Eliza said. "I'll not bring any more embarrassment to Mr. Brennan, and I'll not have you clinging to the child in me that you once knew." She tossed her horsehair brush into the bag. "You all deserve to be left alone, to live a peaceful life."

Fiona stopped Eliza's busy hands. "You know it will hurt me. But you will hurt Mr. Brennan and Ethan as well."

Eliza shook her head.

"Mr. Brennan understands grace and mercy, and that we all have fallen short in our lives before God. He understands forgiveness. Do you not see the agonizing guilt he has lived with, that he could not save the lives of his wife and baby? Then you came along—he told me you were his saving grace. He does not expect perfection."

With Fiona's hands on her shoulders, Eliza looked into her eyes, her own filling with tears. She knew what Fiona said rang true. But she'd left out one thing. Eliza's reputation had spread from Havendale through the countryside. She could not ask Mr. Brennan to sacrifice his own for her. She would not let him.

"I will not be the cause of Mr. Brennan's good name being dragged through the mire, Fiona." She turned away and closed the clasp on her bag.

The sound caused Fiona to moan. "I will tell him." And she headed to the door.

Eliza grabbed her arm. "You will not. I have never ordered you to do anything in my life. But I will now. You will not tell him."

Tears glistened in Fiona's eyes, and her parted lips trembled.

"Forgive me for being abrupt. But you mustn't say a word."

"It will break his heart. You know that?"

Eliza hung her head. "I do. But he and Ethan shall forget me soon enough."

"I doubt it, my girl. Moments ago, he told me that his heart ached for what just happened, and that he saw Mr. Langbourne speaking to you. He wanted to come upstairs and have a word, but I advised him to leave you be for a time. You need to go downstairs and speak to him."

"I need to go somewhere where no one knows me," Eliza said. "I have saved enough of my wages to live on for a short time until I find employment."

"I cannot let you go . . . not without me."

Grieved to see her old friend so upset, Eliza put her palms upon Fiona's cheeks. "Then promise me you will say nothing to Mr. Brennan."

Fiona nodded. "Oh, it seems wrong, but I will do as you ask."

"Are you strong enough to do this?"

"I crossed the ocean, my girl, and walked all the way to Fairview to find you. If I can do that, I can do this."

✍

A full moon hung in the sky that night, and owls hooted to one another in the trees. By candlelight, Eliza penned a letter to Mr. Brennan.

> Dear Sir,
> By the time you read this letter, I will be gone. You have given me no cause to quit Fairview, and it grieves me to leave this place where I have found healing and peace, and a dear friendship with you and Ethan. I shall always be indebted to you for saving my life that day you found me, for giving me a position in your household, and for showing me God's love is greater than my faults.
> Please understand that as long as I live among people who know my past, I will bring shame and embarrassment to you. I shall find a place where no one knows me, and where I can begin anew. God willing, I shall someday find my way back to my darling Darcy. Until then, pray for me, and forgive me for leaving Fairview in this way. I had not the courage to tell you face to face.
> With gratitude,
> Eliza

She folded the letter, dripped the sealing wax upon it, pressed the wax firmly, and inscribed his name on the front. Then she stood up in the gown she had worn the day she set foot back on English soil. After she drew on her cloak, she picked up her bag and closed the door to her room. She went down the servants' stairs and slipped out a side door. Before the scarlet dawn could break, she reached the end of the lane and looked back at Fairview with a heavy heart. All the windows were dark. But the moon streaked the glass and glazed the facade.

She turned away and walked on. Before her stretched a road dimly lit by moonlight. Crickets chirped in the weeds alongside it, and the stillness frightened her. Had she made the right decision? Or had she sentenced herself to a life of dire poverty?

When Mr. Brennan rose from a restless night, he went downstairs to his study and drew back the curtains. Sunlight dazzled his eyes, and he paused to admire the green fields and the budding trees. After a moment's pause, he noted his house seemed unusually quiet. Not a creak on the floor above. No smell of coffee wafted in the morning air. Not a hint of what would be served for breakfast. He had hoped for a large one— eggs and English sausages, creamy porridge, and biscuits.

Roscoe mewed and weaved around Brennan's legs. "Ah, you are hungry too. It appears everyone is still asleep. Not even a mouse for you to catch." He crossed the room and went out into the foyer. He called Fiona. No one answered. Then he strode back to the kitchen and saw that the coals in the hearth were gray, cold ash.

A frown creased his brow, and he left to go up the stairs. Down the corridor, past his room, to a shorter flight of stairs he went. A slow trickle of dread stirred within him as he climbed.

He rapped on Fiona's door first, opened it, and looked inside to an empty room. His anxiety grew stronger. Raising his fist, he knocked on Eliza's door twice. And when no one answered, he turned the door handle and stepped in. The curtains over the windows fluttered, and a breeze blew through the open window. He flung open the doors to her armoire. Empty. He went to her dressing table. Her brush and comb—missing.

And there lay Eliza's letter.

This time dread reached a breaking point. He snatched up the letter in his hands and stared at it. Had he been wrong about her? His pulse pounded as he broke the seal and unfolded the pages. It had been years since he last cried, when Emily died with their baby girl. His hands shook as he read Eliza's letter, and that old, familiar pain of loss twisted inside him.

After he finished reading—once he had comprehended her words—he pressed his fist against his eyes and shoved the letter into his pocket. He paced the floor and then fell to his knees. His locked fingers turned white.

"Help me, God. Show me what to do. Must I be deprived of her as well? She has become a daughter to me, a sister, a close friend. I am too old to ask for her love, and I would not, for she is wedded. But the husband who should care for her is not here. Allow me to take care of Eliza. I pledge I shall do right, Lord God."

He got to his feet and dragged himself to her window. And as he pulled down the latch, he spotted Fiona out on the lane. She trudged along at an anxious pace with her hands clasped at her breast. She stopped, turned full circle, and seemed confused.

Bewildered, Brennan hurried away from the window. Through shadow and light, he rushed downstairs and out his front door. Moving at a sprint, he called out to Fiona. She looked toward him, pale and terrified, and stood stark still, her hands still clutching the edge of her cloak.

"Where is Eliza? And why are you out here?"

Worry filled her eyes. "Oh, Mr. Brennan." The words caught in her throat, and she began to weep.

"What has happened? She is not in her room, and I cannot find her inside the house."

"She made me promise not to tell you, sir. She told me she could not allow your good name to be dragged through the mire or to see you humiliated. I was certain she would change her mind. Bear it with all forgiveness, if you can."

"Forgiveness for not telling me, yes. But bearing it, I cannot do if you are about to tell me she has gone."

On the last word, Fiona went silent and gazed at Brennan with sorrow. He turned away. How could Eliza have done this? She had to have known he'd not allow any word against her to stand.

Fiona moved up to him. "I begged her not to go, sir, but she could not be persuaded."

He nodded. "She has a strong will, I know."

"She agreed to take me with her, but when I woke at daybreak, the time we had set to steal away, I found a letter slipped under my door from her. I panicked and went down the road as far as I could. Then I grew afraid I might lose my way and came back to get your help."

Brennan stared forward. "She left me a letter as well."

"She's out there alone, sir."

Distraught, Brennan wrung his hands. "Foolish Eliza," he muttered. "Foolish, foolish Eliza."

Fiona's face flooded with desperation. "What shall we do, sir?"

The fear in his heart tugged harder. He imagined her treading down a road alone with little money to sustain her for long. "Where did she say she would go?"

"To a place where no one knows her, and then she hopes to sail back to Maryland, to Darcy. I can assure you, sir, Hayward Morgan has seen to it that she will not see the child. He will let her live in poverty and shame, even prison, if she should make any attempt."

Silver layers of sunlight entered the forest nearby, and then sunk from the heavens. A southern wind rose, rustled limb and vine, and whipped across the fields into the lane. "I will saddle my horse. I put my son in your charge, Fiona, until I've returned with Eliza."

Brennan rushed to the stable and pulled his horse out of its stall to saddle him. Shoving his boot into the stirrup, he swung up onto the horse's back, held him with a firm grip on the reins, nudged him with his knees, and galloped off at a violent pace to find a wayward soul.

36

*W*hen the sky threatened rain, Eliza drew the hood of her cloak over her dark hair and trudged on. Not a soul confronted her along the way, for the road remained desolate for miles. Thirsty, she paused upon the bank of a stream that purled down a slope. She sat in the moss, removed her glove, and dipped her hand into the cold water. It tasted sweet and reminded her of her river so far away and the child left behind.

"I am tired, Lord. But I must find my way." She gazed up at the clusters of leaves above her. She thought about her father. What he would tell her to do, and what he would think, to see her sitting beside a stream, all alone?

A verse he had read to her many times came back to her, and she whispered it. "Stand ye in the ways, and see, and ask for the old paths, where is the good way, and walk therein, and ye shall find rest for your souls."

Minutes later, clouds subdued the sun. She stood, brushed off her cloak, and glanced around her. Which way to the road? Her bearings lost, she passed through the woods. They grew thicker, darker, and the wind murmured louder than the birds that sang. She looked for the sun and determined another way. Fretful moments went by until she spotted the road at the bottom of the hill.

With care, she sidestepped down the slope, slipped, regained her footing, and trudged on. As the light waned, she pondered what she would do for the night. If she could find a kind farmer who would allow her his barn and a bed of hay, she'd be grateful.

Not far from the stream, she recognized the path that led away from the road, where the land opened up to grass-covered downs. Eliza gazed at the expanse of land before her, the rocks and heath, the sheep grazing in the distance, then beyond, to the place where she had grown up and Mr. Brennan had ministered until tragedy struck his life. She had to see it for herself, what was once a happier place, now a charred remnant of the past. The silence seemed unearthly, the dusky light so solemn she was filled with a sense of awe.

In her mind, she envisioned the horrid scene—smoldering beams, blackened stone, and tongues of flame. All that remained were the smoke-marred limestone walls and the glassless windows of what had once been a house where the Word of God was loved and reverenced, where care for the poor in body and soul were a way of life, where families had supped, laughed, and cried together.

Were the tears in her eyes brought on from the wind? Dull, sick revolt gripped her belly, and her head ached. No longer could she try to imagine what Mr. Brennan had faced that terrible day, what unbearable agony had consumed him. *Oh, his unfortunate wife and baby. Poor, poor Ethan, to have them not.*

Sorrowful, she headed back down the path above the downs to the road. The quiet that permeated the land broke of a sudden when she heard the trot of a horse drawing near.

She stepped off the road into a thicket and there backed up against the trunk of a large tree. The rider came on, and she saw his face and a pair of keen and urgent eyes.

For a moment, she stood stark still with her hands at her breast. His horse pricked its ears and slowed. Brennan pulling on the reins, waited, and listened. He had come all this way in search of her. How could she stay hidden and not face the man? Away from the tree, she came forward and stood alongside the road before him. Arms at her side, the tendrils of her hair lifted in the breeze. His horse side-stepped, and he steadied him. Then he dismounted and walked toward her.

Pity for her showed in his eyes. About his shoulders hung his hair, damp from the ride, clinging to his forehead. "Eliza. What do you mean by running away like this?"

Feeling ashamed, she lowered her eyes, bit her lower lip, and forced herself not to cry. "I . . ."

"Eliza, look at me." He came closer, and she obeyed him. "Do you really want to leave us? Is running away the answer? Will it end scrutiny, judgment, and rejection from others? I have done none of those things to you. I have accepted you as you are, and loved you—even now when you have left me, thinking it will somehow save me, when all it will do is destroy me."

"I do not want to hurt you, or Ethan, or Fiona," she murmured.

"Then you must see God brought us together—two people with broken hearts, both of us losing a mate and a child. I love you, Eliza, no matter your past or your future. I want to grow old knowing I have my companion, my friend, at my side, to have and to hold until I die."

His words grieved her. "How? You are a man of faith. You cannot . . ."

"I can," he interrupted with haste. "We will live out our lives quietly at Fairview, you and I, Fiona and Ethan. Come back with me, Eliza. We are your family now. If I have to beg, I will do it."

Her hair blew across her eyes, and she brushed it back. Hayward wanted a wife to build his estate and legacy, whether it was she or Miss Marsden or someone else. It did not matter. At one time, she had believed he loved her. But his love had been conditional. As for Langbourne, he wanted her out of pride, vengeance, and lust. She had rejected him, and shocked him into seeing her as a challenge. And how cruelly he would have treated her if she had accepted him.

Brennan looked past the violet eyes and raven hair to a place no other had seen. He treated her as an equal, and he understood spiritual things, the Lord's quickness to forgive, the sacrifice for her sin and his. He'd brought her beauty for ashes, joy for tears. Is this not what she had longed for? To be loved for who she was, not what she was?

Through his expression he pleaded with her, then held out his hand. His warm eyes bid her come home, and at that moment, Eliza knew what love really meant. She saw in him understanding, sacrifice, patience, and forgiveness, gracing a man who had been broken and imperfect.

She took the hand he offered, and she was shielded against wind and rain, safe at last.

" 'He sent from above, he took me, he drew me out of many waters,' " Brennan said. "You are not lost, Eliza, nor forsaken. Tell me you believe that."

"I do. More than anything I have believed in my life."

"Then let us leave this grim place. I have no doubt Fiona will have supper on the table for us, and Ethan will be waiting impatiently by the door."

He climbed into the saddle and lifted her up behind him. In silence, they rode homeward. She did not look back to the ruins, nor to the south where far away the sea met the shores of Cornwall. Instead, she turned her face toward Fairview.

Discussion Questions

1. How did you feel when Eliza lost her father and brother, and was turned out of her home by Mr. Morgan?

2. What expectations did you have for Eliza when Hayward agreed to wed her?

3. Do you believe people can have an immediate connection to each other like Eliza had with Hayward?

4. Did Eliza make the right choice in marrying Hayward? How different would her life have been if she had married Langbourne instead?

5. What were Eliza's character strengths and weaknesses?

6. What were Hayward's character strengths and weaknesses?

7. Was Sarah's choice to raise Ilene as her child made out of love for Eliza and wanting to protect her, or was it for another reason?

8. Why was Hayward unable to forgive Eliza?

9. How did you feel about Eliza and Mr. Brennan being close friends without it being a romantic relationship?

10. What were some of the spiritual themes of this book, and what did they mean to you?

Want to learn more about author
Rita Gerlach and check out other great fiction
from Abingdon Press?

Sign up for our fiction newsletter at
www.AbingdonPress.com/Fiction
to read interviews with your favorite authors, find tips
for starting a reading group, and stay posted on what
new titles are on the horizon. It's a place to connect
with other fiction readers or post a
comment about this book.

Be sure to visit Rita online!

www.ritagerlach.com
http://ritagerlach.blogspot.com

What They're Saying About...

The Glory of Green, by Judy Christie
"Once again, Christie draws her readers into the town, the life, the humor and the drama in Green. *The Glory of Green* is a wonderful narrative of small-town America, pulling together in tragedy. A great read!"
—Ane Mulligan, editor of *Novel Journey*

Always the Baker, Never the Bride, by Sandra Bricker
"[It] had just the right touch of humor, and I loved the characters. Emma Rae is a character who will stay with me. Highly recommended!"
—Colleen Coble, author of *The Lightkeeper's Daughter* and the *Rock Harbor* series

Diagnosis Death, by Richard Mabry
"Realistic medical flavor graces a story rich with characters I loved and with enough twists and turns to keep the sleuth in me off-center. Keep 'em coming!"—**Dr. Harry Krauss, author of** *Salty Like Blood* and *The Six-Liter Club*

Sweet Baklava, by Debby Mayne
"A sweet romance, a feel-good ending, and a surprise cache of yummy Greek recipes at the book's end? I'm sold!"—**Trish Perry, author of** *Unforgettable* and *Tea for Two*

The Dead Saint, by Marilyn Brown Oden
"An intriguing story of international espionage with just the right amount of inspirational seasoning."—**Fresh Fiction**

Shrouded in Silence, by Robert L. Wise
"It's a story fraught with death, danger, and deception—of never knowing whom to trust, and with a twist of an ending I didn't see coming. Great read!"—Sharon Sala, author of *The Searcher's Trilogy: Blood Stains, Blood Ties,* and *Blood Trails.*

Delivered with Love, by Sherry Kyle
"Sherry Kyle has created an engaging story of forgiveness, sweet romance, and faith reawakened—and I looked forward to every page. A fun and charming debut!"—Julie Carobini, author of *A Shore Thing* and *Fade to Blue.*

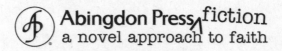

Abingdon Press ˄fiction
a novel approach to faith

AbingdonPress.com | 800.251.3320

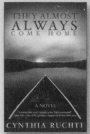

FBM112220001 PACP01002597-01